"That's all that matters to you, isn't it, Jesse?"

Carly asked accusingly. "Beating your father."

He met her eyes with a cold, brief stare. "You don't understand," he said gruffly.

What was there to understand? she wondered. He needed something with which to fight his father, and he had found it in the Sioux people. Just as she thought she was getting to know the man, he became more of a stranger than she ever could have imagined. Her voice split the dense silence between them with a ring of sad resignation. "I'll be leaving in the morning."

If she had been looking, she would have seen the flash of genuine surprise in his dark eyes. "But I thought—"

"You thought what, Jesse? That I would stay here with you forever?"

He would never admit it, he knew, but yes, that was exactly what he had thought.

Dear Reader,

Over the years, we at Silhouette Books have taken advantage of this space to do many things. We have introduced whole new lines of books; we have told you what kinds of stories to expect; we have alerted you to future appearances by some of your favorite authors. Last month we told you about an exciting group of new authors coming from Silhouette Intimate Moments, and now the time has come for them to make their appearance.

Nancy Morse may be familiar to those of you who also read historical romances, but this is her first—but not her last—contemporary romance. Our other three authors this month—Sibylle Garrett, Paula Detmer Riggs and Marilyn Pappano—are all publishing their very first books with us. Let them take you on a trip around the world, from the deserts of the American West to Hollywood, from an Indian reservation to Afghanistan, proving that no matter where you travel, love is always the same.

On their behalf, as well as the editors', I hope not only that you enjoy this month's Silhouette Intimate Moments novels, but also that you will take the time to write to us with your comments. Your opinions and suggestions are always important to us, and I thank you in advance for sharing them.

Sincerely,
Leslie J. Wainger
Senior Editor
Silhouette Books
300 E. 42nd St.
New York, NY 10017

Nancy Morse

Sacred Places

Silhouette Intimate Moments

Published by Silhouette Books New York

America's Publisher of Contemporary Romance

SILHOUETTE BOOKS
300 East 42nd St., New York, N.Y. 10017

ISBN: 0-373-07181-7

First Silhouette Books printing March 1987

America's Publisher of Contemporary Romance

Printed in the U.S.A.

NANCY MORSE

is an avid reader of everything from novels to cereal boxes. Her love of reading has inspired her to write and keep writing, and she is also the author of several historical romances. Her passion for books is also responsible for her deep interest in Native American history and culture. She is the proud possessor of many Indian artifacts and considers her collection not just as a hobby, but as her link with the past.

When she is not working or writing her current novel, she enjoys traveling. Although she is a native of New York, she and her husband have toured Europe and northern Africa. Other favorite activities include the theater, working up a sweat at aerobics class and being with friends.

Chapter 1

A panorama of tawny plain and cloudless blue sky was broken only by a huge, coal-fired electrical generator, whose plume of gray smoke was visible for miles.

Jesse Blackmoon applied his foot to the accelerator of his rented car and sped on past, not noticing much except the stagnant heat, which made him perspire unmercifully under his gray three-piece suit, turning his shirt damp and sticky. With an irritable flick of the wrist Jesse loosened the knot in his tie as he drove down the serpentine road that seemed to go nowhere. For the hundredth time he asked himself what he was doing so far from New York.

He was eager, of course, to close the deal with the Laramie Fork Power Company by selling for an unprecedented sum, two hundred of his ten thousand coal-rich acres bordering the Pine Ridge Indian Reservation in South Dakota. His business associates back east were calling the sale quite a coup. To Jesse, it was just another business deal. If Laramie Fork wanted the coal beneath his land, they were welcome to it. After all, what were two hundred acres to him when he owned so much, most of which he had never even seen until now? And judging from what he saw as he looked around him, it was just as well.

With sun-wearied eyes Jesse traced the horizon. The landscape was dull. Rolling grasslands were marked by creeks lined with stands of trees and low-growing brush. The ridges were studded with pines. To the north, where he was headed, lay the tableland, a vast area of erosion unsuitable for anything but mining. Deal or no deal, Jesse cursed the circumstances that had forced him out of a comfortable air-conditioned apartment in Manhattan and brought him to this dismal place.

After a long, uncomfortable ride that had left him edgy and thirsty, Jesse reached his destination. He brought the car to a halt and shut off the engine before a shack, held together with tar paper and old boards, that stood crumbling from neglect on a dying patch of land. He got out and walked to the front door. He balled his strong, brown fist and rapped.

Emma Huggins was hunched from a lifetime of hard work. With a bony hand whose joints were swollen with arthritis, she gestured for Jesse to enter and have a seat. He sat down on a rickety chair that did not look as if it would sustain the weight of his six-foot frame and looked around.

He saw no sign of electricity or running water. A battered kerosene lamp sat on the table, its smoke-blackened glass shade sitting askew on its base. A bottled-gas stove was shoved up against one wall of the single-room dwelling. The charred bulk of a wood-burning stove was the only visible source of heat for the cold South Dakota winters. There was no refrigerator, just a tiny antiquated icebox, which probably accounted for the abundance of canned goods and boxes of cereal stacked in odd places.

The old woman regarded Jesse, suspicion in her ebony eyes. In English, her second language, she said, "I know why you come here." She smiled, showing that several teeth were missing. "I am glad they sent a young one this time. And an Indian, too. Now maybe we will get somewhere, eh?"

Jesse looked at her. Her age was hard to guess, for her face was deeply seamed from countless years in the sun. He began politely. "Actually, Mrs. Huggins, I'm only part Indian." Although how she'd been able to tell was beyond him. Lucky guess, he surmised. "But that's not why I'm here."

She gave him a quick shake of her head and said with a grimace, "Never married."

"*Miss* Huggins," he corrected. "As I was saying, I'm not one of the men from the power company. My name is Blackmoon. Jesse Blackmoon. I own most of the land surrounding the reservation, and I want to sell some of it—"

"Blackmoon," she echoed, a sudden brightness leaping into her eyes. "Ahh." A strange, knowing look came over that weather-lined face as though something suddenly made sense.

Jesse proceeded tactfully. "I would like to sell some of my land—*this* part," he emphasized, gesturing around them, "to the power company. But the people at Laramie Fork tell me you won't move off the land so that they can begin their work. I understand they've even offered to find you a new house—a *better* house—somewhere else, but you've refused their offer."

As Jesse was speaking, the old woman strayed to the window and looked out. For many long moments she was silent. When next she spoke, it was as if she had not heard a word he had said. Wistfully, she muttered, "I want it to be like I was living a long time ago. It used to be such a beautiful place. Only the mountains in the distance." She jerked her thumb at the power plant that scarred the western view. "Today we have *that*. And *that*," she added sourly, looking to the east, where the strip mine on land leased by the Laramie Fork Power Company lay. "And *that*," she said bitterly, her gaze shifting southward, to where the pumps of the generating plant sucked at the creek. She snorted with contempt. "Look at them out there. Those pumps you see bring no water to this house. Those power lines bring no light. Everything, but most of all the money, goes right past this place like it was invisible."

"All the more reason to move to a house that has those things," Jesse was quick to point out.

"Why should I move from this place?" she asked. "This land is mine."

It was hot, and Jesse's patience was melting like an icicle in the heat. The woman was a squatter, damnit, having taken up residence, such as it was, on private land, *his* land, when she could as easily be living on Indian land a few miles away. He grew impatient, and while he showed only a polite tolerance, still he could not help but challenge her. "Can you produce a deed?"

Flatly she replied, "I have no deed."

"Then by what right do you claim ownership of this land?"

She turned from the window and looked into his eyes from across the room. "This land belonged to my grandfathers. It is mine by ancestral right, not because some piece of paper says so."

Jesse heaved a sigh and rose. He was getting nowhere fast. The men at the power company had warned him that she was stubborn, but he had not expected this. Now he knew why they had come to him in desperation, asking that he intervene and settle the matter. He decided to try a different tack.

Picking his words carefully, he began, "Miss Huggins, this land has belonged to my family for many years. My grandfather bought most of it during the Depression. It's not Indian land. As I understand it, the reservation is just a few miles away. *That's* your land." Then a slier thought came to him. "Besides, my ancestors were Indian, too. So, you see, not only do I have the law on my side, but I have, as you put it, ancestral right as well. Look, I'd be happy to offer you a reasonable sum for it."

"Reasonable?" she said as she shuffled back to her seat. "There is no such thing when it comes to dealing with Indians. Tell me something, Mr. Blackmoon. What do they pay you for your coal?"

He thought for a moment, then answered, "One fifty per ton. But I don't see what that has to do with anything."

"If they pay you one-and-a-half dollars for every ton of coal they take out of your land, how come they pay the Indian only fifteen cents? Your coal must be better, eh?"

"I have nothing to do with that," Jesse grumbled, growing annoyed.

"You have everything to do with it."

"If you mean because I own this land—"

"Man does not *own* the land," she said sharply. "The earth is our mother. She owns us, not the other way around. No, I meant because you are Indian." She glanced up slyly at him, adding, "Even though you try to hide it."

Her eyes traversed Jesse's face slowly, deliberately, taking in the tanned skin, the straight nose, the determined line of the jaw. No hint of anything Indian there. But the eyes— ah, the eyes—as black as the deepest recesses of a cave, eyes that gave away his Indian heritage as surely as if bugles had blared. There was something rocklike and unrelenting about him. Yes, she knew who he was and why he was here. In a low voice she said, "Black Moon would never have sold the land."

Jesse looked up in surprise. "That's funny. My great-great-grandfather was a Sioux warrior named Black Moon." He dismissed the remark with a shrug. "But I guess there must have been many men by that name."

She shook her head. "There was only one." She smiled. "Come, there is something I want to show you."

Jesse followed her out into the blinding daylight. As he trailed her around back, the wind that blew constantly on the plains kicked up a gust of arid soil at his feet. "Damn this wind," he griped.

From over a hunched shoulder Emma told him, "The wind is the breath of the universe."

"Where are we going?"

She did not answer but led the way along a rutted path that took them to the top of a grassy knoll. "There, do you see it?" She pointed west with a gnarled finger over the plains to the precipitous pine-studded slopes that rose thousands of feet. "The Paha Sapa," she said softly, a sort of reverence in her tone. "The sacred Black Hills of the Sioux. Long ago the Paha Sapa was where the women went to gather the lodgepoles and the men went to speak with the Great Spirit." She expelled a beleaguered sigh. "There are no more lodgepoles to gather. Now we have tar paper and green timber from the mill. But for many, the Paha Sapa is still where the Great Spirit lives." She looked up into the handsome face of the man at her side, his vital, strapping frame dwarfing her crippled form. "To the white man the land is just a number. So many acres for so many dollars. But to those who first walked this land, and to those who still do, it is life and death and everything that passes in between."

Jesse grew uncomfortable at her stare. Why was she looking at him like that? Why was she speaking to him as though he knew what she was talking about? It was true that he was part Sioux Indian, but he was too far removed from his Indian heritage for it to matter. He'd been raised on TV and processed food, surrounded by the wealth he had come to take for granted. There were regular workouts at the health club, weekends of tennis and sailing, black-tie parties and staid board meetings—hardly the stuff that Indians were made of. As far as Jesse was concerned, his life was fine the way it was.

Why, then, was he shifting uncomfortably from foot to foot beneath the old woman's probing gaze? It was something in her eyes. Jesse had seen it before, a very long time ago when his uncle Jesse, for whom he'd been named, had come east to say goodbye before he shipped out for Korea. Jesse had heard the things they whispered about his uncle. They called him wild and unpredictable and scoffed at his preference for living on the unforgiving land instead of surrounded by the family wealth. An Indian, they called him, as though it were something to be pitied. Maybe it was, but there had been something in the man's eyes that had set the young boy to wondering about things he had never dared wonder about before. Like why there was this place inside him that had no name or shape yet ached with emotions he could not define? It was the only time in Jesse's life when his need to learn about his heritage had surfaced. He had vowed to learn more about it when his uncle returned from the war. But the man they had called an Indian—the warrior—had died in a foreign land, and the boy had grown up a white man. The feeling was still there, though. Every now and then it rumbled around inside of him, reminding him of its presence deep in the core of his being. Somewhere within him was a place as dry and as empty as this stretch of South Dakota.

Jesse looked down at the old woman and shivered despite the air that scorched his lungs. Something in her eyes reminded him of what he had seen in his uncle's. It was as if she knew.

Emma turned away and started down the hill. "It is only a two-hour drive to the hills in that shiny red car of yours," she said. "On the way I will tell you a story."

Jesse glanced at his watch. He shrugged out of his jacket, rolled his shirt sleeves up past his elbows, slung his jacket over his shoulder and followed Emma.

Hours later, as the sun sank in the west, Jesse drove away from the shack, feeling strangely calm, although he had accomplished absolutely nothing. He was oblivious to the fading light as he steered the car around the ruts of the dirt road. Scanning the countryside as he drove, he gave an unimpressed snort. The sun had parched the land all around, bleaching it of any life it had had in the springtime. His ancestors had fought and died for this?

But if the land was not exactly beautiful, there was something about it that worked subtly upon his senses. Perhaps it was the vastness of it, the wide-open expanse that was unbroken by the city skyscrapers he knew so well. It was empty, like himself inside, and in a strange way Jesse felt a kind of kinship with this land.

He had to admit that he had never seen a sunset quite so lovely as the one that fired the western sky. Manhattan, unfortunately, was short on sunsets. At times he might catch a glimpse of the sun sinking beyond the horizon from the window of his office. Occasionally he saw an orange ribbon of sun reflected in the Hudson River as he drove by, but there was always the distraction of the tugs moving like alligators through the water and of the smoke spewing from the stacks across the river in New Jersey. Here there were no sounds to intrude upon his senses, no objects to obstruct the view, nothing to detract from this pervading sense of aloneness.

Jesse leaned forward to switch on the radio but stopped when something up ahead caught his attention. Even in the fading light of dusk he could see that she was beautiful as she came toward him astride a dark horse. Her body rocked rhythmically to the gait of the horse. A stream of dark hair fanned out behind her in the breeze. As they passed on the narrow dirt road she looked at him briefly, and Jesse barely caught a flash of blue from her eyes before she was gone.

He turned his head and craned his neck out the window, staring after her. Was she truly as lovely as he thought, or was it a trick of the twilight? He was still looking behind him when the car suddenly tilted, the steering wheel spinning through his fingers. He snapped his head forward, too late. He had driven up the side of an embankment. He jammed his foot on the brake and down-shifted, but the momentum carried him up over the embankment, and the angle of the car made it impossible for Jesse to gain control.

The car tilted over the top, flipping over several times before coming to a halt on its roof, its wheels spinning idly in the air.

At the sound of the crash, Carly McAllister spun her head around. She could not see the car, but it was easy enough to read the dust cloud that rose from the other side of the embankment. Jerking hard on the reins, she wheeled her horse around and galloped back. She reined up sharply at the top of the rise and gasped at the grim sight that greeted her. She was out of the saddle and dashing the rest of the way on foot before her horse even came to a halt.

She ran to the car and looked inside, but there was no sign of the driver. Glancing around, she spotted him sprawled on the ground several yards away. She rushed to him and knelt at his side. Placing two fingers firmly against the side of his neck, she checked for a sign of life. The pulse beneath her touch confirmed that he was alive. But he was far from safe, for the smell of gasoline was strong in the air. Carly glanced back anxiously at the car. It could blow at any moment. She knew it was dangerous to move him, but she had no choice.

She placed both arms under him and carefully dragged him away from the wreckage.

She dropped to her knees beside him and with grim determination set about examining him. She began with his arms, gently probing the well-defined biceps, then her hands traveled slowly, purposefully, down to his rib cage, where she kneaded the taut flesh, and lower still, up and down the length of each muscular thigh.

Jesse came to. Except for a knot at the back of his head that throbbed without mercy, he felt okay. He lifted himself onto his elbows and watched with a lopsided smile as she poked and prodded him.

"Do you always manhandle your victims this way?"

Carly froze and looked up from her work. "Victims?"

"Yes. If you weren't so pretty, I wouldn't be lying here near death."

Her mouth dropped open. If that was a compliment, it was the most arrogant one she'd ever heard. Wryly, she asked him, "And do you always drive looking backward?"

"Not generally," Jesse admitted. "Are there any broken bones?"

"No."

He started to rise. "Good, then I'll be on my way."

"Not so fast," she said. "No broken bones doesn't mean there isn't any internal bleeding."

He gave her a skeptical look and laughed. "What are you, a doctor or something?"

"As a matter of fact, I am."

"Oh. Well, look, Doc, I feel fine."

"Don't kid yourself, mister," said Carly. "If you were thrown clear of the car, it means you weren't wearing your seat belt, and if you weren't wearing your seat belt, you must have bounced around inside that thing like a Ping-Pong ball. You could be injured in ways you don't even know. I'll bet by this time tomorrow you'll be feeling muscles you didn't know you had. ''

But Jesse was insistent. "I'm all right, I tell you."

"A minute ago you claimed to be near death."

His look turned sheepish. "That was just—"

"I know that was just the male ego straining for sympathy after the male libido ran amok."

With an exasperated sigh Jesse sank back to the ground. "I've got to tell you, Doc, your bedside manner stinks."

"Sorry," she said. "I haven't had much time to cultivate one. I've been too busy convincing my people that my power to heal is as great as the tribal cures and spiritual remedies."

"*Your* people?" He gave her a quizzical look. "I've never heard of a blue-eyed Indian before."

"My great-great-grandmother, a Brule Sioux, married a French-Canadian trapper. The white blood in my family shows up every other generation or so."

And what a striking combination it was, thought Jesse. The fading light captured features that were more than lovely. They were radiant—at least to his eyes, which were admittedly still a little fuzzy from the accident. His gaze moved over her admiringly. "So, you're a doctor, huh?"

There was that tone of skepticism that Carly had heard all her life. "Yes. And I've had a hard enough time convincing them. I don't need to convince you." She started to rise, but his hand clamped over her arm, pulling her back down. His touch was like a flame along her flesh.

"Hey, I'm sorry," he said. "I didn't mean to offend you."

Carly sighed. "Oh, that's all right." She hadn't meant to be short with him. The truth was she'd been on edge for days, ever since they'd brought old Johnny Starbuck in with a bullet hole in his chest. There hadn't been much Carly could do for him with her limited facilities, so she'd driven him to the hospital in Pine Ridge in Luke Lightfoot's old pickup. Death was common in Carly's profession, but Johnny Starbuck's had shaken her up more than she cared to admit.

Misreading the expression on her face, Jesse observed, "Judging from that look, I'd say I don't have much longer to live."

Carly's thoughts snapped back to the present. She gave him a faint, unconvincing smile. "You'll live."

"You don't sound too pleased about it."

"Look," she said, "I saved your life, didn't I?"

"How? By feeling me up for broken bones?"

Carly opened her mouth to protest, but the words were lost amid the explosion that rocked the ground as the car burst into flames, shooting metal and chrome into the air. They stared at the flaming mess, mouths agape. When Carly turned back to him, the fire's glow tinting her skin with amber light, she said, "No. By pulling you away from that."

Jesse looked at her. There was a strange brightness in her eyes that was difficult to read. He felt like a jerk. In a grumble low enough to mask his foolish feelings, he said, "Thanks. I owe you one."

"You don't owe me a thing."

"Why do I get the impression that you don't like me?" he said.

Carly looked at him. She could tell from the way it fit his body so well that the suit he was wearing, though torn and soiled, was custom-made. His car must have cost more than the people in these parts made in a lifetime. She'd seen his type before, wealthy businessmen who came to buy up Indian land cheaply. She could tell he wasn't from the power company, though. The Laramie Fork men were down-home boys. This one had a city slickness about him and an intelligence that Carly suspected bordered on dangerous. No, she didn't like him very much at all.

Still, there was something compelling about him, and much to her dismay, she found herself reacting to him the way any red-blooded woman reacts to a good-looking man.

His face was hard-boned and handsome. There was toughness ingrained in those features, and although there was no suggestion of cruelty about him, there was the distinct feel of something quick, hard and dangerous. Carly guessed that any strains of gentleness within him were deeply guarded. Shaking herself loose from the impact of his looks, she got to her feet and asked, "Do you think you can walk to my horse?"

"I think so."

She held out her hand. "What's your name?"

"Jesse Black—" A gasp of pain tore from his throat, cutting off the rest of his words. He fell, clutching his leg.

Carly saw instantly what was wrong. How could she have missed it before when she was checking him over? She'd overlooked the deep gash in his left calf. The blood still spilled from it, seeping into the fabric of his pants. She ripped the cloth wider to get a better look. It was a deep and ugly wound that required immediate attention.

Carly looked around for something to wrap around his leg to staunch the flow of blood. Finding nothing suitable, she acted automatically, pulling her T-shirt up over her head.

Jesse smiled appreciatively at the sight of her flesh so unexpectedly revealed to his eyes. The generous curves of her breasts were confined to a lacy bra that commanded his gaze.

Carly knew that he was staring, but what could she do except try to ignore the flame of embarrassment that licked her cheeks? When the T-shirt was securely wrapped around his leg, she searched the ground for a stick of suitable size and strength. When she found one, she positioned it in the tourniquet and gave it a twist, forcing a grunt of pain from Jesse. The job done, she stood up. "I'll take that."

He looked up at her blankly. "Huh?"

"Your jacket, please. I'll take it now."

"Oh. Sure. Here." He struggled out of his jacket and tossed it to her. But instead of slipping it on, Carly rolled it up and tucked it beneath his leg to elevate the limb. With that, she turned and strode to where her horse waited in the shadows.

"Hey," he called out to her, "where are you going?"

"To get help."

"And what am I supposed to do while you're gone?"

Carly slid her boot into the stirrup and mounted in a fluid motion. Grasping the reins in one hand, she turned the horse's head back around and guided it over to where Jesse lay on the ground, looking pale in the growing darkness. "Lie as still as you possibly can," she advised him.

He let out a groan. "Thanks a lot, Doc, but you don't really expect me to bleed to death if I move, now do you?"

His sarcasm was met with blatant disapproval as Carly's blue eyes flashed from above. "I mean it, Mr. Black," she told him in a no-nonsense tone. "Don't move. It's not that I think you might bleed to death, but you see, the diamondbacks come out at night, and if they find you squirming around, you're going to scare the daylights out of them. A frightened rattlesnake usually attacks," she added matter-of-factly before she snapped the reins and set her horse to a gallop down the dark road.

Chapter 2

The town of Broken Bow, South Dakota, lay in the extreme northwest corner of the Pine Ridge Indian Reservation. It consisted of a church, a small café, a supermarket and a filling station. The Public Health Service Hospital, the government office complex, the schools, even the seat of the Sioux tribal government, were all located far to the south, in the town of Pine Ridge. By contrast, Broken Bow was a mere skeleton, a scattering of bleached-out bones beneath the blistering sun.

On the outskirts of town, at the end of a narrow lane, stood a small frame house that had once served as an Episcopal mission during the nineteenth-century frenzy to Christianize the Sioux. Today there was a garden of wild flowers, vegetables and weeds around back, and parked out front was a red car that had seen better days. The boughs of a giant cottonwood shaded the house, rustling with affection against the weathered timbers.

It was unbelievably hot. The burned morning air seemed to evaporate in Carly's mouth as she sat at the end of the porch, her back pressed up against a splintered post, bare legs stretched out before her, smooth skinned and golden brown. The sunshine glistened on her hair, which was styled in two ebony plaits that fell like thick ropes over her shoulders. Her ancestors had used bear's grease to make their braids shine, but Carly was blessed with an abundance of natural highlights that trapped the light in varying shades of red and gold. Her flesh gleamed with perspiration. One bright drop escaped the rolled-up bandanna she wore about her head, and trickled down the side of her face.

Carly lifted her gaze from the page of the book in her lap and fixed it on the steamy, undulating horizon. A troubled frown marred her expression. She was thinking about poor old Johnny Starbuck again.

He was an old Indian who had lived by himself in a shack near the Black Hills. They were calling it a hunting accident, but how could you shoot yourself in the chest with a shotgun? Carly wondered. The coroner's report was plain enough. Even Johnny's last words seemed to corroborate that he had somehow shot himself. Carly shook her head in bewilderment. It just didn't make sense. But then, none of the others did either.

The first had occurred three years ago, shortly after Carly had arrived in Broken Bow. A man named Dan Sittingbull, a descendant of the famous Sioux leader, had been found dead in a drainage ditch on his land. They said he'd been drinking and although the man did have a history of alcoholism as, unfortunately, many of his kind did, Carly had found no evidence of alcohol that day upon examining the body. In her opinion, he had drowned, cold sober, in less than two inches of stagnant water.

Then there had been Mary Yazzie, an old woman found dead in her kitchen. Old age, they said. But when Carly went back to Mary's place to look around, she had noticed a cup of brown murky liquid on the kitchen table. Carly had lifted the cup to her lips and taken a cautious sip of the liquid, which until then had passed for tea, only to spit out what was in her mouth when the acrid taste of foxweed touched her tongue. Foxweed was a useful medicine when the leaves were properly brewed and applied as a poultice, but when taken internally, it could be fatal. How could Mary Yazzie, a woman skilled in healing with plants, have made such a dreadful mistake?

Since then the death toll had risen sharply. Ten at last count. Word had spread through the reservation. Some blamed the water. Others pointed accusingly to the generator that spewed thick gray smoke into the air they breathed. Several families had gone away, leaving their houses and land to the scavengers who came in company-owned cars to pick over the leavings.

Little by little, Indian land in these parts was being taken over by non-Indians. Wills turned up in which the deceased had left their land to local politicians and power company executives. Local courts declared several adult Indians incompetent, while minors who stood to inherit the land of their fathers were made wards of the court. Johnny Starbuck was just the latest piece to an ever-frightening puzzle. And now, with the Laramie Fork Power Company threatening to buy up even more land, there was no telling what would happen.

A dust cloud on the horizon drew Carly's thoughts away from the uncertain future. A faint smile touched her lips when she recognized the big black Lincoln that came gliding smoothly over the pitted road. Who but George Gonzalez would have the nerve to drive around in a thing like that?

As chairman of the Council on Indian Rights, an appendage of the Sioux Nation, George Gonzalez, an Oglala

Sioux, was not a typical man of his people, not entirely liked or trusted by his Indian allies but nevertheless, indispensable to them. A Marine veteran of World War II and an electrical engineer who had once worked in missile design, he was adept at playing by the white man's rules. He was, Carly supposed, the perfect man to spearhead the only Indian rights organization that had achieved any progress for her people. He had been helpful to her when she first arrived in Broken Bow, introducing her to many people and sending her her first patients. He was the closest thing she had to a friend in this lonely place, and if at times she sensed something vague and unsettling about him, she attributed it to the difficult task he had in uniting a people who by history and nature had never come together under one leader.

Carly laid her book aside and rose to greet him as he pulled the car to a stop in front of her house.

George got out, dabbing at his brow with a white handkerchief. "Hi, Carly, how's it going?"

"Pretty much the same, George. And you?"

"You know how it is," he answered. "No rest for the weary."

Carly gave him a sympathetic smile. "I can't say I envy you. You sure do have your work cut out for you."

He whistled softly through his teeth. "Don't I know it."

"Making any progress?"

He shrugged. "Well, if you believe everything you read, we're all millionaires. We're taking back the whole eastern United States, starting with Maine and working our way down the Easter Seaboard. We're destroying tourism in the Northwest by asserting our fishing rights, and we're holding the entire Southwest hostage with our water rights and energy resources."

They both laughed. George went on. "Americans find it useful and convenient to believe that we Indians are rich. It wipes out any need for them to feel guilt or concern. It provides a justification for taking our resources, destroying our tribal sovereignty and ignoring our problems. The media project our feeble efforts to pull ourselves up by our own bootstraps as the biggest menace since Little Bighorn." He swept his own frustrations aside with a wave of the hand, saying, "But why am I telling you all this when you know it as well as I do?"

"There's something else I know, too, George."

"Now, Carly, what have I told you about stirring up trouble?"

"Trouble? I'd say the trouble has already started. All I'm trying to do is find out who's causing it."

"Yes, and look at what you've gotten for your efforts."

George was right. Her attempts to alert the sheriff in Pine Ridge about her suspicions had resulted in a curt reply that she leave the law to the lawmen. The chief resident at the Public Health Service Hospital had no comment to make on the unusual number of unexplained accidents that had filled his emergency room these past three years. He clearly did not wish to get involved. The people at the Bureau of Indian Affairs office told her bluntly to concentrate on healing live Indians and leave the dead ones to them. No one, it seemed, would listen to her. The only person she had managed to convince that something was wrong was George, who had promised to look into the matter for her.

"Have you found out anything?" she asked him now.

He shook his head. "These things take time, Carly."

But she noticed that his eyes had darted away as he spoke. Did he, too, think she was off her rocker? "Sure, George," she said with a dismal sigh.

"Look, I've got to run." He climbed back into his shiny black car and started up the engine. "Don't forget, there's a meeting tomorrow night over at my place."

"Huh? Oh, sure, right." She watched the dust cloud grow as the wheels of the car churned up the arid Dakota soil far out onto the prairie, then turned around and went inside.

It was much cooler in the house. In the kitchen Carly filled a glass with iced tea, plopped in a couple of ice cubes and carried the drink into the living room. On the way she bent over to stroke the black cat that sometimes wandered in. She murmured something to the feline, then straightened up and turned around.

She gasped to see him standing there, leaning indolently against the bedroom doorjamb, dressed in nothing but his underwear and a smile. His arms were folded across an expanse of bare chest. One long, leanly muscled leg was crossed lazily over the other. His near-nakedness was a heated demand for action.

"How long have you been standing there?" she asked, feeling the blood rush to her face and trying hard to hide it.

It had been only a minute or two, actually, but the sight of the dimpled backs of her knees, the well-turned calves and slim ankles exposed by her denim cutoffs had glued Jesse to his spot in silence.

"And what are you doing out of bed?" she scolded him.

"I thought I heard a car," he said.

"You did. I had a visitor. Come on, let's get you back into bed." She came forward, turned him around and steered him back into the bedroom, warning him, "There's always the possibility of a concussion."

"All I did was get out of bed for a couple of minutes," he complained. "I wasn't planning on running the Boston Marathon, although, come to think of it, I feel good enough to do that, too." Still, he allowed himself to be led back to bed. On the way something caught his attention. He sniffed the air. "What's that?" he asked, speaking of the intoxicating aroma that seemed to grow stronger the nearer she stood to him.

"Sweetgrass," she answered. She pointed a stern finger at the bed. "In you go."

He climbed reluctantly back into bed.

Carly did her best to ignore the masculine body that was stretched out, practically naked, before her. In her line of work she saw lots of naked bodies. Granted, this one was in far better condition than most, but that was no reason for her to be feeling like a schoolgirl. She cleared her throat and, assuming her most professional manner, said, "Turn over, please. I want to check that leg."

Jesse rolled onto his hip and propped up his head on his elbow. "How long was I out?"

Carly carefully removed the bandage on his leg. "Since I got back to you last night."

"How'd you get me here?"

"By pickup."

"You don't look strong enough to lift an unconscious man into a pickup truck," he said.

She laid the old, red-stained bandage aside and examined the sutures she had put in late the night before. "I had some help."

Jesse scrutinized the wound. There was no sign of infection, and already it looked to be healing nicely. He was particularly impressed by the neat bit of stitching. "Nice work, Doc."

"You sound surprised," she remarked.

"Uh, no, not at all."

But Carly wasn't fooled. She had been battling skepticism all her life and recognized it when she heard it. Sometimes it was like that for a woman. Always it was like that for an Indian. "I did my clinicals at Jacksonville Memorial, my electives at Sisters of Mercy in Los Angeles, my internship at New York University Medical Center and my residency at Boston General. I was offered a place on the surgical staff at Boston General, but I turned it down to practice here.''

He was visibly impressed by her credentials. Still, he exclaimed, "You turned down Boston General to practice *here*?''

"Yes. What's wrong with that?''

He shrugged with exaggerated indifference. "Nothing. I just think it's a waste for someone as . . .'' He'd been about to say "beautiful'' but changed it quickly. "As resourceful as you to be out here in this infernal place.''

Carly looked up from the dressing she was applying to his leg, her blue eyes heating up. "And *I* think it's a waste to devote yourself to the things that destroy the earth.''

"What?''

"I know why you're here,'' she charged.

"You do?''

"Sure. You're here to buy up the land. Just like all the others.''

"Well, actually,'' Jesse began, "I'm here to—''

"You're no different from the others,'' she went on, ignoring him. "Oh, sure, you're better-looking than any man has a right to be, but you've got the scent of money about you. Either you have so much of it that you think you can buy anything, or you want it so bad you'll do anything to get your hands on it.''

A smile crept across Jesse's full lips, but it did not reach his eyes. "You've got it all figured out, haven't you?''

"I've seen it all my life,'' she assured him. "The government officials whose hands are bound in red tape, the greedy power company executives who trick my people out of their land with clever contracts that contain even more clever fine print, the local politicians who double-deal the land away for a few more votes.'' With a disparaging sigh and a voice grown grim, she added, "And men like poor old Johnny Starbuck who wind up dead because of *that*.'' She jerked her thumb toward the window and turned to gaze disapprovingly at the panorama beyond the glass pane. "Whoever owns that land out there ought to come have a look at what they're doing to it." She shook her head in disgust. "It looks like some huge beast is eating it up alive." For several moments she was silent, then voiced her thought. "What do you think he's doing right now?"

From the bed Jesse ventured, "Who?"

"The rich bastard who owns most of the land surrounding the reservation and keeps selling off parcels to the Laramie Fork Power Company. The miserable, insensitive brute who's forcing people to move. That's who."

Jesse stiffened, the hairs at the back of his neck standing on end. He did not like hearing himself described in such terms. "What makes you think the guy's so bad?"

"Isn't it just like a man to side with another man?" Carly huffed. "Do you know what will happen if Laramie Fork buys that land? It will trigger a land grab on the reservation itself the like of which hasn't been seen in these parts since Custer found gold in French Creek. How many Indians do you think will be forced out of their homes and off their land?"

In a low grumble he answered, "I hadn't thought about it."

"Of course not. Why should you? You're not paid to think about it. You're just the one he sends to strike his dirty bargains. You're just the messenger. And the message is clear, isn't it? Sell or else."

Jesse bolted upright on the bed at the accusing innuendo. "Now wait just a minute, lady!"

Carly sprang to her feet and stood glowering at him from the foot of the bed. "No, *you* wait just a minute, Mr. Black. How much did you offer Emma Huggins to move?"

If he was surprised that she knew about it, he gave no indication of it. Obviously, news traveled fast in these parts. He answered. "I didn't."

"Okay then, how much are you *going* to offer her?"

For a long moment blue eyes clashed with black, striking with enough force and fury to cause sparks. From the bed issued a low growl. "As much as I have to."

"And if she still won't move?"

"That's private land she's living on," he countered.

She could have told him that it didn't matter whether it was private land or reservation land. The result would be the same. She could have told him about all the other people who had been forced off Indian land. Instead, she said, "You haven't answered my question."

Jesse made no reply, but the uncompromising look behind the taut silence spoke volumes.

"Just as I thought," said Carly. She turned on her heel and walked to the door.

"Now where are you going?"

She paused to look back at him. "I'm taking a ride out to the Starbuck place to have a look around."

"Starbuck? You mean the old man who died?"

"He was killed," she corrected him.

"By whom?"

"I don't know."

"What for?"

"My guess is he was killed for the two hundred and forty acres of reservation land he owns over by the Black Hills."

"How do you know?"

There it was again, that tone of mocking doubt that made Carly bristle. "I don't. I said it was a guess."

"How are you getting out there? Horseback?" He recalled the sight of her astride the brown horse, breasts bobbing to the gait of the horse, legs open wide to accommodate the animal's girth. Even now he found the thought arousing.

She didn't notice his intent gaze. "It's too far to the hills to go by horse. I'll have to drive."

Jesse's black eyes lit up. "You have a car?" he asked eagerly. But whatever hope he had of getting out of this place any more quickly was dashed by Carly's reply.

"Yes, I have a car, and one day maybe I'll get it to run. I think it's the carburetor, but—" She shrugged. "Who knows?"

Jesse expelled an irritated sigh and grumbled, "Great. What about me?"

"Sleep if you can," she suggested.

"In the middle of the day, with the temperature hovering around 110? Fat chance. Where are my clothes?"

"I threw them out."

"You *what*?"

"They were a mess. On my way back I'll get you something to wear."

"How long will that take?"

The cross-examination was beginning to irk her. "I don't know, Mr. Black. I also have some rounds to make. Maybe early evening."

"Would you quit calling me that?" said Jesse in an exasperated tone from the bed. Secretly, his conscience was smarting. She obviously did not know that his name was Blackmoon or that he owned the private land surrounding the reservation—or, for that matter, that it was his company, Blackmoon Industries, known internationally as BMI, that was leasing the land to Laramie Fork. Surely the Blackmoon name was known in these parts, and, he guessed, not entirely liked. For that reason he let her continue to think his name was Jesse Black, saying simply, "My friends call me Jesse."

"I wasn't aware that we were friends."

He rolled his eyes and groaned. "Would it make any difference if I told you that I'm part Indian?"

Carly studied him from across the room. So *that's* what it was. There was something vaguely familiar about him, something she'd not been able to put her finger on. Still, she wasn't sure it made any difference. He would not be the first Indian to turn his back on his heritage. Here in Indian country they were called apples—red on the outside and white on the inside. Part Indian? Yes, she saw it now when she looked closely at him. She ventured a guess. "Sioux?"

"Yes, as a matter of fact. From what I understand, my great-great-grandfather was an Oglala war chief." He thought back to the story Emma Huggins had told him about his ancestor Black Moon, and a strange look came over his face. For the first time in his life a name and a man had been attached to the past where before there had been only a void filled with unanswered questions.

The sound of tires approaching outside turned their heads in unison toward the window. A battered Ford pickup came rumbling into view, spitting up gravel as it pulled to a halt.

"There's my ride," said Carly. "Look, Mr. Black—" She stopped at the look she received and reluctantly acquiesced. "All right, Jesse. I have to go out for a while. Sorry there's no TV, but I have some cassette tapes in the other room. Vivaldi, Sinatra, Springsteen—there should be something in there to suit you. Help yourself. If you get hungry, there's food in the refrigerator."

"Do you have a phone?" he asked.

"Inside on the desk. Be my guest. I'm sure you must want to make arrangements to get away from this 'infernal' place as quickly as possible."

When she was gone, Jesse got out of bed and went to the window. He watched her run out into the bright sunshine. The light bounced off her dark braids as she swung her tall, slender frame into the seat beside the driver. Jesse squinted to get a better look at the man behind the wheel, but a cowboy hat pulled down over his head shielded his features. Was that who had helped Carly last night? he wondered, recalling her mention of a pickup truck. What was that guy to her, anyway? And what difference did it make to him?

The pickup disappeared down the dirt road, leaving a funnel of dust in its wake. Jesse strolled into the living room and spotted the phone on an old rolltop desk. It had a rotary dial, not the slim-lined touch-tone buttons he was accustomed to. It seemed to take forever to dial New York City.

His deep, resonant voice filled the receiver. "Russell Blackmoon, please." There was a static pause as buttons were pressed on a distant switchboard and his call was transferred to the executive offices of BMI. To the familiar voice that answered, Jesse said, "Hi, beautiful, it's Jesse. Is my father in?"

Helen, his father's secretary, had been with the firm for twenty-five years. Her devotion to the senior Blackmoon was awe-inspiring, for she guarded his private office like a junkyard dog, and with as much temerity in her bark. With Jesse, however, it was different. Maybe it was his charm, or his good looks, or the fact that she had known him since he was thirteen, but for him she pulled strings and bent the rules whenever she could. Today, though, not even Helen's influence could put his call through any faster when his father was tied up on another line.

Jesse sighed deeply. "Thanks, Helen. I'll hold."

He picked up the phone, and with the receiver cradled between his ear and shoulder, he walked as far as the cord would allow. He looked around. The house was small but comfortable, efficiently furnished and tastefully decorated in warm earth hues with an occasional burst of brilliance from a vase of bright wildflowers. A wood-burning stove, which must serve as a furnace in the winter, was abloom with greenery in its converted state as a summer planter. Plants hung in the windows, winding spidery tendrils along the wooden frames. Lush furry-leaved African violets sat on the sill. The place seemed a tiny oasis in the midst of the parched Dakota landscape.

He roamed around, looking here and there at the curious odds and ends Carly had collected over the years. Scattered about on the walls and on shelves and encased in a glass cabinet were impressive examples of a tribal past. He saw intricately beaded bags, fringed pouches, quilled fetishes and carved utensils that resembled the modern ones he used. The striking colors, the soft, supple feel of leather tanned to whiteness, gave the place an earthy, primitive feel. Something churned deep inside of him, something he did not understand.

He moved restlessly to the window, where he stood for a long time, looking out. Carly was right about his wanting to get away from this place as fast as he could. There was something about it that disturbed him. First there had been the old woman with her knowing stares and strange tales. And then the accident that had left him with ten stitches in his leg, a lump the size of a golf ball at the back of his head and nothing to wear. He had every reason to want to get out of there. But Jesse knew he would not be leaving, not yet anyway. For one thing, he wanted to go back and speak to the old woman. There had to be *something* he could do to persuade her to move.

But it was more than just the old woman that made Jesse decide to linger in this place. It was Carly McAllister, with the eyes of blue and the sweet-grass fragrance that made his throat go dry. She was not like the women he was used to. Despite the medical education and the keen intelligence that brightened her eyes, there was no pretense about her. She was proud—to a fault, it seemed—and just pugnacious enough to delight him. But Jesse could not help but wonder whether she was aware of the powerful enemy that lay in wait in the form of BMI. Against such an entity she would be helpless, in spite of all that marvelous courage and the fiery temper.

But BMI was no threat to Carly and her people, Jesse reasoned. All his company wanted to do was sell some of the family land for the coal beneath it. Surely there was nothing so important about coal that anyone would kill for it. It was not worth as much as oil. It lacked the glamour of gold. And there was no shortage of it to skyrocket the price. Why on earth Laramie Fork was willing to pay such a handsome sum for a mere two hundred acres was beyond him, but that was their business.

Jesse's dark eyes swung away from the window and his thoughts came into sharp focus when he heard his father's voice on the other end of the line. Jesse spoke a few quick words into the receiver, then listened in taut silence, handsome face set in a scowl. At length he muttered, "No, not yet. I know. Yeah. Okay." He hung up.

Conversations with his father were like that, brief and excruciatingly to the point. "Get that woman off that land. Do whatever you have to," his father had ordered. He could still hear his father's staccato voice grating over the phone as he walked to the front door and opened it. A gust of hot, dry air hit him in the face when he stepped outside. Dressed only in his shorts, he stood on the porch, dark eyes squinting against the sunlight as he scanned the horizon.

There was nothing out there to distract Jesse from the swarm of aching emotions that suddenly overwhelmed him. As always, there was a rift within him. On the one side stood Jesse Blackmoon, president of BMI, at the age of thirty-eight a strong-minded man and a shrewd one. A man patterned in his father's own image, or so it would seem. On the other side stood an enigma, a mystery, something even Jesse did not understand. It showed itself in flashes of arrogance that his father clearly abhorred. It had been the cause of many heated arguments between father and son. It was at times like that that Jesse saw in his father's eyes something he could only describe as hatred. As a boy he had never understood it. As a man he no longer gave a damn. He had stopped trying to win his father's favor a long time ago, when he realized that it would not come if he stood on his head and whistled Dixie.

Russell Blackmoon was a formidable force, and it was true that Jesse's arrogance inflamed his ire. Jesse thought that was only because his arrogance reminded his father of his Indian blood, something Jesse knew the elder Blackmoon preferred not to think about. But if Jesse's father was able to obliterate his Indian heritage from his awareness, Jesse was not. It was at times like these, after speaking with his father and hearing the hostility in his voice, that Jesse realized how different they were. He used to blame it on other things, like coming from different generations. He used to think it couldn't possibly have anything to do with the fact that they both had Indian blood running through their veins. If anything, that should have brought them closer together. In truth, it only drove them farther apart.

When word had come that the men at Laramie Fork were having a hard time getting the old woman to move off the land, Russell had stormed into Jesse's office, demanding that he fly out to South Dakota to settle the matter. Russell knew what he was doing in sending his son to do the job. Jesse, after all, had a way with women. If that didn't work, then maybe the fact that he was part Indian might do the trick. Even that was worth a try. At first Jesse had bristled at his father's command, but in the end his own shrewd business sense told him that if he didn't get out to South Dakota, the whole deal could fall through.

With a sigh Jesse now turned his gaze from the horizon and looked down to the end of the porch where something

caught his eye. It was the book Carly had been reading earlier. Its pages flapped in the breeze. A medical text, no
doubt. But when he went to it and picked it up, he smiled.
There on the front cover were two lovers wrapped in a
steamy clinch. So, this was how the pretty doctor wiled away
the hours. There was something about the thought that
pleased him, for it told him that beneath the professional
demeanor beat the warm heart of a romantic, a woman who
dreamed and who was not afraid to indulge in fantasy. Still
smiling, Jesse carried the book back inside and flopped
down on the couch.

Carly found him like that when she returned many hours
later, long after the sun had gone down and the day had
cooled off. He was sound asleep, broad chest rising and
falling softly in time to his breathing, dark lashes fanned
over tanned cheeks. How strange it was to see a man sleeping on her sofa. In the three years she had been living in this
house she had been the only person here, with the exception of Luke Lightfoot when he helped her in with the groceries a couple of times, and only then for a minute or two.
And it suddenly occurred to Carly how lonely it was living
alone like this. As much as she hated to admit it, the truth
was she had come to South Dakota looking for refuge from
a broken heart. She had foolishly thought that you could
run away from a broken heart the way you could run away
from home, with nothing but a knapsack on your back and
a pocketful of optimism. But she'd been wrong about that,
and God knows what else. You couldn't run away from a
broken heart. Like a dark shadow, it followed you everywhere.

Carly watched the sleeping man, her physician's acute eye
observing him. Deciding that he looked okay, she tiptoed
from the room. Several minutes later she returned with a
sheet and placed it over him, careful not to awaken him.
Then she stood back to watch him.

What a handsome man he was. Asleep, he looked almost harmless. Surely a misleading impression, she thought, basing the uncharitable assessment on the hard lines that etched his eyes and the uncompromising quality in his look. Still, she could not deny that she was intrigued by him for a reason that went beyond those arrant good looks. Maybe it was because he was part Indian. Or perhaps it was the pervasive loneliness that she sensed about him. It was easy enough to spot it in someone else when she recognized it so well in herself.

Later that night Carly lay in bed, unable to sleep, gazing out the window at the bright moon. Her thoughts were haunted by the past and tormented by the present. The only safety seemed to be in the future, where nothing seemed certain, but Carly was afraid to think too far beyond tomorrow. She turned her face to the pillow and inhaled deeply. The scent of Jesse clung faintly to the cool cotton pillowcase. It was an erotic combination of male musk and lingering traces of expensive cologne. Something inside of her stirred, something Carly thought had died three years ago. She closed her eyes in anguish when the image of Grant Hastings loomed before her mind's eye.

Her mother had encouraged her to marry Grant, the intern she had met and fallen in love with during her clinicals. "Forget about doctoring," her mother had advised. "Marry Grant and have lots of babies." What they did not know, of course, was that marriage to Grant Hastings was out of the question. Grant already had a wife, and while ancient Sioux custom permitted a man to have more than one wife—preferably sisters, for the sake of harmony in the lodge—these were the 1980s, and Carly's devastated heart found little comfort in the practice of her ancestors.

New to affairs of the heart, Carly had been too naive to suspect the truth. Never had she felt such emotion for a man, or now, three years later, such utter contempt. She supposed she had become gun-shy, and she had sworn to herself that she would never fall in love again. And if it looked at times that at the age of twenty-eight she was well on her way to becoming an old maid, then so be it. As far as Carly was concerned, it was infinitely preferable to the pain of loving. Whoever said that being in love was wonderful should have their heads examined! Love was nothing but a sickness full of woes.

But there it was again, that scent, faintly stirring, playing upon her senses in a covert manner, making her remember things she had sworn to forget. Was it possible that it was still there, that old feeling that had once flamed within her? Was it there right now, radiating like a warm ember, waiting only for the right spark to make it flare anew? Carly could not stop herself from thinking about the man sleeping in the next room. What difference did it make? she asked herself with a sigh. In the morning he'd be gone.

That thought firmly in mind, Carly rolled over and fell asleep.

Chapter 3

W hat do you mean you're not leaving?''

Carly's voice rose an octave the following morning when she went to the kitchen for a cup of coffee and found Jesse already there.

He stood before her, blocking her way into the kitchen. His tall frame seemed to fill up the doorway. With one arm positioned up against the jamb, he looked downright imposing.

Imposing was not the way he felt, however, and for a moment he could not answer. All he could do was look at her. Her jaw was tilted up at him, full lips parted in momentary confusion, delicate nostrils flared. The tilt of her head made it look as if the weight of the ebony hair that fell loose and flowing down her back was too heavy for the slender white column of her neck. The kimono-styled robe she was wearing was a stirring contrast to the wild, disheveled look of a woman just arisen out of bed. A delicate water-lily pattern shimmered over the folds of silk so blue that it matched the color of her still-sleepy eyes.

"I...uh..." He tested his voice. It sounded okay. "I've got some business to finish."

He was referring, she knew, to his unfinished business with Emma Huggins. The thought bristled her composure. Surely, though, she could be civil to him for the length of time it took to drink a cup of coffee. But it made her angry. Ducking beneath his outstretched arm, Carly gained entry to the kitchen and went to pour herself some coffee.

"I hope you don't mind," said Jesse as he followed her into the room.

Mind? Why should she mind that he wasn't leaving? Because his presence shook her up in a way she preferred not to be shaken up? Because he reminded her of things she wanted to forget? Because it had been so long since she had felt a man's strong arms around her? The silk of her robe rustled when she forced a shrug and said, "Why should I mind?"

"About the coffee, I mean. I needed a cup, so I went ahead and made a whole pot."

She felt suddenly foolish for having misinterpreted his comment. To hide her embarrassment she turned away and busied herself with pulling a mug from the cabinet and filling it with the piping-hot brew. The coffee burned her mouth when she took a sip, loosening from those lovely lips a string of Indian swear words.

"Now, now, is that any way for a lady to speak?"

Carly glared at him, her mouth still on fire. "How do you know what I said? Do you speak Lakota?"

The glint of laughter lurking in his dark eyes turned to momentary befuddlement. "Lakota?"

"That's what the old buffalo-hunting Sioux used to call themselves. Some of us still call ourselves that."

"No," he answered, "I don't speak Lakota, or Sioux. I just know a curse when I hear one."

She moved to the counter and pulled out a stool. With a graceful motion she slid onto it. "Actually, you did me a favor."

"Huh?"

"The coffee. It usually takes two or three cups to get me going in the morning."

"Then I'm glad I could repay the favor. You sure did one for me when you brought my clothes back. Where'd you find them?"

Carly's gaze flicked over him from over the rim of her coffee mug. His jeans rode low on his hips. The sleeves of his shirt were rolled up past the elbows, exposing well-defined forearms. On his feet he wore a pair of scruffy sneakers. A sudden, impulsive thought flashed through Carly's mind. He must have lots of women in his life, she dared to think. "About a hundred yards from the wreck. Fortunately, you weren't the only thing that was thrown clear."

She had spotted the red and black nylon roll-type bag on the ground not far from the burned-out shell of his car when she and Luke had driven by it yesterday afternoon. Suspecting that it contained his clothes, she'd been only too glad to retrieve it for him. Since she had promised to get him something to wear, it saved her the awkwardness of having to ask Luke for something to borrow. As it was, Luke, in his typical jealous fashion, had questioned her endlessly about the man from the East. Finding that bag had been a favor to them both.

"How about a briefcase?" asked Jesse. "Dark brown, about so big?"

"Sorry, no briefcase. It must have gone up with the car."

Jesse issued an oath under his breath.

"Important papers?"

Only the contract with Laramie Fork and the quitclaim deed prepared for Emma Huggin's signature, he groaned inwardly. "Of course they were important. Now I'll have to phone New York and have my secretary prepare new documents and mail them to me. That could take days." He expelled an impatient sigh. "I hate this kind of thing."

Carly ran a hand through her hair, which was still rumpled from sleep, and remarked, "Something tells me that all it would take is one phone call to get everything you could possibly want or need within the hour."

"What I need, maybe, but not what I want. That's already here."

Ignore him, Carly commanded herself. She had no reason to think that he was referring to her, even if the look in those black eyes said as much. No doubt he was talking about that chunk of land Emma Huggins was sitting on.

"And anyway," he went on, "you overestimate my power."

She looked into those coal-dark eyes and saw once again the uncompromising quality in their depths. No, she did not think she was overestimating him at all. "So, where do you plan to stay?" she asked.

"I was thinking of a motel."

"Think again," she told him.

He cringed. "No motel?"

"This isn't New York City. Broken Bow doesn't get many tourists."

"A boardinghouse?"

She shook her head. "Sorry."

"Here, then?" he ventured, quickly adding, "I wouldn't be in your way. I promise."

Carly gave him a withering look and said, "How did I know you were going to ask that?"

"Come on, Carly, what do you say? It'll only be for a few days. And I'd be happy to pay you for your trouble."

Trouble? That was a laugh. As it was, she'd barely gotten enough sleep last night from the troubling memories he had awakened in her. Oh, well, what were a few more sleepless nights? "All right," she heard herself say. "But you don't have to pay me. I'll tell you what you can do, though. You can buy some supplies instead—penicillin mostly, and insulin for Emma Huggins. Oh, and I can use some—" She ticked off a list of medical supplies as long as his arm.

"Sure," he said. "Anything. But tell me something. Doesn't the Public Health Service or the Interior Department or *someone* provide medical supplies for the reservation?"

"I have an arrangement with the hospital in Pine Ridge for the supplies I need," she explained, "but I'm sick and tired of going begging to them for what I need." What she did not tell him was that the flow of medical supplies into Broken Bow had abated considerably since she had called the hospital administrator some unflattering names over the way he was ignoring the rising death toll on the reservation. "I've been using my own money to pay for supplies, but—" She expelled a dismal breath of air and shrugged.

"Don't your patients pay you?" he asked.

"Oh, sure, with home-baked bread and henhouse eggs."

"How about good old American money?"

"Money? You mean that green stuff with the pictures of presidents on it that I've always heard we doctors make so much of?" She threw her head back and laughed with genuine amusement.

It was good to see her laughing. Her teeth flashed against her dark skin, and the blue of her eyes was as bright and clear as the sky on the cloudless July morning. "We don't see much of that in these parts," she said, grinning. "This is Indian country, remember?"

"You make it sound like the far side of the moon."

Her laughter dwindled to a tinkle, then died away. "It might as well be." She swallowed the dregs of coffee in her mug and poured herself some more. "But I'm going to change all that," she announced between sips.

"Are you, now?" His dark eyes were bright with amusement.

"Um-hmm. I'm going to open a clinic right here in Broken Bow. It'll have surgical facilities and an ER and an ambulance."

"That's going to take a lot of money," Jesse remarked.

Her face held no trace of the laughter that had brightened it only moments before. "Yes, it is." She did not mention, of course, that she had a plan to get the money she needed for the clinic. There was no sense in telling him; he would not understand about the land. Not the selling of it—*that* he would understand only too well. He could probably even give her a few tips on how to get the most money for it. But the feelings that battled within her over it—that was the part she did not trust him with.

The 240-acre tract of land that the government had allotted to her family back in 1887 under the General Allotment Act was hers now to do with as she pleased, even if it meant selling it for the money to establish the clinic. But inwardly Carly shrank from the thought of selling the land. She was Indian. She *was* the land. No, she didn't expect a man like Jesse to understand something like that.

From where he stood leaning against the counter, Jesse watched Carly slip deeper into thought. Her splendid eyes smoldered with a barely suppressed anger that seemed to change into some unfathomable emotion even as he stared at her. His gaze dipped to the folds of her robe that had come open across her knees and slid to either side of her legs, exposing the long columns of smooth bronze skin. Jesse was astonished by his body's lightning-quick response. Blood pounded through his veins, and he felt an uncontrollable stirring of desire against the tightness of his jeans. Get hold of yourself, Blackmoon, he told himself. Still, he could not help but wonder what all that black hair would feel like wrapped around him in the heat of passion, and whether her legs were really as silky as they looked.

Carly glanced up just then to find Jesse's black eyes scorching her. She awkwardly pulled the robe back over her legs. She slid off the stool and, snapping the electrical tension crackling between them, said, "If you will excuse me, I have to get dressed now. I've got a busy day ahead of me."

Jesse followed her into the living room, eyes mesmerized by the sway of her hips. "Where are you off to?"

"I'm taking a ride out to Emma's."

His eyes jerked up at that. "Can I come?"

"I don't think so. I only have one horse." She wasn't about to make his dirty job any easier for him by giving him a lift out to Emma's.

"We could ride double," he suggested.

"Janey's sturdy, but she'd old. I'd like to spare her the extra weight, if you don't mind."

"How about the car, then?"

"It's not running, remember?"

"Maybe I can fix it. Where is it?"

Carly came to a halt just before her bedroom door. She closed her eyes, counting to ten before she spun around to glare up at him. "Are you always this persistent?"

He stood so close that she could feel the warmth of his breath against her cheek when he replied in a low, grating tone, "Only when I have to be."

Carly groaned. His infernal persistence was beginning to get to her. Summoning as much composure as she could muster, she decided on a different tack. "I'll tell you what. If you can get that thing running in the time it takes me to shower and get dressed, you can come along. If not, you can stay here."

"Alone?" he exclaimed.

"Of course alone. I offered you a place to stay for a few days. Constant companionship was not part of the bargain."

He tilted his head closer to hers and dazzled her with a smile. "What's wrong with companionship?"

"Nothing. I'm sure it has its moments."

"Particularly in a place like this. It must get pretty lonely out here, especially at night." As he spoke he reached out to grasp some strands of ebony hair and bring them over her shoulder, where he released them to fall softly over her breast. He leaned forward and placed the flat of his hand on the door beside her head. "The lovely Pocahontas must have lots of braves coming to call," he whispered teasingly.

She felt the warmth rush to her cheeks. "No, there's no one."

"Well, then, like I said, it must get pretty lonely."

Carly managed an elegant shrug. "Like hot summers and cold winters, you learn to live with it."

Jesse's gaze traveled over her face, dark eyes glinting with a dangerous warmth as they studied her. High cheekbones, tanned and hollowed, petal-soft skin begging for his touch. He could see the pulse at her throat. He lifted his hand and rested a finger at the slightly fluttering point in the column of her neck. "You're very beautiful," he said matter-of-factly.

"Thank you."

"Don't thank me," he said. "I had nothing to do with it." He moved his head closer to hers, his gaze wandering to her lips, where it lingered.

The breath caught in Carly's throat so that her voice emerged a ragged whisper. "I have to get dressed."

"What's the hurry?"

"I—"

"Carly, Carly..." He crooned her name. "We both know what's happening."

"Happening? I don't know what you mean."

"C'mon, be honest." He was referring to the vibrations, of course, the ones that raced like currents of electricity back and forth between them, but there was no need to say it out loud. She knew what he was talking about even if she wouldn't admit it.

The sound of her gasp filled the still morning air. "You're insufferable," she said into his face, which was now only inches from her own.

"Maybe. But at least I'm honest."

"And presumptuous."

"Presumptuous?" he echoed in his own deep voice.

"Yes! And you're...you're going to be left behind if you don't get out there and fix that car," she blurted out. She turned to go and reached for the doorknob, but she felt a rough hand clamp over her arm and spin her back around. One strong arm wound like a serpent around her waist, pulling her hard up against the wall of his chest. For one incalculable fraction of time his lips hovered and smiled above hers. And then time stopped. They stood locked in eternity, lips melded, breathing blended, heartbeats synchronized into one strong, fast drumbeat.

Suddenly Jesse released her and stepped back. Carly took a deep breath as reality returned. They watched each other for a moment or two, neither speaking, both assessing what had just happened. Jesse swallowed low in his throat and said, "Now, *that* was presumptuous." It was his turn to spin on his heels and stride from the room, leaving Carly surrounded by dead silence broken only by the frantic beating of her heart.

Minutes later, in the haven of the bathroom, Carly stood naked beneath a stream of hot water. The action of the water worked to massage the tension out of her. Slowly her

breathing returned to its normal rate and she began to un-
wind. The water was hot, the way she liked it. But today as
it touched her body intimately, it brought an unaccustomed
sensation. She closed her eyes to it. For a moment it felt like
strong, probing fingers gently kneading her flesh, touching
her all over. She felt dreamy in the wake of Jesse's kiss, and
it was easy to lose herself to the fantasy. So strong did it become that when she opened her eyes, she expected to find
him standing in the steam-filled bathroom, one strong hand
holding back the shower curtain. But when she stepped from
the shower there was no one there except her own hazy image in the steam-streaked mirror.

Wrapped only in a towel, Carly peeked out the door.
There was no sign of Jesse. Just then she heard a clang as
metal struck metal, followed by a sharp expletive from Jesse
outside. Knowing that it was safe to leave the bathroom
without being haunted by his stare, she nevertheless ran to
her bedroom and closed the door quickly behind her.

Carly let the towel drop to the floor, where it settled in a
gentle heap about her feet. She stepped daintily out of it and
walked to the dresser. From the top drawer she pulled out a
pair of white lace panties and a matching bra whose demi-
cut cups allowed an ample curve of flesh to brim over its top.
She had a weakness for lace and silk and satin and ruffles.
They made her feel like a woman beneath her jeans and
compensated, in her imagination at least, for her otherwise
drab existence in Broken Bow. When she had silk or satin
next to her skin, it was easy to lose herself in a romance
novel and imagine she was in the court of a king or on the
yacht of a rich playboy. And even if no one else knew what
she was wearing beneath her jeans, the mere thought of the
lacy undergarments made Carly feel sexy. It showed in the
way she moved, though she herself was not aware of it.

Carly slid easily into a cool cotton shirt whose sleeves she
rolled up past the elbows and a pair of washed-out jeans

frayed at the knees. She was pulling on a pair of boots when the sound of the engine sputtering to life outside brought her head up. She smiled, then quickly frowned. She wasn't sure she liked the idea that Jesse had gotten the car started. Now she would have to take him with her as she had foolishly promised.

She sat down at the vanity to brush her hair. When the tangles were out and the tresses flowed smoothly to her waist, she deftly pulled the dark mass all away from her face and wound it into a long braid that started high on her crown and trailed midway down her back. She slipped two silver hoops into her ears, applied a dab of gloss to keep her lips from burning in the hot sun and left the room. She was just snapping her medical bag shut when Jesse came in.

A slow smile curved his lips. Even in jeans she was lovely.

"I see you got the car started," she said.

His face split into a proud grin. "It was nothing," he said as he wiped grease from his hands with an old rag he had found in the trunk. "The spark plugs were dirty, so I cleaned them up. Ready to go?"

"In a minute." She went into the kitchen, where she downed the last of the coffee before turning the automatic coffee maker off and following Jesse from the house.

A static silence settled like dust over them as they sped past the huge generator of the Laramie Fork Power Company. Jesse ran the back of his rolled-up sleeve across his brow to absorb the moisture that dampened his black hair and trickled in tiny glistening beads down the sides of his face. He whistled softly through his teeth and remarked, "Sure is hot." Inwardly he cringed. Here he was, talking about the weather.

One bare arm resting on the rolled-down window, Carly steered the cherry-red Mustang over the pitted dirt road that turned off the main stretch of pavement. The hot breeze picked up a loose strand of her hair and flicked it about. For as long as she could remember the summers had been hot. She was used to it, though. And if she dreamed wistfully of white sandy beaches and blue-green water at times, well, dreams were a necessary ingredient of life. Besides, this was home. She swept the errant strand of hair from her face and said, "I don't mind the heat." She did indeed appear to be unruffled by the soaring mercury.

"We get heat like this sometimes in New York," said Jesse. "But the air's so thick with humidity it's unfit for human consumption. We have something called the air quality index. During a midsummer heat wave it can fall well below the healthy level."

Carly took a deep breath of air into her lungs. "It's hot, but at least it's pure . . . for the time being, anyway. In San Francisco there was so much smog at times I felt like I was strangling."

"San Francisco?" he questioned. "I thought—"

"What? That I was born and raised on the reservation?"

"Well, yes."

"Born, yes. Raised? Well, sort of. Actually, I was too young to remember the reservation before I moved with my mom to the Bay Area as part of a voluntary relocation program of the Bureau of Indian Affairs in the early sixties. It was shortly after my father died. Because of the memories, Mom couldn't bear to be around the reservation, and the Bay Area has a large Indian community, so we fit right in."

"With those blue eyes?" he teased.

"Blue eyes notwithstanding," she said, "I'm Indian through and through; make no mistake about that."

"How'd your father die?" he asked.

"He broke his neck when he fell from his horse." She said it without emotion. "The white man my mother met and married in San Francisco is the only father I've ever known.

His name is Henry McAllister. He's the hospital administrator at Mercy General."

"Did he have anything to do with your studying medicine?"

"He had everything to do with it. He's a good man, kind, honest, intelligent. When I was growing up, I admired those qualities enough to want to emulate him."

From Henry McAllister Carly had developed those first sparks of interest that ultimately led to a medical degree from the University of Illinois Medical School. "Dad provided most of the funds. Despite the odd jobs I picked up here and there to pay for my tuition, a medical education is an expensive proposition. I couldn't have done it without him. I consider myself fortunate. Few of my own people have the means or the luck to get this far."

"Why here, though? Why South Dakota?"

"You mean why not Boston General?" How could she explain to him that this was where her heart was? How could she describe those summers she had spent on the reservation with her mother's people and the things she had learned from them—the language of the people, the myths, the legends, the healing remedies, the ceremonies? How could she convey the deep, abiding love she had come to feel for this parched land? Or the way she craved the hot, dry wind moving through her hair whenever she galloped over the prairie on her horse? Softly, she said, "This is where I belong. This is home." She glanced over at him. "And you?"

Jesse settled back and slung one arm over the seat, fingers so close to her that he could almost stroke the soft brown flesh of her shoulder. "I never had much of a relationship with my father. There was always this distance between us. I stopped trying to figure it out a long time ago. I guess I just remind him of something he'd rather forget."

"Have you always lived in New York?"

"Yeah. In the summer we'd go up to Martha's Vineyard or out to the Hamptons, or wherever else the rich white people went on their summer vacations."

Did she detect a faint denigrating ring to his tone? She studied his profile for confirmation, but his look was unreadable. To Carly's shock she heard herself ask, "Are you married?"

He took the question in stride, not nearly as surprised by it as she was. "No, but I came close once."

"Close but no cigar, huh?"

"I think the thing she liked most about me was the fact that I'm part Indian. I think she expected me to show up in a loincloth, carry her off to my tepee and ravish her. When I didn't do that, she lost interest." It was his turn to inquire, "And you?"

Carly shifted uncomfortably in the worn seat. The conversation was treading dangerous waters where memories, like sharks, cut the surface all around her. "No," she replied, "I've never been married."

"It's hard to imagine that a woman like you would never have come close, though," he observed.

"I didn't say I'd never come close."

"What happened?"

There it was, the dreaded question. "It . . . it just didn't work out."

Dark eyes squinting against the glare of the sun, he said, "I see. Is that why you've holed up in Broken Bow, South Dakota, population three hundred and fifty?"

"They'll have to change that sign as you come into town," said Carly. "I delivered twins the other day."

"Okay, three hundred and fifty-two. Why the evasion?"

"Perhaps," she told him, "it's just none of your business."

"You've got a point there." But just when she thought he was going to let it go at that, he asked bluntly, "So? How long has it been?"

His direct approach disconcerted her. "I, uh, three years."

Jesse whistled at that. "Three years is a long time to waste feeling sorry for yourself."

Her blue eyes flashed at that. "I stopped feeling sorry for myself a long time ago when I realized it no longer mattered. Since then I've learned that if it's sympathy you want, you'll find it in the dictionary—not too far from sucker."

After that she fell into a silence that chilled the air inside the car in spite of the one-hundred-degree temperature. Jesse shifted his gaze out the window and watched the rutted road pass endlessly beneath the wheels of the car. This was the same stretch of road he had driven down two days ago on his way to see Emma Huggins. As they drew near the old woman's house, Jesse began to grow nervous. He glanced over at Carly, who drove in tight-lipped silence. "How'd you know I was out to see Emma the other day?"

"No one comes out this way unless it's to see Emma. In case you haven't noticed, there's not much else out here."

He cast a dispassionate glance at the terrain and muttered, "Yeah, I see what you mean." He looked back at her. "When you saw her yesterday, did she mention my visit?"

"What makes you think I saw her yesterday?"

"You brought my bag back from the wreck, so I figured you'd been by to see her. Like you said, no one comes out this way unless it's to see Emma."

"Actually, I asked Luke to swing by the wreck just in case there was anything that was salvageable."

"Then you didn't speak to Emma Huggins?"

"No. Why?"

He offered a careless shrug in reply. "Just curious." Privately, Jesse was relieved that she had not spoken to the old woman. Emma Huggins knew who he was and the corporation he represented, not to mention his link to Laramie Fork through BMI. No doubt she would have passed the information on to Carly. Of course, he had no idea what he would do or say once they reached Emma's shack and his identity was revealed to Carly, but he'd worry about that later.

The tawny plains rolled up to the green meadows and swept the precipitous pine-covered slopes of the Black Hills in the distance. Jesse was thinking about the spot Emma had taken him to the other day. They had sat beneath a birch tree and she had given him a history lesson unlike any he had learned in school. She had not read from a textbook or spoken from notes. In words and memories handed down to her by her father and by his father before him she told Jesse about his mighty Sioux ancestors, the ones who had defeated Custer at the river the Indians called the Greasy Grass, better known as the Little Bighorn. She told him about men like Crazy Horse and Sitting Bull and others whose names he recognized from old Westerns. And most astonishingly of all, she told him about an Oglala warrior named Black Moon, whose courage and valor had helped dictate history. Jesse had found himself listening with a new found rapture to her tales. Something had quivered to life within him; something theretofore undefined had a name at long last. The name was Black Moon.

It was past noon when they arrived at Emma Huggin's tar paper shack. Carly got out of the car and knocked lightly on the door. There was no response from inside. She called out, "Emma? It's Dr. McAllister, Emma." She tested the door. It was not locked. She pushed it open, and they stepped inside.

Dust swirled up in eddies at their feet, particles of it hovering like tiny flies in the beam of sunlight that came in through the window. Carly glanced about. "Hmm, that's funny."

Jesse's strong voice questioned behind her, "What is?"

"She's not here."

Plausibly, he offered, "Maybe she went out for a while."

From over her shoulder she gave him a sardonic look. "Without a car, where would she go?"

He lifted his shoulders in a haphazard shrug. "Does she have any relatives?"

"She has a nephew who lives about sixty miles from here."

"So there. He must have come by and driven her somewhere."

Carly mulled over the possibility. "It's possible. Okay, I'll just leave a note telling her I was here and that I'll be back tomorrow." From her black bag she pulled out a writing pad with a familiar physician's Rx at the top an scribbled a hasty note, which she placed on the table. Then she carefully withdrew two vials of clear solution and placed them in the small battered icebox.

Jesse asked, "What's that?"

"Insulin. Emma's diabetic. I taught her how to use the syringe so I wouldn't have to drive out here every day to give her a shot. I got this old icebox for her, too, since insulin has to be refrigerated. I'd wanted to examine her on this trip, though." She slipped the notepad back into the bag. "I'll come back tomorrow. Now that you've got the car running, it'll be no trouble."

Minutes later they were back in the car. The seats burned their legs after the car had sat baking in the noonday sun. Jesse let out a low expletive. Carly gave a little yelp of pain as she started the car.

They had not driven more than a quarter of a mile when a sharp report rang out.

"What was that?" asked Jesse.

"It sounded like a gunshot to me." She brought the car to a halt alongside the road.

They got out and climbed the steep embankment. They stood at the top for a few moments, watching.

A figure stood in the ravine below, feet braced in a combative stance, arm outstretched, the muzzle of a pistol aimed at the burned-out shell of Jesse's rented car. Into the charred and lifeless body he fired another bullet, then another. It sounded like corn popping in a deep pan. Jesse's strong hand clamped over Carly's forearm as he pushed her to safety behind him.

"You wait here," he told her. He took one long stride forward when Carly darted out in front of him. "Jesse, wait. I'll handle this."

She walked to the edge of the embankment and cupped her hands to her mouth. "Luke Lightfoot!" she shouted. "What are you doing down there?"

The man whirled, startled by the sight of the visitors. His hand dropped to his side. The muzzle of the gun, aimed now at the ground, was still smoking when they approached.

"What's going on?" Carly demanded.

"Nothing," he replied. "Just taking some target practice, that's all."

"Yeah, pal, well, take it on somebody else's car," snapped Jesse.

Luke aimed a scornful look at the wreck and scoffed, "She ain't much good for anything else."

It was then that Jesse looked at what was left of his rented car, *really* looked at it. It was hard to imagine that he or anyone else could have walked away from a mess like that. The closeness of his own demise stunned him, and for the moment he was rendered uncharacteristically silent. It was only the sound of Carly's voice from behind that snapped his gaze away from the flame-blackened remains of the car.

"What are you doing here, Luke? It's a long way to drive just for target practice, isn't it?" Her gaze shifted past him to his vehicle, parked about fifty yards away. "Hey, what happened to your old pickup?" she exclaimed when she saw the shiny new model sitting there.

"I was tired of that beat-up old thing," said Luke. "So I got a new one."

Her astonishment turned to mild suspicion. "Where'd you get the money for it?"

Luke shifted uncomfortably from foot to foot before answering. "I won a bundle Monday night in a poker game. Bought this here beauty from Willie Nighthawk. It's only got three thousand miles on it."

Jesse, whose keen ears were trained to detect lies spilled from the shrewdest of lips, regarded Luke Lightfoot with instant hostility. So, this was the guy who had come by yesterday to pick up Carly in that rolling relic. He scrutinized Luke with a keen and critical eye.

Luke Lightfoot was a good-looking man with the typical characteristics of an Indian—prominent nose, high wide cheekbones, full lips, dark hair and eyes. It was easy to see what Carly might see in him from the standpoint of looks, but the guy was drunk. Jesse had tied one on himself on more than one occasion, and he knew a man who'd been drinking too much when he saw one.

Luke regarded Jesse with a like intensity. Carly felt sandwiched between two opposing forces as she stood there. It was like a sudden meeting of two mongrels. She spoke up quickly to break the tension. "Luke, this is Jesse Black, the man I was telling you about. Jesse, this is Luke Lightfoot."

It might not have been the wisest thing to do under the circumstances, but it was all she could think of. From Jesse there came a low grunt of acknowledgment, from Luke a slight inclination of the head. Carly breathed easier. "Do me a favor, would you, Luke?"

He tore his belligerent gaze from Jesse's face. "Sure, Carly, anything."

She smiled tenderly at him. "Don't use Jesse's car for target practice, okay?" She gave a little shrug as if to suggest that Easterners had strange quirks that could not be explained, then turned back to Jesse, saying, "C'mon, let's go."

"Hey, Carly," Luke called out. "You gonna be at George's tonight?"

She had scheduled an appointment with one of her patient's, having forgotten about the meeting at George's house this evening. Usually, she tried to work her patients in around these meetings, at which she and her Indian friends discussed reservation problems. As the only doctor within a hundred-mile radius, Carly felt it her duty to attend. She hedged. "I don't know, Luke. We'll see."

Luke's dark eyes slid to Jesse. "Unless, of course, you got better things to do tonight, huh, Carly?"

She could feel Jesse stiffen at her side. "Ignore him," she whispered.

They walked back to the Mustang. "Is he always like that?" asked Jesse as he swung his lean, muscular frame into the bucket seat beside her.

Carly thrust the key into the ignition. The engine made several feeble attempts to turn over before finally starting up. No doubt there were many women on the reservation who would have loved to trade places with her in Luke's affections. But there was something about Luke that bothered Carly. It was a sort of hopelessness that dulled his eyes. It was the frequent bingeing on beer and whiskey. Sadly, Luke was typical of many men at Pine Ridge, men whose hopes did not go beyond the invisible boundaries of the reservation and ultimately withered and died like so many weeds beneath a blistering sun.

Carly expelled a little sigh and said, "Luke's harmless enough."

But Jesse was not convinced of Luke Lightfoot's harmlessness. He had seen the look in those black eyes. It had been the feral intensity of an animal stalking prey, the desperate, grasping need of a man for a woman. Luke Lightfoot had set his sights on Carly; that much was obvious. And Jesse knew that the combination could be a dangerous one.

Chapter 4

Carly finished scribbling onto the prescription pad and turned back to the man seated on the edge of the examining table. "Take this to the pharmacy in Pine Ridge," she told him. "It should help that cough. But I'm telling you, Willie, it's the drinking and the smoking. If the one doesn't kill you, the other surely will. And working that mine day in and day out isn't doing your lungs a whole lot of good either."

Willie Nighthawk finished buttoning up his short-sleeved shirt and slid off the table, rustling the strip of white paper that covered it. "But Doc," he began.

"No buts about it," she told him. "The air down in that hole isn't fit to breathe."

"I'm telling ya, Doc, I'm this close to making a strike." He held up his hand with his index finger and thumb just barely apart to emphasize his point.

"You've been saying that for as long as I've known you," Carly chided him. "And what are you going to do if you *do* strike a vein of gold?"

He grinned mischievously. "I'm gonna buy myself a bottle of the best Irish whiskey and celebrate."

She shook her head and laughed too. "Just as I thought."

"Seriously, Doc, I cut back on my drinking."

"I'll bet. And I suppose you didn't touch a drop the other night at the poker game either."

"Poker game?" His look went blank. "There weren't no poker game the other night."

She glanced up, surprised. "There wasn't?"

"Nah. Couldn't round up enough of the guys. Sam was down at Wind River, visiting his wife's people, and Luke weren't nowhere around."

Carly's mind did an abrupt backtrack to yesterday afternoon. Hadn't Luke told her he won the money for the truck in a poker game? It was common knowledge that Luke and Willie and Sam and a few of the others played five-card stud together.

"Something the matter, Doc?" Willie asked when he saw the frown that was troubling Carly's expression.

Uncertainly, she answered, "No, it's nothing. Tell me something, Willie. How much did Luke pay you for the pickup?"

"More'n it was worth," he said, smiling broadly.

"Did he say where he got the money for it?"

"Nah, you know Luke. Keeps to himself mostly. I didn't ask. Ain't none of my business."

And it was none of hers, either. Most likely Luke had played cards with another group of men. Maybe he had gone over to Rosebud or down to Pine Ridge. Carly took Willie by the arm and led him to the door. "Well, Willie, if you're going to strike it rich, I hope you do it soon. I don't know how much more of that black hole your lungs can take."

The old Indian laughed. "Don't worry about me, Doc. I'm sitting on a prime piece of land."

She gave him a questioning look. "Thinking about selling?"

"Nah. But it's like having money in the bank, if you know what I mean. Had an offer for it. Twenty-five thousand."

"I should have the results of the X rays in about a week," said Carly. "I'll call you to set up an appointment. Good night, Willie."

"'Night, Doc." He ambled off into the darkness.

Carly returned to the examining room to jot down some notes in her file. A couple of minutes later the door opened and Jesse poked his head in. "Can I come out now?"

"Oh! Jesse, I'm sorry. I forgot all about you. Of course you can come out."

He walked into the examining room, grumbling his dissatisfaction at having been forgotten. "Thanks a lot." He flicked a cursory glance over the room. It was small but efficiently stocked. He watched as she placed a fresh sheet of white paper over the examining table and returned Willie Nighthawk's folder to the metal file cabinet. "What was that all about?" he asked. "How come I had to wait in the bedroom?"

Carly shrugged out of her white coat and hung it on a hook behind the door, explaining, "There's no reason for people to think I have a man living with me. I have a reputation to think about. People in these parts don't have much faith in a doctor who... you know."

"Who what? Who has needs and desires the same as they do? Maybe it's time they—and you—realized that doctor's aren't gods. You're only human, Carly, the same as the rest of us poor mortals."

"That's not fair," she wailed. "Look around you, Jesse. Do I live like a god?"

He rolled his eyes and made a face as if to suggest that there was no reasoning with her.

Ignoring him, Carly strode into the living room, picked up her handbag from the coffee table and headed for the door.

"Hey," he said, "I'm sorry. Is it something I said?"

"No."

"Then what's wrong? Where are you going?"

"Nothing's wrong. There's a meeting at George Gonzalez's house tonight. I'm late as it is."

"But it's going to rain. Have you seen those clouds out there?"

Carly opened the front door and looked out. "You're right. It's going to rain. I'll see you later. Don't wait up for me."

Outside, the car made some gurgling sounds when she tried to start it up.

"Don't give it so much gas," suggested Jesse, who had followed her from the house and was sliding into the seat beside her.

She looked at him. "Where do you think you're going?"

"With you."

"Oh, no, you're not. You'd stand out like a sore thumb, make too many people uncomfortable or unwilling to talk openly. People in these parts don't take easily to strangers."

"Maybe it's time they learned," he flatly suggested. "Come on. What would be the harm in letting me come along?" The truth was he was curious. And besides, he didn't feel like spending the evening looking at the walls of Carly's house all alone. "I promise I won't say a word."

Carly relented only after extracting repeated promises from him that he would not interfere.

She gave the engine another try. Nothing.

"The gas," Jesse repeated.

Carly sank back into the worn seat and scowled at him. "Maybe you'd like to try it?"

"Sure. Shove over."

With a breath of exasperation she got out and trudged around to the other side of the car while Jesse climbed over the gearshift and seated himself behind the wheel. Adjusting the seat to accommodate his six-foot frame, he gave the key a twist in the ignition, saying, "All it takes is a gentle touch and not so much gas."

But when the engine failed to respond, Carly murmured a sardonic "Um-hmm."

"There are two things a man's got a way with," he said. "Women and cars."

She was about to issue a loud protest when the engine flared to life. The sight of Jesse's arrogant I-told-you-so smile was too much to bear. "Just drive," she told him.

It was a half-hour drive to George Gonzalez's house down the dark, winding roads of the reservation. As they approached, they could see the house, pale yellow light shining from the windows.

George answered Carly's knock at the door and showed them into the living room, where several people were gathered. Carly made some quick introductions and left Jesse to fend for himself while she took a seat on the couch and joined the conversation. The others regarded Jesse with suspicion, dark eyes appraising him from across the room. After a while his presence was not so much forgotten as tolerated. At George's suggestion Jesse helped himself to a cold beer from the refrigerator. With the can grasped lazily in his hand he leaned indolently against the wall, dark, inquisitive eyes scanning the faces in the room.

There were the grizzled faces of the older men and the rigid faces of the younger ones who did not think the older leadership was aggressive enough. In the bold and innocent conceit of youth they raised sharp objections to the issues at hand.

George Gonzalez held their anger in check with the defiant, unflinching, but calm tone of a modern warrior. His voice was uniquely his own, bold, blasphemous, fiery, articulate, saying things no one else dared say in public, certainly no Indian, and far too outspoken for some of the quieter folk, but just what the young activists seemed to need.

Jesse listened intently to their talk as the hours passed, and soon astutely summed up the situation for himself. It centered around a recent court ruling that upheld a previous ruling citing the 1877 sale of the Black Hills to the U.S. Government as a valid agreement, despite the fact that it had not been approved by two-thirds of all Sioux men as stipulated in a previous treaty. The fight for the land did not end with Custer at the Little Bighorn, it seemed, and these modern-day warriors had taken up the battle.

Jesse left them arguing among themselves and went to the kitchen for another beer. When he popped the top off a cold can and turned around, he found George Gonzalez standing in the doorway, watching him closely.

"You must find all this talk pretty boring," said George.

Jesse gave a shrug of his broad shoulders. There was something about Gonzalez he did not like, something he could not put his finger on. Maybe it was the way those eyes did not look straight at him but hovered on the periphery of making contact. "It sounds to me like you could use some organization. What are you doing about it?"

The directness of the question was accompanied by an unflinching look from Jesse's black eyes. It made George uncomfortable. "My theory is simple," he said. "If the government wants the resources beneath Indian land, it's not going to deal with only the Sioux or only the Navajo or only the Crow; it's going to deal with *all* of us."

"Strength in numbers. That makes sense. But what have you done about it?"

"I once contacted some Arab oil experts for advice on how to best develop the reservation's oil resources. Damn if it didn't start suddenly raining money on Pine Ridge. From out of nowhere two million in federal grants poured in. True, it was only to divert us from forming an alliance with the Arabs, but what the hell, we can always use the money.''

There was a shrewdness about this man that warned Jesse not to underestimate him. His tenacity and hard wit were discernible in those intense eyes.

George pulled a beer out of the refrigerator and the two men walked back into the living room.

"It's the money," one of the young Indians was complaining. "It's been five years since the Supreme Court upheld millions of dollars in compensation for the Black Hills and we still haven't seen any of it.''

"The hills are not for sale!" Carly argued. "We shouldn't even be *thinking* about taking that money. They can't force it down our throats if we don't want it. Besides,'' she pointed out, "with sixty thousand people spread over eight reservations, the money wouldn't amount to very much per family anyway, once it was divided.''

"Maybe not for you," the young man objected. "But I've got a wife and two kids to support.''

"Yeah," another put in. "We've got almost seven thousand people living on state and federal aid. Housing is scarce. Businesses don't take root on the reservation. All our land is held in trust for us by the federal government, which means that while the banks can't foreclose on the land, they also won't make any loans that consider the land as collateral. We don't even have a bank on the reservation, because there's no money to put in it. We're stuck between a rock and a hard place. Some of us can use that money.''

"But it's more than the money," Carly contended. "The land is sacred. Our ancestors once ranged across these northern plains praying, fasting, seeking visions in the Black Hills. Now we must pay user fees and endure tourists in our holy places. It's like someone taking a church or a synagogue and giving it away to private parties. It's unconscionable!''

From the doorway where they stood listening, George gestured toward Carly as he said to Jesse, "When I think of all the talk we used to hear in the sixties. Just listen to her. She gets right to the heart of the matter. They need me because I know how to think like a white man, but they need her because she knows how to think like an Indian."

Jesse's eyes fixed upon Carly. Her blue eyes flashed with angry determination. The tilt of her chin was evidence of the defiance that ran hot through her blood. She was lovely when she was all fired up like this, when her cheeks were flushed with warm color and her slender body was vibrant with life. He was only dimly aware that George had left his side, strode across the room and rejoined the conversation until he heard his voice.

"There's something you aren't considering," said George. "If the Bureau of Indian Affairs had invested the award—even if it represents only the 1877 value of the land—it would now be worth—" he paused for some quick mental calculations "—more than $145 million plus interest. That's a hell of a lot of money. On a reservation virtually without private enterprise, that money could finance new businesses and create jobs. It isn't like they're asking us to move out of our homes. Hell, no one actually lives in the hills. Meanwhile all that money is accruing interest and we can't touch it until we all decide what to do."

There commenced a flurry of excited conversation. George used the opportunity to take Carly aside. Gesturing to Jesse across the room, he asked, "Where'd you find him?"

"I didn't. He sort of found me."

His gaze flicked over the other man with obvious contempt. "How much do you know about this guy?"

His tone, thick with suspicion, brought Carly's eyes up to his. "Not much. Why?"

"Be careful," he warned. "There's something about him. I don't know. Something."

Was there anyone George trusted? Carly wondered. Born of a Paiute mother and a Sioux father, he'd been raised on the Walker Reservation in Nevada. The land there was a rocky wasteland, a desolate, dismal region of thorny undergrowth and scrawny trees. Here and there across the barren land were ghost towns and prehistoric geological sites. Growing up in the desert, he'd eaten everything from jackrabbit to potatoes to chow mein. In his youth he had done everything from cow punching to construction work through swampland and desert, eventually working his way off the reservation, only to return in adult life, having come full circle. It was no wonder, she supposed, that he was wary of strangers to whom the better things in life were as common as the scenery. But there was an unforgivingness about George that made Carly uneasy. She could not help but think that he just might like people—and perhaps himself—a little better if he could only learn to forgive.

"Have you made up your mind about your land?" George asked.

The question diverted Carly's thoughts from George's particular shortcomings to her own. How could she speak convincingly to these people about the sacredness of the land when she was thinking about selling her own land for the price it would bring? Sure, she wanted a clinic for her people, but did the end justify the means? Jesse had teased her about her blue eyes, but the blood that ran through her veins was Sioux. She might have grown up in the hills surrounding San Francisco Bay and studied medicine far from the reservation, but her mother and her mother's people had instilled in her a deep sense of heritage. She was Indian, and to her the land was sacred, not to be bought and sold or bartered away. She gave George a helpless little smile and said with a deep, uncertain sigh, "I don't know, George. It's not an easy decision to make."

"Just remember what I told you. When you're ready to sell, come to me first."

George was the only person who knew that Carly was contemplating the sale of her land. When she had confided it to him, she had half expected him to try to talk her out of it. His easy compliance had, frankly, surprised her.

"I hope you have that deed in a safe place, Carly. That's an expensive piece of real estate you have there, so close to the hills as it is. We wouldn't want it to fall into the wrong hands, would we?" As he spoke, his eyes shifted with fox-like mistrust to Jesse.

Carly saw the look in George's eyes and shuddered. He was right, she supposed, to mistrust Jesse. Jesse was, after all, a stranger, and as a man, a threat. In this fight there could be only one leader, and George fancied himself it.

Carly's eyes met Jesse's from across the smoke-filled room. He left his spot against the wall and approached.

"Jesse, it's late," she told him. "I think we should be going."

At the door Jesse shook hands with George and thanked him for the beers, noting once again the way George's eyes avoided his. Outside, he took a deep breath to clear his head of the stale cigarette smoke that had filled the room. He was trying hard to quit, and being around smokers didn't make it easy. "Who's driving?" he asked.

Carly gave him a wry look and said, "Since you have such a way with cars, why don't you drive?" The fact was she was tired and wanted to lean back, close her eyes and fall asleep.

But whatever sleep Carly thought she would get on the drive home was short-lived; when they were halfway there, the storm that had been brewing all day broke with fury. In minutes the narrow dirt road was a morass of mud. Rain pelted the windshield, and with visibility hampered, she sat erect in the worn bucket seat, scouting the wet darkness for ditches.

Jesse steered the car cautiously in the driving rain, muttering an occasional epithet under his breath at his inability to see more than ten feet ahead. Suddenly, the car listed to one side as the right front wheel sank into a water-filled ditch. Jesse thrust the gearshift into reverse and gave it some gas in an effort to back out. The rear tires spun noisily but made no headway to move the car. "Damn," he grumbled. With practiced control he worked the gearshift, rocking the car forward and back in an attempt to dislodge it from the rut. But the road was so filled with mud that the spinning tires only made things worse.

Carly looked over at Jesse's frowning face and asked, "Got any suggestions?"

"Yeah," he said flatly. "I could get out and push."

"Are you kidding? I didn't put those stitches in your leg so that you could rip them out by putting too much stress on those muscles. Do you have any better ideas?"

He didn't. Just then a shaft of white lightning split the dark face of the sky, followed by a hideous crack of thunder. Jesse was losing patience. He reached again for the gearshift, but before he could move it, the car stalled. Angrily, he gave the key a sharp twist in the ignition. The engine made one grinding effort to turn over and then died.

Carly crossed her arms over her chest and huffed, "Dirty spark plugs, huh?"

He shot her a furious look, warning her with it not to push him any further.

Averting her gaze toward the rain-spattered window, Carly muttered, "Now what do we do?"

"We wait," came his deep-throated reply. "It can't rain forever."

The minutes ticked by as Carly and Jesse, tense and expectant, waited in silence for the rain to end. Jesse reached over and turned on the radio, but the sound of static forced him to switch it off in a hurry. At least the battery wasn't dead. Maybe he had flooded the engine trying to back out of the ditch, he thought. Well, it could have been worse. He could have been stuck out here alone. Another flash of lightning lit up the interior of the car. In that moment he saw Carly's profile, clear, distinct and beautiful. He studied her in the darkness. What a paradox she was, a twentieth-century woman on the outside with old-fashioned principles on the inside.

"What is it you want?" he asked.

The sound of his voice drew Carly out of private thought. Her eyelids fluttered open and she turned her head to look at him. "Want?"

"Yeah. For yourself. For your people."

It was a question she had asked herself a hundred times. She knew it was not possible for her people to hold on to their tribal past without also embracing the new, and what was new was white. It had been that way for more than a century. But how could you combine the two when one was at such odds with the other? She pulled in a ragged breath and let it out in a long, slow sigh. "I don't want to hold on to the tribal past," she said softly. "Living in fading nostalgia as a walking museum piece isn't what I want."

"What *do* you want?" he reiterated.

"I want to live as a contemporary Indian in a modern world. I want to modernize the old tribal ways so that they will not only survive but will be revitalized."

"How does Gonzalez fit in, with his rhetoric and that expensive Lincoln sitting in his driveway?"

She knew how it looked to outsiders. She tried as best she could to explain it to him. "There are many others who feel as I do. Unfortunately, there's this disparity among us that has plagued us throughout our history. Few men are able to unite the once-mighty Sioux nation the way Crazy Horse did over a hundred years ago, and then only briefly. Today the Crazy Horses and the Sitting Bulls are gone. In their places are men who wear three-piece suits and drive expensive cars. Organizations have sprouted like weeds over the reservations. Each claims to have the power and the leadership to set things straight. But all organizations do is rearrange history. It takes movement to write history, and that's where George fits in. He knows how to make things move."

Bluntly, Jesse said, "I don't like him."

Carly smiled at that. "He said the same thing about you."

"What else did he say about me?"

"He told me to be careful around you."

His eyes were bright and intense upon her face. "He's right, you know."

Those dark eyes burned with the hot fire of eagerness, of raw, primitive lust that made Carly's heart thump in her chest. "And you? What do you want that brings you to a place like this?"

He answered simply, "To do my job."

"At whatever the cost?"

"Look, Carly, we all do what we have to to get by. You tend the sick, and in your spare time you make fiery speeches about the land. Me, I make money. Whatever works, you know?"

"Call it whatever you want," she replied. "But men bent on plunder usually find ways to get it. We've seen it before. We're seeing it now." She was thinking of the ten lives lost in the past three years, and God knew how many others she wasn't aware of.

"I've never plundered anything in my life," Jesse said defensively. "I pay a fair price for what I want."

"Fair? Before the white man came the Indians lived in harmony with nature. They depended on no one but themselves. In the past few hundred years we've seen the destruction of that harmonious life. In its place is a dependency on the government that provides only a marginal existence at best. Is that fair?"

"Life isn't always fair," he told her. "Besides, you make it sound hopeless."

"It must have seemed pretty hopeless a hundred years ago to our grandfathers, but *they* never gave up."

"Are you suggesting that *I* have?"

She replied with a shrug that said it all.

"My great-great-grandfather and my uncle may have been warriors, Carly, but I'm just a businessman. Why should *I* fight for the land?"

"Because you're an Indian. And because the war isn't over."

He arched a dark brow at her and observed, "You seem to have fared pretty well."

"Indians display a miraculous resiliency," she responded. "It's because we are Indians first and all else second that we've survived."

"Yes, but if you want to go on surviving, maybe you'd better consider what it takes to live in this world."

"And what is that?"

"Money," he answered. "Plain and simple. It takes money to eat, money to put a roof over your head. You can't ignore those facts, Carly."

Her blue eyes flashed at him through the darkness. "Figures! Is that all you can think about? All right, I'll give you some figures. Indians were remarkably healthy, even disease-free, before the arrival of the European settlers. Today, Indian life expectancy is about seven years less than that of non-Indians. The Indian death rate is one-and-a-half times that of the total U.S. population. About six percent of the country's population are problem drinkers, but estimates for Indians range from twenty to eighty percent. The

Indian death rate from alcoholism is five times that of the American population. Shall I go on?''

Tersely, he replied, ''I get the point.''

''If you do, then surely you must see what you're doing when you come out here trying to buy land that doesn't belong to you, or when you make it easy for the power companies to take over.''

''It's my job, damn it!'' His angry bellow crushed her voice. ''And I don't need you to tell me how to do it!''

Carly sucked in her breath and turned away, hot tears stinging her eyes. She was a fool for trying to make him understand. She fumbled with the latch on the door, fingers shaking treacherously in an attempt to get it open.

''What are you doing?'' Jesse exclaimed.

Without answering, she flung the door open.

''Are you crazy?'' he shouted. ''It's pouring out there!''

But Carly was beyond hearing him as she jumped from the car. Instantly, she sank ankle-deep in mud. She looked down at the dark slime that had swallowed her feet. She pulled one foot out with a sucking noise and set it down, then did the same with the other as she hurried away from the car as rapidly as the driving rain and sucking mud would allow.

In seconds she was soaked clear through to her skin. Her clothes were matted to her body and her hair was plastered to her face in thick clumps. But Carly was oblivious to her discomfort as she stalked off down the road. Somewhere above the roar of the storm she heard Jesse's deep voice shouting after her, but she didn't stop. She hated him, his insensitivity, his blind determination to do his job no matter what the consequences. Let him sit in that infernal car until hell froze over!

She stumbled along, not caring that her shoes were ruined or that she had a good three miles to go before she reached home. She wanted only to get away from him.

Suddenly Carly felt rough fingers close around her arm to spin her around.

It was Jesse. He had come after her. She could see the fury that turned his dark eyes hard and cold. She struggled to break away from his painful grip, but he only held tighter. In her own blind fury she fought him, raining blows against his chest with her balled fists. "Let go of me!" she cried.

He pulled her close, so close that she could hear his voice above the storm, in a harsh whisper close to her ear. "Go ahead," he told her. "Fight me. Say no all you want. It won't change what's happening or what's about to happen."

In the hard, driving rain he pulled her savagely into his embrace and crushed her mouth beneath his. They fell to the ground together, and his lips bruised hers with fierce kisses as they rolled over and over in the mud.

The rain felt like pebbles pelting their bodies. A lance of lightning lit the sky, illuminating the forms on the ground below, which were covered in mud. And then the sky went dark again, sealing them off from the rest of the world so that none but they would know that she had ceased to struggle and lay still beneath him, heart throbbing, as he kissed her.

Chapter 5

The sound of a bird chirping outside the window awakened her. Her eyelids fluttered open and she stirred. Her black hair was spread like a fan against the pillow. Arching her back like a contented kitten, she yawned and stretched her arms over her head. Into her nostrils wafted the scent of the earth, which was still damp from last night's downpour. She could hear the leaves of the big cottonwood rustling against the weathered timbers of the house.

Carly was smiling without knowing it, feeling strangely content as morning came upon her. And then she remembered last night, the kiss in the rain, the feel of the mud swallowing her body, the heat from within that had threatened to consume her, and she bolted upright in bed. It was just a kiss, she told herself, no more than that. And yet it had scorched her down to her very soul, leaving her weak and uncertain and shamefully wanting more.

She swung her legs around to the side of the bed and sat there for a few moments, recalling the kiss in the mud that had sucked the breath from her lungs. There had been no tenderness in him, no gentleness, as his mouth had plundered hers. He had kissed her savagely, exploringly, hungrily, in every conceivable way, it seemed. And if it were possible to be taken by a kiss alone, then that was the way she felt. The warmth of his body pressed to hers had been like the heat from a forest aflame, burning through the soggy fabric of her clothes, past her skin, setting her insides on fire.

There had been no words, only needs, only feelings. As his mouth had closed over hers, he had given her no choice but to want it as much as he did. His mouth had demanded so skillfully that she was giving before she'd even been aware of it. She'd known he would feel like that, strong, lean and smooth. What she hadn't known was what he would taste like. She had found out last night. Her cheeks reddened at the thought of how she had responded to his forceful kisses—not with outrage—but with a forcefulness of her own. She had wanted his strength—not just the muscles and the brawn but the inner strength she had sensed in him from the beginning. And he had given it. In those few furious minutes in the mud, he had given her a glimpse of the strength beneath the arrogance. It had both excited and frightened her. If his kiss had the power to drain her, what would it be like, she dared to wonder, to make love with him? They had not spoken a single word the rest of the way home. What had there been to say?

She glanced apprehensively toward the bedroom door. What could she say to him this morning? "Good morning" seemed somehow inappropriate. "Did you sleep well?" No, that would not do.

Carly got up and went to the vanity, where a look in the mirror revealed a faint flush to her cheeks. Hoping that Jesse would not notice it, she pulled on a robe and left the room.

She expected to be greeted by the aroma of fresh-brewed coffee permeating the house, but there wasn't any. Nor was Jesse's masculine form stretched out over the sofa. A sudden sense of panic shot through her. Would he have left without saying goodbye?

Carly had a feeling of something missing as she quickly showered and dressed. Could it be that she had gotten used to his abrasive, forceful presence in just a few short days?

The sun was shining brightly when she left the house, dark braids swinging about her shoulders as she made her way to the barn to saddle Janey for the ride to Emma's. She entered the musty barn and stopped short. The brown mare was not in her stall. Tacked to a splintered post, however, was a note. In a large, sweeping stroke that she knew had to be Jesse's she read, "Gone to see Emma Huggins. See you later." It was signed simply "J".

Carly's face went pale. How dared he help himself to her horse! And how dared he assume that his business with Emma was more important than hers! Carly stalked from the barn in a fit of rage.

Back in the house she went straight to the phone. Fingers shaking, she dialed Luke Lightfoot's number. There was no answer. Slamming down the receiver, she tried George Gonzalez. Again no answer. Where were your friends when you needed them? she wondered. Without a car or a horse she had no way to get to Emma's—or, for that matter, anywhere else. She was stuck there until Jesse decided to return. And to think that she had let him kiss her last night! This time when Carly's cheeks burned scarlet, it was with pure anger. Maybe George was right about Jesse after all. Maybe he was the kind of man who could not be trusted. She could just picture his eyes brimming with triumph.

Those same dark eyes that Carly cursed were moving over the land, taking in the subtle changes that otherwise would have gone unnoticed except to one who was watching. His body moved rhythmically to the gait of the mare as he surveyed the surrounding country. There was a primitive kind of beauty about the land, a raw and hungry ruggedness not unlike the people who inhabited it.

The wind whispered through the dark needles of the pines. His nostrils filled with the pungent scent of the sagebrush. A cry from overhead lifted his gaze skyward. A hawk circled the clear blue sky in a slow, wide arc, wings spread to capture the currents of air. With its crystal-sharp vision it spotted something moving on the ground below, and, drawing its wings close to its body, it dived with balletic grace and disappeared from sight beyond the trees. The sun was like hot, soothing fingers against his skin, massaging the tension out of his muscles as he rode on into the lengthening day.

In his pocket he carried a checkbook. His father had said to do whatever he must to get that woman off the land. All right, then, everyone had a price. He'd write her a check for as much as she wanted. And if that didn't work, well, he'd worry about that later.

But there was something about this whole thing that left a sour taste in Jesse's mouth. Why were those two hundred acres so important? Why not another two hundred acres, or five hundred, or a thousand? Did the men at Laramie Fork know something he didn't? And why him? Why was *he* the one given the dirty job of forcing the old woman to move from the only place she'd ever known as home? Oh, sure, he knew what the answer was, for he'd asked his father. The old man had given him one of his rare smiles and alluded to Jesse's way with women, even old ones. "And if that doesn't work, you can always impress her with your being part Indian." He had uttered the word with a snarl, his smile disappearing behind a scowl. Why? Jesse wondered. Why did his father hate not only his own Indian heritage but every-

thing Indian? Russell's father had been half Sioux, so it
wasn't that there was even all that much Indian blood in the
family. But it was there, and Russell did not like it. Jesse had
no doubt that if the Blackmoon name had not come with the
family business that Russell had inherited, his father would
have shortened it to Black long ago. There was no sense
changing the name of an internationally known company,
though, and Jesse guessed that his father carried the Blackmoon name around with a measure of extreme tolerance.

The night before he left for South Dakota, Jesse had
spoken to his mother about it, but as always she'd been
strangely reticent on the subject of her husband's preju-
dice. Jesse gave a derisive snort when he thought of how
ironic it was that she, a white woman, had borne no preju-
dice when she married a man who was part Indian.

Jesse had always felt a little sorry for his mother. It could
not have been easy for her, living with a man who was married to his business and who'd had countless affairs with
other women. Somehow, she had endured. Indeed, the years
only added to her ability to withstand her husband's harsh-
ness. Something—Jesse knew not what—kept his mother's
spirit alive. Something burned strongly in her still-lovely
eyes, something that refused to dim no matter how lonely
she became. Jesse had often wondered how she could love
a man like his father. Who knew? Maybe she didn't. But the
look that came over her face when she thought no one was
watching could only be described as love. Jesse shook his
head in wonder. What a strange dichotomy his parents represented, one filled with unexplained hatred, the other
brimming with unexplained love.

And where did he fit in? At times there seemed to be two
people inside him battling for supremacy over a divided
soul. Emma had told him that somewhere inside him was a
third person who was the best of both worlds. Could it be?
Would the day ever come when he would actually feel at

peace with himself, when he would be comfortable inside his own skin, red, white or whatever color it was?

There was something about the people he had met out here that he envied. Despite the poverty and the cultural repression that Carly spoke of, at least they knew who they were. The truth was, he didn't know who he was or what he was doing here. What had he said to Carly about the importance of making money? He had to laugh. It was as if he'd been trying to convince himself of it. There had to be something more important than making money. There *had* to be.

But what? Land? Love? A woman? Something suddenly churned inside him, and he thought of the kiss in the mud last night. Carly McAllister was all those things. Her body did things to him that drove him wild with desire. But it was more than the physical need a man has for a woman. She was vibrant and alive in ways he had not thought existed. She was filled with a purpose that he, with all of his wealth and cunning, envied and admired. He had been handed things all his life—money, position, women. She'd had to struggle every inch of the way. He had become jaded, disillusioned. She refused to give up on her dreams. There were a few things about the cold, hard world that he could teach her, but he also had much to learn from the Indian woman with the flashing blue eyes and the sweet-grass fragrance.

The sight of the tar paper shack in the distance tugged Jesse's thoughts back to the matter at hand. With grim determination he urged the mare into a trot. He reined up before the shack and climbed down from the saddle. His legs felt rubbery when they hit the ground. It was a long time since he'd been on a horse. Three sharp raps on the door brought no response. He called out to her. Still nothing. He looked around, squinting against the glare of the sunlight. The place was eerily quiet. He walked around back and climbed to the top of the grassy hill. In the distance he saw the pine-covered slopes of the Black Hills. He caught himself wondering what visions waited in that place, which was supposed to be so sacred. Dismissing the thought, he looked around for a sign of Emma, but she was nowhere to be seen. Muttering to himself, he walked down the hill, went back to the front door and tested the knob. The door opened and he stepped inside.

Carly sat on the ground cross-legged, oblivious to the little crawlings and scratchings of insects around her as she worked in her garden. She was, to put it mildly, fit to be tied, venting her anger on the weeds, pulling them out by their roots and tossing them into a heap to be cleaned up later.

It was hours since Jesse had ridden off, leaving her without any means of transportation to make her rounds. This wasn't New York. She couldn't very well hop on a bus or take the subway. She couldn't even stick her arm out and hail a taxi. Leave it to him to have gotten himself good and lost by now. Well, it served him right.

She could just imagine him wiping the sweat from his brow with the back of his sleeve, muttering harsh epithets in that deep, growling voice of his as he wandered around in aimless circles, looking for the way back to Broken Bow. There were no air-conditioned cafés to run into out there on the plains, no swimming pools to cool off in. If he was lucky, he'd find his way back before the hottest part of the day. If he was smart, he'd get Janey into the shade. If, if, if, Carly thought as she tugged furiously at the weeds. *If*, the most useless word in the English language.

Consumed as she was by her ire, Carly did not hear the sound of a horse's hooves approaching the house. It was only a familiar whinny that brought her head up and spun it around. She jumped up and raced around to the front of the house. There was Janey, looking tired but none the worse for the wear. Astride her was Jesse, his dark eyes fixed on Carly.

She took a step forward, then stopped. Something was wrong. She felt the anger wash out of her like water from a broken dam, leaving her cold and weak and unable to move. One word scratched at the back of her throat. "Emma."

Jesse nudged the mare forward and brought her to stand before Carly's frozen form. He looked down into her wide, frightened eyes and said, "Emma's dead."

Carly placed the receiver back in its cradle and turned away from the telephone. Her voice throbbed painfully in her throat. "The autopsy report will tell us for sure, but it's too soon for that. There preliminary findings point to insulin shock."

Jesse rose from the sofa and went to her. "Insulin shock?" His dark eyes were bright with questioning. "But how?"

She gave a dull shake of her head. "I don't know."

She moved past him and went to the front door. Outside the moon was bright and full in the dark sky. Carly moved as if in a dream to the edge of the porch and stood for a long time looking out into the fathomless night. What a day it had been, filled with the kind of things nightmares were made of. Once the initial shock of the news of Emma's death wore off, she had made a frantic call to Luke. She was thankful he had just gotten in. He had come racing over in his new pickup truck, and the three of them had gone back to Emma's shack. Luckily, Jesse had had the presence of mind not to move the body. After Carly conducted a perfunctory examination, they'd carefully placed Emma's body in the truck and driven to the hospital in Pine Ridge.

Hours later Luke had dropped them off at Carly's place. At that point the cause of death had been still unknown, although Carly's trained eye had recognized the signs. The preliminary findings had only confirmed the fears churning in her stomach. Insulin shock. The words seemed to make no sense.

Had Emma taken too large a dosage? Had someone tampered with the vials Carly had put in Emma's ice-box the other day? Once again there were too many unanswered questions. And another Pine Ridge Indian had become a statistic.

Carly sensed Jesse's presence behind her even before she felt his strong hand upon her shoulder. The heat of his fingers penetrated the cool cotton of her shirt. She turned around to face him. In a fading voice she told him, "You should have no trouble turning that land over to Laramie Fork now."

Through the moonlight he searched her wan face. "What are you talking about?" He knew what she was saying, but there was something in her tone that made him question her.

"That land was as good as Emma's. We all knew it, even if she had no deed."

"Carly, that's private land," Jesse asserted. "She had no claim to it." Emma's death had shaken him up, more so than he cared to admit, but it changed nothing.

"What difference does it make now?" Carly shook her head in sad disillusionment. "You can go back to New York now and tell your boss, whatever his name is, that your mission was a success."

Jesse's hand dropped to his side as if he'd been struck. His black eyes flared at the accusing tone, no matter how softly her words had been spoken. "Are you saying that I had anything to do with Emma's death?"

"Of course not. Not you. But everything you stand for. Don't you see, Jesse?" She searched his handsome face long and hard. A cry welled up in her throat. "My God, you don't, do you?" Turning, Carly fled from the porch out into the waiting night. Minutes later she reappeared astride

Janey's bare back, galloping far out onto the moonlit prairie.

She needed to get away from it all, from him, from his eyes, which followed her everywhere and had the unnerving ability to unhinge her. She needed to breathe in the clear, fresh air of the prairie, to clear her head so that she could think rationally. She rode with abandon, black hair streaming out behind her in the night breeze, listening to the earth reverberating as the horse's hooves struck the dry ground, feeling the wall of her chest throb with the beating of her heart. Nothing made sense anymore, least of all her feelings for the dark-eyed Easterner. Who should she trust? George, who'd told her to be careful of Jesse? Jesse, who hinted that she should be careful of George? Luke, whose lies had left her with too many questions? Her own heart, which had deceived her once before?

He was sitting on the porch waiting for her when she returned many hours later, long after midnight. She led Janey into the barn, rubbed the horse down and joined him on the porch. For a long time they both sat there without speaking. The air was still and warm. Crickets chirped in chorus, and the bullfrogs croaked from the creek. After a while Carly's voice infiltrated the tense space between them; it was a whisper filled with bitterness and pain. "It's the sacred places. More than a hundred years ago our forefathers fought and died for this land. Today our people are still dying for it. Look around you, Jesse. Emma Huggins died for it."

He wanted to come close to her, but he knew that any attempt to touch her would be met with resistance. "Talk to me, Carly," he whispered. "Tell me what's wrong. What's going on out here?"

"I don't know. It's the land. Something about the land." She drew in a breath, and with her back pressed up against a post, she told him about the shocking pattern she had unearthed. When she was finished, she looked down at her hands that lay limp in her lap. "You must think I'm crazy. Everyone else does."

He used this moment of painful vulnerability to move closer to her, if only just to inhale the sweet fragrance that emanated from her long, dark hair. "No, I don't," he said. "I don't think you're crazy at all." If anyone was crazy, he was. Crazy for feeling the way he did about her. "Is it only at Pine Ridge?" he questioned her. "Are they dying on the other reservations as well?"

She shook her head. "The people in these parts have always considered themselves lucky because they live so close to the sacred Black Hills. Now it seems that anyone who owns land within a hundred-mile radius of the hills has reason to fear for his or her life."

"Does anyone else know about this?"

"Sure. Everyone knows what's happening, but no one wants to admit it. They all make up excuses, and bit by bit we're losing our land. Private land is one thing, Jesse. As angry as I get at times over what your boss is doing to his land, still, it's his land to do with as he pleases."

There was an imperceptible tensing of his muscles as she said this. What would she think if she knew whose land it really was? Was she even familiar with the Blackmoon name? Judging from the innocence of her expression, he guessed not. Well, that wasn't so unusual, he surmised. His family had always kept a low profile in the area, having scarcely anything to do with the land except to lease it to Laramie Fork. No, he decided, it was possible she had never even heard the name Blackmoon.

"But Indian land is something else," Carly was saying. "In 1871 the U.S. Government ceded the land of this reservation and the hills to the Sioux nation because it considered the land had little value. Then Custer found gold in the hills, and ever since then we've been fighting for what's rightfully ours.''

"But why? What else beside coal and gold is under this land?"

"I don't know. Nothing, as far as I know. Certainly the gold is no secret. They've been mining it for more than a hundred years."

"And you're absolutely certain those people were killed for their land?"

She looked up at him with pleading eyes. "Yes. I'm absolutely certain of it. At first I thought it was just a gruesome coincidence, but not anymore. It was something Johnny Starbuck said as he lay dying. I paid no attention to it at first. It sounded like he was saying 'Shoot self.' So I figured that the coroner's report was right after all, and that Johnny really did shoot himself in the chest with his hunting rifle. But the more I thought about it, the more it bothered me. How, Jesse? How can you shoot yourself in the chest with a rifle? A shot at such close range would have blown his body to pieces, but it didn't. There was just a hole, a neat, round hole smack dab in the middle of his heart. No powder burns. Nothing. Just that awful little hole with a red ring of blood around it. And then I realized what Johnny had really said that day. It was 'Shoot . . . sell.' He was trying to tell me something about selling his land. He wouldn't sell, so someone shot him."

Jesse ran a hand through his thick black hair, sweeping some loose strands from his eyes. "Carly, I just don't know. Do you have proof?"

Proof was the one thing she did not have. She did not tell him about her suspicions where Luke was concerned, how Luke's stories didn't add up. Maybe she just didn't want to admit to herself that Luke was somehow involved in all of this grisly mess. "Anyone who's smart enough to kill ten people isn't about to leave proof," she said.

"Eleven," Jesse corrected her.

She got to her feet, bringing him to his beside her. As she turned to go, she felt his touch, ever so light, upon her arm. In that moment she knew what would happen, but she did not have the strength to stop it. She was in his arms, feeling their warm strength going around her, pulling her close. He softly kissed her fragrant neck and buried his face in the pliant flesh as he fit his lean, tall body to hers. He mumbled something as his mouth edged to the corner of hers, where it lingered for an instant before covering hers fully.

Carly felt smothered by the warm lips moving over hers, drugged by the taste of him, wonderfully alive as if infused with sudden electric energy. Her own mouth began to stir beneath his, hesitantly at first, then boldly, and suddenly all her fears were forgotten as she stood captive in his embrace.

He groaned deep in his throat and spoke something into the dark hollow of her mouth. His lips moved with the same urgency as hers, an urgency born of suppressed emotions and hunger too long denied. He could almost pinpoint the precise moment when the last of her resistance gave way to surrender. Her lips parted easily when his tongue thrust forward, seeking, needing a closer intimacy.

Carly's breathing was labored, painful in her chest, but it was an exquisite pain that tortured her now. She moaned softly when his lips burned hot across her cheek to her neck, which was achingly bared to him.

"Carly, what are you doing to me?" he whispered raggedly against her flesh.

Her response was to draw his mouth to hers again and kiss him. It was so good to be in his arms, to feel warm and protected, safe, wanted. To feel the passion that ruled the moment without fear of the consequences. His kisses took her to a place far from the reality of Pine Ridge, light-years away from Johnny Starbuck and Emma Huggins and the others. For a few turbulent moments none of that existed as Carly surrendered to her need.

In the next moment the need was gone, like dust in the wind, when Jesse pulled his head away and looked at her expectantly. She had no trouble reading the look in his eyes. It was asking for—no, demanding—more. Carly blinked and blushed deeply. Into her still-spinning mind came the sound of his voice the night he had caught up to her in the rain. *"Say no all you want,"* he had told her. *"It won't change what's happening or what's about to happen."* Maybe it was the thought of precisely what was about to happen that spiraled Carly back to earth. She was suddenly all too conscious of her surroundings—the hot, still night air, the weariness in her limbs, eleven unsolved murders.

By the light of the stars he saw the expression on her face change, and he knew he had lost her for now. The blood still surged through his veins, and the arousal she had elicited in him would not be so quick to subside, but when he saw the fears return to trouble her beautiful face, he knew not to press the matter.

She spoke in a low voice, not trusting it to remain steady. "I'm tired, Jesse. Really tired. I'm going to bed."

Jesse remained outside long after Carly had gone. By degrees his breathing returned to an even pitch as he stood on the porch looking out at the night, thinking. Now that Emma Huggins was dead and the problem of getting her to move off his land apparently solved, he no longer had a valid reason to stay in Broken Bow. Now the deal with Laramie Fork could go through without a hitch. Still, there was something that bothered him. He thought about what Carly had told him. Could it be gold that Laramie Fork was so interested in? He expelled a frustrated sigh. Forget about Denmark; something was rotten right here in Broken Bow.

There was only one way to get to the bottom of this. The answer, he knew, was back in New York. Somewhere within the vast files of BMI lay the reason Laramie Fork Power Company was willing to pay such a high price for a tract of land not much good for anything.

Chapter 6

Carly rolled over and opened an eye at the clock beside the bed. Eleven o'clock! She never slept this late! Nor had she ever slept quite so soundly. She hadn't even dreamed. It was as if she had been tossed into a silent void without images, memories or pain, a void so quiet it had a sound all its own.

She lay there staring up at the ceiling, following with her eyes a crack in the wooden beam as it snaked out of sight, when the shrill sound of the telephone intruded upon her consciousness. She didn't move, hoping that Jesse would answer it. But the phone kept ringing. Carly pulled the pillow over her head and scrunched down deeper in the covers. When she could stand the sound no longer, she threw the pillow aside and jumped out of bed, muttering some choice Sioux swear words.

The man must have nerves of steel, she griped as she hastened to put an end to the awful caterwauling of the phone. She rushed to the desk.

Rubbing the sleep from her eyes, she said, "Hello?"

"Hi, Carly. It's me."

Her eyes snapped open, and her head spun in the direction of the couch. She expected to see Jesse's masculine form beneath the sheet and a hint of his dark head from beneath the pillow, but the couch was empty. "Jesse?"

"Yeah."

"Where are you calling from?"

There was a pause, then, "New York."

Carly gave a little laugh. Surely he was joking. "New York? What are you doing there?"

"I live here, remember?"

He lived there. Of course. How simple. Still, she did not understand. "When did you—"

"I didn't want to wake you."

She could feel her muscles beginning to stiffen. Like well-trained soldiers they came to attention. "I see," she said evenly. "When did you leave?"

"Before dawn."

"But how?"

"You said it yourself once. Don't you remember? You said all it would take is one quick phone call to get me everything I need within the hour."

Silence.

"So, anyhow," he went on, "I didn't want you to think I had run out on you."

"Sneaking out in the middle of the night certainly has all the appearances of it, though, doesn't it?"

He responded sharply to the accusing tone. "Look, I'm sorry. Really. I had to get back to the office. I'll explain it later. Right now there are some business matters I have to take care of."

Her voice sounded strained, a bit too high-pitched to be convincing. "Sure, Jesse, whatever you say. Hey, what difference does it make? I mean, it's not like we owe each other anything."

"Carly, I—"

"Forget it. You don't need to explain to me. Like you said, we all do what we have to to get by. Take care of yourself, Jesse."

She hung up and for several minutes just stood there, staring down at the phone. Then her bottom lip began to tremble and a glistening teardrop appeared at the corner of her eye, followed by another and another, until the warm, salty tears were streaming down her cheeks and her slender shoulders shook with sobs.

When the phone rang again, Carly grabbed for it. "Hello? Jesse? Oh, I'm sorry. Yes, Doctor, what was that? Yes. Thank you."

It was the hospital in Pine Ridge calling to tell her that the medical supplies she needed were on their way. Jesse's handiwork, no doubt. But then, it was easy to throw your weight around when you had all that money behind you. If Carly didn't need the supplies so badly, she would have refused them. As it was, the fact that she was forced to swallow her stubborn pride for the sake of her empty medical supply cabinet only made her feel worse.

She'd been a fool to trust him. No wonder he'd left before the break of day, stealing away like a thief in the night. Murder had a way of scaring people off. For some crazy reason, though, she had thought Jesse was different. He didn't seem to be the type who scared easily. But maybe it wasn't the murders that had scared him off. Maybe it was her. Had he been able to tell that she was falling in love with him? Or was it his style to entrance a woman with his good looks and then leave her? She forced herself to remember that he had not promised to love her. All he had promised were the medical supplies, and those he had delivered. Still, she hated him for the ease with which he had manipulated her heart. She hated herself even more for having let it happen.

* * *

Sixteen hundred miles away, Jesse turned away from the Manhattan skyline that was emerging into the daylight through the window of his Upper East Side apartment. He was angry with himself. Here he was, the guy who'd always been in control, suddenly reeling out of control where this woman was concerned. She had every right to be mad at him for the way he had left without saying goodbye. But he knew she would have asked too many questions. He had grappled with himself over whether to awaken her as he had stood over her bed, watching her sleep. He had leaned close to brush a strand of ebony hair from her face and to breathe in the sweet ambrosia of her skin, which was pink from sleep. He had been gripped by the desire to take her in his arms and make fierce love to her. But to do so would have been to disturb the peace he guessed was a rare commodity for her these days, judging from everything she had told him. He could have left a note, but he decided against it. The first thing he wanted her to hear upon waking was his voice, even if it did come from sixteen hundred miles away. Anything less would have been cowardly.

Yet where had his bravery been on the phone just now, when he should have told her how he really felt? Telling a woman how much he wanted her had come easy to him in the past. Most of the women he knew expected to hear it anyway. But this woman was different, and maybe it was because he did want her so much that he had a hard time saying it. It scared him a little, too, for it went far beyond the flesh. Yes, he wanted to feel her soft skin pressed to his, wanted to taste the sweetness of her—but he also wanted to know the essence of her, to experience in her the fulfillment of his needs that went deeper than mere physical desire. Where Carly McAllister was concerned, Jesse's emotions were giving his libido a run for its money. But it was more than his own fears that led him just shy of telling her how he felt. It was the mixed message he was getting from her. It was driving him crazy with frustration and anticipation, for despite the frost in her voice on the phone just now, there had been compliance in her lips that night they had kissed in the mud on the lonely road to Broken Bow, and a momentary surrender when he had held her in his arms on the porch beneath the stars.

Jesse showered and shaved, dressed in a tan summer suit, light blue shirt and dark blue tie, and took the elevator to the lobby. The doorman greeted him when he strode out into the humid morning air. "Good morning, Mr. Blackmoon. Can I get you a cab?"

"Morning, Ernie. Yes, thanks."

The shrill whistle of the red-capped doorman brought a taxi to the curb. Jesse climbed inside. "The BMI building, Park between Fifty-second and Fifty-third," he instructed the cigar-chomping driver.

The yellow taxi sped down Second Avenue. At Fifty-third Street it made a sharp right, cutting off another cab in the process and bringing a string of expletives their way. At Park it turned left and pulled up to the curb before a glass building that bore the letters BMI in black marble over the revolving doors of the main entrance. Jesse paid the fare and hurried inside.

His nerves were on edge and the day had barely begun. The effects of the city traffic, the heat rising from the pavement, the bodies rushing to and fro in the midst of the morning rush hour, his phone call to Carly, all converged upon him as he stepped off the elevator on the forty-fourth floor. With long, tigerlike strides he walked to his office and closed the door behind him. He stood there for a few moments with his back pressed against the door, catching his breath, steeling himself for the day. Then he went to his desk and buzzed his secretary.

"Bring me in the file on Laramie Fork. Then get my father on the line."

Minutes later a manila file folder was placed before him. He rustled through it but found nothing unusual. But then, he hadn't really expected to. The intercom buzzer brought his head up. He recognized the voice of his father's secretary when he answered it. "Hi, Helen. Yeah, I'm back. Is he in? Good. I'll be right up."

The gray-haired woman in the silk print dress looked up from her work when Jesse walked in. He leaned on her desk with both hands and flashed a disarming smile. "Egad, woman, you get more beautiful every day."

"Oh, hush, you scamp," she said, laughing. Then, gesturing toward the heavy oak door of Russell Blackmoon's office, she said, "Go on in. He's expecting you."

"In a minute. First, tell me something, Helen. Is there anything going on with Laramie Fork that I don't know about?"

"Why, no, Jesse, not that I know of."

"Do me a favor, would you? If you hear of anything— about Laramie Fork, I mean—will you let me know?"

Although she answered to the elder Blackmoon, she rarely denied Jesse a favor. It was the mother hen in her, she supposed, for she had known him since he was a boy. She answered without hesitation. "Of course, Jesse."

Russell Blackmoon was on his private line when Jesse walked into the wood-paneled office. He went to the mirrored bar and leaned back on one elbow, looking bored and disinterested while his father wrapped up his conversation.

When the older man hung up, Jesse sauntered over to the oversize mahogany desk and sat down in one of the armchairs before it. The chairs before the desk were of such a height that the occupants were seated slightly lower than the man behind the desk. One was left with the distinct feeling of being somehow beneath him, as though he were looking down his strong aquiline nose at one. It gave Russell the undisputed edge. But Russell knew it took considerably more than the seating arrangements to manipulate his son the way he did clients and business associates. He hadn't been successful, though, at breaking that streak of arrogance, something the elder Blackmoon had been trying to accomplish for thirty-eight years. It was there now in the tone of voice and the casual lifting of one corner of the mouth in a travesty of a smile. "It's good to see you, too, Dad."

Russell hid his feelings well. It was one of the reasons he was such a wealthy and important man. There was no sense in letting one's emotions show in the boardroom. Perhaps that was why he was able to continue in the same level tone despite the fact that his son's sardonic reply made him boil inside. "I was expecting you to call. What's the matter? Don't they have any telephones out there?"

Jesse said, "I got tied up."

"With what?"

He flinched inwardly at the commanding tone. "With something you wouldn't be interested in."

Russell snorted at that. "You're right. I wouldn't be interested in your sex life. But I am interested in the land."

"The land's all yours."

"You mean you got the old woman to move?" Russell's green eyes lit up.

Those green eyes were Russell's saving grace, the one thing that showed he was no Indian. They had come to him by way of his great-grandmother, a white woman whom the Oglala warrior Black Moon had married. Irish, she had been, with hair as red as the setting sun and eyes as green as the Black Hills in the springtime. There they were now, the same emerald eyes that had captured the heart of a fierce Sioux warrior, staring back at Jesse with eagerness.

Jesse replied, "Not exactly."

"But you said—"

"The old woman's been taken care of?"

"How much did it cost us?"

"Is that all you can think about?"

"I'm running a business here, Jesse. Whether you like it or not, money is what it's all about." Those green eyes narrowed with suspicion. "Why the sudden aversion to money? It never used to bother you before."

"Let's just say I've discovered a few things it can't buy."

Russell waved his hand at the ridiculous thought. "Nonsense. There's nothing money can't buy. I'm surprised you haven't learned that yet. Which brings me back to my initial question. How much did it cost us?"

"Us, Dad? It didn't cost *us* anything. It cost that old woman a hell of a lot, though." He rose and said, "There's something funny going on with Laramie Fork. I think we ought to check into it before we go ahead with this deal."

"That's impossible," scoffed Russell. "The papers are ready to be signed. Of course, they would have already been signed if they hadn't gone up in smoke along with the rest of your car. I heard about the accident from your mother. Apparently, you saw fit to tell her about it, but not me. Well, that's as it may be. But as far as Laramie Fork is concerned, I've had a new set of documents drawn up. The men from Laramie Fork are flying in themselves this week to sign them."

"Just give me a few days," Jesse urged. "Let me check into this thing. If everything's okay, then we'll go ahead."

Russell rose from his leather swivel chair to glower at his son from across the massive desk. "I said *no*! This deal will go through when *I* say it will go through. Do you understand me, Jesse?"

As always, Jesse refused to back down to his father's furious look but chose to meet it head on. "Maybe there's something *you* don't understand. People are dying out there, and it has something to do with the land and with this deal.''

"That's ridiculous. What's the matter, Jesse? Have a few days under the hot sun fried your brains? The men at Laramie Fork aren't killers. Besides, this deal is worth millions to us in the long run. Millions."

Something fierce was welling up in those dark eyes. "You don't give a damn, do you?"

"About those people? There's nothing I can do to help them."

"You're wrong, Dad. You can do something. You can wait to sign those documents until I get to the bottom of this thing."

Green eyes clashed with black, neither giving way for several furious moments. Slowly, stressing each word, Russell told his son, "I said no."

Jesse tore his gaze away from his father's and strode angrily to the door. It was impossible to be involved with a man like his father and not be manipulated to some extent. Business associates and employees were more easily manipulated, but even the lesser extent to which Jesse was subject had grown too much for him. This was where it stopped. With one hand grasping the doorknob, knuckles whitening under the pressure, he turned to look back at Russell over his shoulder. "There's a meeting of the board of directors tomorrow. You may as well know that I plan to bring this matter up before them."

Russell sat back down and folded his hands across his chest. There was a smugness about him as he replied, "You can tell them whatever you like, but I should warn you, they never forget who owns most of the voting shares in this corporation. *I* am BMI, and I suggest that you not forget it either, Jesse."

"That's right, Dad; you are BMI. But don't *you* forget what BMI stands for. It's Black Moon, Dad. Black Moon."

There was the slightest wince behind those green eyes, which would have gone undetected except for the fact that Jesse was watching so closely. It gave him a small measure of satisfaction to know that there was something he could do to bring about a reaction in his father—something other than anger, that is. With that, he turned and strode from the office, leaving the door open behind him.

Helen watched Jesse stalk out. She could not remember a time when those two had not argued like that. She shook her head sadly. That boy sure had a way of angering his father. Just then, at the sound of her name shouted gruffly from the inner office Helen turned toward her boss's door, which was still partly ajar from Jesse's hasty exit. From her desk she whisked up her steno pad and pencil and hurried to answer the call. Ordinarily, he summoned her via the intercom. She knew when he shouted like that, he was angry. "Yes, Mr. Blackmoon?"

"Take a letter to Laramie Fork," he said. When he finished dictating, he ordered, "Remind my son that he is expected to dinner tonight. Tell him his mother will be very disappointed if he is not there."

Russell watched Helen go from the room, a thin smile pressed on his lips. He had not finished with Jesse on this subject. Perhaps in the atmosphere of the house in Great Neck, over dinner, with his mother present, Jesse could be convinced not to go snooping where he shouldn't. He'd speak to Lucy about this, that's what he'd do. He would have her talk Jesse out of this damned-fool plan he had to check out Laramie Fork. Jesse had a softness for his mother. She had a way of getting him to do things when others couldn't. If she were to ask, he would not refuse.

There was something different about him. She knew it the moment he set foot in the room. She took his hand and pressed a kiss to his cheek before accepting the bouquet of lilies he had brought for her. She'd always had a fondness for lilies, and he had always known.

"Jesse," she said softly, smiling into her son's dark eyes, "it's so good to see you again."

He laughed in that deep, mellow voice that set the memories spinning wildly in her mind. "I've only been gone a few days, Mom."

"I know. It's just that I always miss you so much when you go out of town. It's as if..." Inwardly, she thought it was as if she would never see him again. "It's as if months have gone by," she said.

Jesse followed his mother into the kitchen, where she pointed to a crystal vase on a top shelf and he got it down for her. At the sink she filled it with water, then placed the flowers in it. Her slim hands moved gracefully over the delicate buds of baby's breath and inserted the slender stalks of each lily carefully into the vase.

"It doesn't feel like months," Jesse muttered as he watched her arrange the flowers at the kitchen table. It felt more like a whirlwind to him. "I see this heat wave hasn't broken yet. I didn't mind being away from this heat and humidity. I can tell you that. It may be hot out there, but it's—I don't know—it's—"

"Clear," said Lucy. "Still, yet moving with life."

Jesse smiled at her. "Yeah, I guess that's it. It's almost as if the clarity of the light somehow brings about a clarity of perception as well." He shrugged. "I know it sounds strange."

"Not at all. At least not to me."

No, it would not sound strange to her, would it? After all, she'd been born in South Dakota. Her father, a Norwegian shipowner, had been forced to give up his thriving maritime business and move to dry South Dakota because of his worsening asthma. Lucy had been born amid all that heat and dry air. Her father's ranch had bordered the Blackmoon property in those days. She had known the Black-moon boys, Russell and Jesse, all her life. Her father and theirs had feuded over the boundary lines of the land. The decades-old feud had come to an end, however, when she married Russell, combining the properties. A year later, at the age of eighteen, she had come east with her husband to begin life in an alien place.

"Do you ever miss it, Mom?" Jesse asked.

She looked up wistfully from the lilies. "Practically every day."

"Think you'll ever go back?"

"Good heavens, no!" she exclaimed. "Your father would never go back to that place again."

"I wasn't talking about him. I was talking about you."

For a moment she looked truly baffled. "But I would never go without your father."

"Why not? Why not do something for yourself for a change?"

She looked away and fiddled with the flowers. "Jesse, let's not start on that again, all right?"

His hand came out to clamp down over hers, stilling her movements and snapping her eyes up to his. "Don't you ever get tired of it?" he demanded. "Tired of running *his* house, managing *his* money, always doing things *his* way? Didn't you ever do anything for yourself?"

Lucy looked into her son's searching eyes, then lowered her gaze and said softly, "Once, a very long time ago."

Jesse loosened his grip and let her go. He couldn't be angry with her. There was still too much of that fair Norwegian beauty lurking in her features and too much tenderness in her heart to inspire much anger. He gave her a gentle smile and put an arm around her waist. "What's for dinner? I'm starved."

They strolled from the kitchen. "I had Mary put a couple of T-bones on the grill."

"Mmm," he murmured. "You must have been reading my mind. But how come only two? Isn't Dad eating with us?"

"No, he's not. He has to work late. He phoned a little while ago."

He felt her stiffen beneath his touch. "Oh, I get it," he said humorlessly. "So, you're the one who's supposed to work on me, is that it, Mom?"

"Now, Jesse—"

"Don't you see what he's doing? He's using you to get to me. I gave him a hard time at the office today."

"Yes, I know," said Lucy as she took a seat at the table, which was set for two. "About that Laramie Fork deal. Jesse, please, can't you let him handle this?"

Jesse sat down and looked at his mother forthrightly across the table. The glow of the candles softened his features, but not his tone. "No, Mother, I can't. This time it's gone too far. This time people's lives are at stake. Did he tell you that?"

"You know I never get involved in your father's business dealings."

He groaned audibly. "Not getting involved is different from not being told the truth."

"All right, Jesse, what is the truth?"

He told her.

She was silent for several minutes as she picked at the food in her plate. Then she looked up at him and said, "This is not your fight, Jesse. The people at the power company are not cheating *you* out of anything."

"But it *is* my fight," he insisted.

"You can't be responsible for what happens to some people who live thousands of miles away. Why not Africa, then? Or Pakistan? Why not feel guilty for the rest of your life because somewhere in the world someone is starving?"

He, too, had stopped eating and was looking into her eyes from across the candles. "This is different."

"How is it different?" she challenged.

"Because they are my people." He snorted derisively and said, "I used to think that my Indianness had been successfully bred out of me the way inferior traits are bred out of white mice. Dad never talked about it, and I never really knew Uncle Jesse, so—" He shrugged and dropped his gaze in time to miss the sudden tensing of his mother's posture. "Don't try to stop me from finding out who I really am."

Lucy's heart skipped a beat in her chest. Now she knew what it was about him that was different. Just as she knew what his next words would be.

"It's the land."

A sob drowned deep in her throat. The land. Always it would be the land. Her father and Russell's father had battled over it—who owned the water rights and where the boundary lines were drawn on their adjacent properties. Russell had never had much use for his land. To him it was a means to increase his wealth, trading in parcels the way Jesse used to trade in baseball cards when he was a boy. The land had been everything to Jess, though. He had lived for it, worked it, ultimately died for it. Jess. Would a day go by that she did not think of him in some way?

Lucy Blackmoon looked into her son's dark eyes and felt herself transported back in time to when she was a girl and had been invited to the Blackmoons' for the first time for Sunday dinner. Looking up from her plate she had found young Jess's eyes upon her, dark, deep and bright. The eyes of an Indian. Remembering made Lucy realize that it was useless to argue with her son. She asked, "What will you do?"

In that growl she recognized so well, he said, "For one thing, I plan to bar the sale of any more Blackmoon land to Laramie Fork. Then I plan to challenge every company that enjoys a cheap lease on reservation land. I may not be able to stop them from leasing reservation land, but I can damned well make them pay fair prices for it. If it comes down to a fight, I'm ready for it."

"You'll be fighting against your father. You know that, don't you?"

Jesse was silent as he contemplated the extent of those words. He had opposed his father before in business matters, but this time it was different. His eyes moved over his mother's still-youthful features. He trusted her judgment.

"What do *you* think, Mom? Do you think I'm doing the right thing?"

Russell had counted on Jesse's going to Lucy. The bond between mother and son was a strong one, and he thought all Lucy had to do to steer Jesse away from the Laramie Fork project was say the right words. But he had not counted on his wife's reaction.

Lucy slid her hand across the table and covered Jesse's with it. Her flesh looked pale against the swarthy hue of his, her fingers almost sickly compared with the strong-boned fingers beneath hers. She gave his hand a reassuring squeeze. There was no talking him out of his stance, she knew, so she told him, "If you do not take this chance, Jesse, you cannot win."

Chapter 7

Luke Lightfoot swallowed the last of his beer and left the bar. Angrily, he thrust the key into the ignition of the pickup and peeled out of Broken Bow.

He drove tight-lipped, cursing himself for coming to town in the first place. What crazy idea had popped into his head that today might be a lucky day to find some work? He'd had a feeling that maybe his luck was about to change. Until now, it had been mostly bad.

It wasn't that Luke hated the reservation, but sometimes, when the sky was crystal clear as it was today, limitless in expanse, endless in possibilities, it filled him with a restless stirring deep inside.

Luke was a Sioux, but he was not a warrior. When the white man had taken away the people's spirit for warfare, the fighting men of the Sioux had ceased to be. Luke wasn't a hunter, for there wasn't much reason to hunt when he got what he needed at the supermarket. He wasn't a holy man, for the logic of technology told him that things like mysticism and the quest for visions don't exist in the real world.

Luke was not quite thirty-two, yet the disappointments of his life were etched in deep lines around his eyes. Like too many of his kind, he drank too much, often just to pass the time that seemed to be always on his hands.

Luke searched the undulating horizon. Why was it that only within the boundaries of the reservation did he feel like a man? Whenever he dared to venture beyond, reality would slap him in the face. Angry and hurt, he would return there, where he belonged and yet where he somehow did not feel at home either. He stood somewhere between two pasts, the one the old ones spoke of and the ones the filmmakers portrayed. He had grown up never quite knowing which to believe.

He was an Indian, yet what was that, exactly? Whatever it was, it was unrecognizable in everything he saw around him. Only in his innermost self did he have an inkling of what it was, and even then, he could not define it in so many words. Something that emanated from an unknown consciousness told him that he *was* a warrior, without lance or shield, for his heart waged a never-ending battle against the restraints of his heritage. He *was* a hunter, without bow or quiver of arrows, for his mind never ceased searching to comprehend it all. And he *was* a holy man, without sacred rattles or medicine pouch, for in spite of what he saw around him, he never really stopped believing.

Luke brought the pickup to a screeching halt and climbed down, feeling particularly sullen and depressed. He cast a dispassionate glance at the parched land and closed his eyes for a moment, and then the moment was gone, as a quick gust picked it up and scattered it in the wind. To hell with it all, he needed a drink. He turned to climb back inside the cab when a movement on the horizon caught his eye. He watched a horse and rider appear, grow bigger.

The rider was Carly. She had become a familiar sight in these parts, astride her brown mare, her black braids swinging against her back, black medical bag dangling from the pommel of the saddle. Luke kicked at the dust with his boot. The sight of her only reminded him of one more thing he wanted but could not have.

She was no longer heading toward him, but had turned aside on a different route. Jumping back into the truck, he took out after her. He caught up with her on the road to Willie Nighthawk's place and slowed to a crawl to keep pace with her mare's easy trot.

"Hi, Carly," he said with a wave. "How's it going?"

"All right, Luke. And you? I haven't seen you in a couple of weeks."

"Yeah, I know. Been busy. Willie's been letting me work the mine with him. You on your way to his place?"

"Um-hmm."

"So am I. Why don't you hitch Janey to the bumper and climb inside out of the hot sun?" he suggested.

It sounded like a good idea to Carly. She pulled up on the reins, hopped down and led Janey around to the back of the truck, where she tied the reins loosely to the chrome bumper. The pickup door was already open when she got there.

Despite the Stetson she was wearing to shield her head against the harsh glare of the sun, the heat was oppressive on this day in early August. Inside the truck Carly removed her hat and placed it on the seat between them. From on top of her head her braids spilled down over the back of the seat. He could not help but notice the way the sunlight danced along each silken strand. There was a predictable tightening in his gut.

"So, Carly," he said, "what brings you out to Willie's?"

It was something Willie had said to her during his examination a few weeks ago that had prompted Carly to saddle

Janey for the ride out here. He had alluded to his property being worth twenty-five thousand dollars. Money in the bank, he had called it. His 240 acres was, in fact, worth far more than that. The price was hardly fair. Still, someone had put that figure in Willie's mind, and Carly wanted to know who was offering dirt-cheap prices for prime reservation land.

Carly saw no reason to say anything about it to Luke. It was possible that she was letting her imagination run away with her, but she thought it best to keep her suspicions to herself until she got to the root of this thing.

"You know Willie," she said with a laugh. "You can never pry him loose from that mine. I have a hard enough time getting him to come by the office to see me, so I thought I would ride out to see him."

Luke had already forgotten about Willie, though. "Uh, Carly," he began. "I was thinking of driving down to Pine Ridge this weekend. You know, go to a movie or something. You feel like going?"

"Gee, I don't think so, Luke. But thanks anyway."

His fingers tightened around the wheel. "How come you never want to go out with me?"

"I've told you, Luke. I'm not much for dating. Besides, I'm dog-tired at night. It's not easy riding these prairies, going from house to house all day to see people who can't get in to see me."

He'd heard her excuses before, and he was tired of them. He scoffed. "What's the matter? You got something against Indians?"

"Don't be silly."

"Maybe you prefer white men, huh?"

A heated blue gaze flashed in his direction. "My preferences are nobody's business."

"Yeah? Well, you seem to prefer the rich, white Easterner type. You know, the kind that comes out here to rob us."

Carly's indignant gasp filled the small cab of the pickup. "How dare you?"

"Have you gone over to see Emma's place lately? They've moved the rigs in. They should start digging it up any day now."

Carly hadn't been out that way since the day Emma died. She had no idea they would have moved in so fast.

"It was you who brought that jerk over to George's that night," Luke accused. "There's no telling what he may have learned that he could use against us."

"If you had bothered to be there yourself," said Carly, "you would have learned whatever he did. But you don't even bother to show up at the meetings anymore."

"Why should I? All I hear's the same old thing. We've got lawyers working on this and lawyers working on that, but so far no one's seen any money. I'll tell you something about money, Carly. It looks damned good to those who've never seen it. And I'm gonna get as much of it as I can."

"And how are you going to do that, Luke? By gambling? Win any more big bundles at five-card stud?"

His brown eyes left the road to turn on her. There was a look in them like that of a creature caught in a snare. "I win a few bucks here and there," he said evasively. "Enough to keep me in beer."

Dryly, she said, "Yes, I noticed."

His gaze swung back to the dusty road. With one arm resting on the open window, the other draped loosely over the wheel, he said, "And I've noticed a few things about you."

She looked at him with a wry, amused expression and said, "Oh? Like what?"

"Like that flush on your face. Like the way you move, all restless-like, as if you were just coming into heat."

It was not what she had expected. She sucked in her breath. She knew the feeling he described, but to hear it said like that embarrassed her. "I don't know what you're talking about. Maybe I'm just getting a cold or a virus."

"Maybe you need a man over at that place of yours," he suggested coolly.

"I'll be the one to decide what I need, thank you."

Luke brought the pickup to a halt alongside of the road. "But that's just the problem," he said as he reached forward to turn off the ignition. "Most women don't know what they need." He turned to level a look at her. He brought one arm to rest upon the back of the seat. With his fingers he played with her hair.

Carly fidgeted against the hot vinyl, trying to keep a lid on her temper. "Luke, I would suggest that you start up the engine and drive."

He slid toward her. "Not yet."

She knew what was coming. In that fraction of time she looked earnestly into his eyes and said, "I don't think you want to do this."

"I think I do."

She turned quickly to the door and fumbled with the latch, but before she could get it open more than a crack, his hand darted past her to clamp over the open window and pull it shut.

He flattened her against the seat, rolling his weight onto her while his lips sought hers. The taste of beer was strong on his mouth. Carly squirmed beneath him, struggling to force his weight from her. In the cramped quarters of the cab there were arms and legs all over the place. In the melee one of Carly's legs burst free from the entanglement of his and with the heel of her boot she jabbed at the horn, raising the shrill sound into the quiet surroundings. He tried to stop her, but each time she managed to get her foot free, she went for the horn.

Luke tore his lips from hers. "Stop that, dammit! You're gonna scratch the paint off the thing."

Carly panted beneath him. "If you don't get off me, I'll kick more than scratches into it," she warned.

Muttering an epithet, Luke heaved himself up and fell back into place behind the steering wheel. "Man, you are the most *un*romantic woman I've ever known."

Carly opened the door and jumped out while she had the chance. She went around back and untied Janey from the bumper. Leading the mare by the reins, she leaned in the window to look at Luke, who was sitting there with a pout on his face. "I may be unromantic, but if you ever manhandle me like that again, Luke Lightfoot, I'll put a quick end to your romancing days." She thrust her boot into the stirrup, mounted and rode off.

She was fuming as she cantered down the road to Willie Nighthawk's place. What was it with men that made them think they could come on like that and get away with it? Did Luke think she would like him any better if he forced himself on her? Frankly, she'd had her fill of forceful men.

Jesse had been forceful about the way he had barged into her life. He, too, had forced kisses upon her, but unlike with Luke, with Jesse, she had found herself wanting more. Luke was right about the flush on her face. For weeks she'd been walking around with a fever, temperature hovering slightly above normal. She could fool Luke with explanations of colds and viruses, but Carly knew the real cause of it. It was the memory of Jesse's lips working magic on her.

Three weeks had passed since she had heard from him. Three weeks of waiting and wondering. What was he doing? Did he think of her as often as she thought of him? His silence spoke volumes, but then, what was there to say? That he didn't care for her in the way she wished he did? What was it he had said when she had accused him of being insufferable? His deep voice came back to her. ''Maybe. But at least I'm honest.'' Where was his honesty now, when it counted? She had not thought him to be a man afraid of the truth. She could imagine him spitting it out and kicking sand over it, but never walking away from it. And yet he did not have the nerve to call and tell her how he really felt. Her heart shuddered with pain, and then sank to new depths when she thought of the rigs that were now in place on Emma's land. That was all she really needed to know about Jesse Black.

It was past noon when she reached Willie's place. She climbed down from the saddle and knocked on the door. As she waited for him to answer, she rubbed her eyes, which were weary from the sun and the dust. After a minute, she knocked again. She shook her head with impatience. Nothing was going right today. With a huff she walked off in the direction of the mine.

Carly climbed to the top of the steep hill that shadowed Willie's house, then loped down the other side. At the entrance to the shaft she cupped her hands to her mouth and called his name. Her voice echoed off the granite walls. When it brought no response, Carly turned away. Back up the hill she climbed, then down the other side back to the house. She walked around back and peered through the kitchen window, which was partly open. Something on the table caught her eye. She glanced one way, then the other. Then, she hoisted herself up and climbed in through the open window.

Carly's mother used to scold her when she was a little girl, saying that whenever she wanted to behave in a questionable way, she would invariably find an excuse for making it the right thing to do. Telling herself that it was in Willie's best interests, that was exactly what she did now as she entered the empty house.

On the kitchen table were a Sony Walkman and a set of earphones. Carly knew that Willie wore them when he worked in the mine, and since they were here, then Willie must have gone off somewhere for the day. Feeling bolder from his absence, she noticed the papers on the table and tilted her head for a better look. It was a deed of some sort covering Willie's property. Upon reading further, however, she noticed that the price had now jumped to fifty thousand dollars—twice as much as originally offered, but still only a fraction of what the land was worth. Upping the offer could only mean that the pressure was on Willie to sell.

Carly flipped up the last page of the document and expelled a sigh of relief to find that it was not yet signed. Nevertheless, she was baffled, for the name typed in under the word Buyer was BMI. Carly's features scrunched into a questioning frown. BMI? What was that? she wondered.

Chapter 8

The mid-August heat beat at the windshield of the black Lincoln as it sped south along the black-topped highway. Inside, the frosty air-conditioning assured a comfortable ride unruffled by the 110-degree temperature outside. A country-western tune played on the radio. In the back seat were the sandwiches and cold beers Carly had packed for this trip to Pine Ridge, for there would be no place to stop along the way for a bite to eat.

Beyond the window, passing by in streaks of drab color, were fields of rolling grassland, interspersed by a series of low, rough ridges, the slopes dotted with pines. This was the Pine Ridge country, extending from the edge of the Black Hills eastward along the northern border of Nebraska. To the north lay the badlands, a vast tract set with a jumble of clay buttes that were carved into fantastic shapes with mysterious and lonesome valleys lying between them. Great alkali flats, snowy white in the sunlight, were strewn with the gigantic bones of prehistoric animals. In the summer heat the hills and buttes seemed to sway as if in an eerie dance. It was the land of the spirits where, legend had it, men were led astray to die of thirst and cold, never to be seen again by their friends.

It was wild and unforgiving country, beautiful in a strange and moving way. Here and there an old car body had been left along the side of the road, attracting the rattlesnakes that liked to take shelter during the day from the hot Dakota sun. Occasionally, some small creature that had tried to scurry across the road could be seen flattened against the asphalt.

Carly had made this trip many times before, usually behind the wheel of her own red Mustang, before it died of exhaustion, that is. Today she had hitched a ride with George, who often drove the hundred miles to the town of Pine Ridge to meet with members of the tribal council. If it were not for the purpose of this trip, she might have been able to convince herself that it was just a routine run to pick up medical supplies. But it was not routine, and as Carly watched the terrain slip past the window, her errand weighed heavily on her mind. After a while she turned to George and took a deep breath.

"George, wouldn't it be necessary to file a legal document, say a deed, with the county clerk?"

"Um-hmm," he answered. "But if you're worried about your tract of land, Carly, don't be. When you decide to sell, I'll handle all that for you. Those things sometimes get held up on someone's desk. In your case I'll see what I can do about moving it along. See, Carly? It pays to have friends in high places."

He said it with a smile on his face and a hint of jest in his tone, but as Carly studied him from where she sat, she wasn't so sure he'd been joking. He often aimed barbs of sarcastic humor at the establishment, but there had been something in his voice just now that made her realize how much like the establishment he had become. It even showed in the way he dressed. The three-piece suits he wore might have served to impress the establishment, but they made little impression on the Indians in these parts. Just once, Carly was thinking, it wouldn't hurt if George took off his jacket, rolled up his shirt sleeves and showed the people that underneath the suit he was just like them, that his skin was just as brown, just as Indian.

"And the county?" she ventured. "It's Shannon County, right?"

"That's right." His eyes left the road to glance briefly at her. "Are you thinking about searching the title on your land?"

"No. I was just wondering about all that land that's fallen into the hands of the power companies these past few years. In order for any land sale to be legal, legal papers would have to be drawn up and filed with the county clerk. Who knows? Maybe a search of the county clerk's records might turn up a clue, a connecting thread, something—*anything.*"

George shook his head and expelled a dismal sigh. "We've been over this thing a hundred times, Carly."

"Yes, George, we have. And you've accused me of having a wild imagination, and when that didn't work, you told me you would look into it. Since then there's been another death."

"I *have* been looking into it," George insisted. "But I've got to be discreet. Something like this takes time."

"Time is something we don't have," she said. "That's why I'm going to Pine Ridge to have a look at those records."

"It's a blind alley, I'm telling you," he argued.

"You may be right, but at this point, there's precious little else to go on."

"And what if you *do* find something?" he questioned. "Then what?"

"Then the sheriff will *have* to investigate."

His expression turned grim. "You realize the repercussions of something like this, don't you? I mean, if you do find something, and if they do investigate? A lot of big people are going to be very angry."

"I don't give a damn how angry they get," Carly charged. "Personally, I'd rather be angry than dead. And I wish you'd stop defending them. They're just a bunch of greedy men who steal Indian land."

"Yes, well, those greedy men make rotten enemies, Carly. I keep telling you, we have to work *with* them, not against them."

"And does working with them mean compromising the position of the Sioux nation, not to mention our own personal integrity?"

He looked into her blue eyes, which were sizzling, and said, "Integrity has nothing to do with it. Integrity is useful when it doesn't get in the way. Nothing—nothing—must get in the way of getting what we want."

Carly turned away from the rock-hard look in George's eyes. The whole thing left a bad taste in her mouth. Still, she assumed George had his reasons for doing the things he did. After all, it could not be easy standing practically alone at the helm of a small nation of people.

It was like that for most of the hundred-mile ride to Pine Ridge, long stretches of silence riddled with bursts of conversation. After a while Carly turned back to George and asked, "Does the name BMI mean anything to you?"

"BMI?" He turned the name over several times in his mind. "No," he said, shaking his head, "I don't think so. Why?"

"I have a hunch it might be behind the recent land sales on the reservation." She was reluctant to admit that she had climbed in through Willie's window to get a look at the papers on his kitchen table, saying with a sigh instead, "I don't know, George. Maybe you're right. Maybe I am crazy."

"Now, I never said that. Impulsive, maybe. Hotheaded. A little daft at times, but never crazy."

"Thanks." She laughed. "I was beginning to think I'd turned into a *witkowin*."

"You'd better not let your patients hear that, Carly. If they suspect that the pretty doctor is a crazy woman, they're likely to go back to the old ways of healing."

"There's nothing wrong with that," she replied. "All I ask is that they don't close their minds to my way of healing, because, I'll tell you, George, in my line of work you see too many things that can't be cured with chanting or plants."

She lapsed into silence, thinking about the deadliest killer of all. History had proved the complex human to be the most violent, volatile force on the face of the earth, possessing the ability to obliterate vast portions of the population with single swipes of warfare and madness. Someone had obliterated eleven lives on the reservation. Not a huge number compared with the tens of thousands of people who had died from disease and pestilence throughout the course of history. Nevertheless, except for the cholera and smallpox that the European immigrants had brought into Indian territory during the 1800s, no virus or disease had taken such a deadly toll on the Oglalas of Pine Ridge as the hand of man.

The town of Pine Ridge was sharply divided into two sections. To the west of Highway 18 on tree-lined streets stood the government buildings, the schools, the hospital and the government-built housing for federal employees. To the east stood the churches, cafés, stores and a filling station. Beyond these were the makeshift homes of the "town"

Indians and the suburban-style housing projects that had been built in the sixties by the tribal government in cooperation with the Federal Housing Authority.

George pulled up to the curb before one of the government buildings. "Are you sure you want to waste your time doing this?" he asked Carly.

"It's my time, George."

"Suit yourself. I'll meet you at Frank's Café at around six. See you later."

The woman wearing the steel-rimmed glasses looked up from her work at the pretty face with the forthright blue eyes that gazed at her over the counter. "Can I see some identification, please?"

"Oh. Sure." Carly delved deep into her bag and pulled out her wallet. From it she extracted her driver's license and a credit card that saw little action on the reservation. It was only when she traveled to San Francisco to visit her folks that she used it. Other times, like now, it came in handy as identification or to jimmy the lock on the front door of her house on those rare occasions when she locked herself out.

The woman seemed satisfied and slid the ID back across the counter. "And you say you want to search some title?"

"Yes. The title to my land. It's up around Broken Bow. I'm thinking of selling, and I want to make sure it's free of liens. That sort of thing. You know." It was George who had unwittingly provided Carly with the perfect excuse to gain access to the county records.

The woman hedged. "I don't know. Usually lawyers do that kind of thing, don't they, Miss McAllister?"

"Yes, except that my lawyer is out of town this week. And that's Doctor McAllister."

The woman hesitated for a moment, then said, "Follow me, please." She led the way to a row of microfilm, machines. Switching one on, she said, "This here makes it go forward. This here makes it go backward. If you need help finding anything, let me know.''

When the woman had shuffled back to her desk behind the counter, Carly sat down at the machine. From this distance it would be impossible for the woman to read what was on the screen unless she had eyes like an eagle, which Carly doubted from the thickness of the lenses in her glasses. Satisfied that her real motives would not be detected, Carly began to spin through the records.

For over an hour she sat there, her eyes growing bleary from the tiny green print against the black background. She squinted from the glare thrown onto the screen by the overhead fluorescent lights. A nerve began to throb at her temple and only grew worse as her eyes strained harder. Soon she had a splitting headache.

Back in time she went, searching the records of Shannon County, South Dakota, looking for deeds or liens or releases similar to the one she had spied on Willie Nighthawk's kitchen table. Her fingers worked the control levers, flipping fast forward, then stopping abruptly and shifting to reverse when something caught her eye.

It was a deed entered into on the twelfth day of September 1982 by and between Mary Yazzie, seller, and BMI, purchaser. The name of BMI set off a warning bell in Carly's mind. The deed covered forty acres of land described as the northwest quarter of the southwest quarter of Section One, Plat 321. She read further. For the sum of twenty thousand dollars—the appalling price of five hundred dollars per acre—BMI had purchased forty acres of prime Indian land. But where did Laramie Fork fit in? Carly wondered, for whenever she had chanced to drive by Mary Yazzie's land, she had seen the huge excavating rigs of the Laramie Fork Power Company digging up the earth.

All trace of weariness vanished as Carly spun through the records. Her fingers froze on the forward mechanism when another document rolled onto the screen. This one was the lease agreement between BMI, lessor, and Laramie Fork Power Company, lessee, covering the same forty-acre tract of land. Well, at least that explained the presence of the mining rigs. What it did not explain, however, was just who or what BMI was.

Carly sat erect in the hard-backed chair, fingers twitching on the controls, working them now the way a seasoned pilot works the controls in his cockpit. Another deed appeared on the screen. Again, BMI had purchased land, this time 120 acres of it, at a dirt-cheap price and leased it to Laramie Fork. And so it went for the next couple of hours. Deed after deed turned up in which BMI had acquired, according to Carly's quick calculations, more than two thousand acres of Indian land and then leased it to Laramie Fork. There was Johnny Starbuck's land and Dan Sitting-bull's and several other names Carly knew, and many more she did not.

A whoosh of air went out of Carly's lungs like deflating balloons and she slumped back in the chair. They were all legal, every last one of them, signed, sealed, notarized and filed with the county clerk. Legal didn't mean right, though. There had to be more to it than this. There *had* to be.

She looked down at the notes she had scribbled onto a pad as each document had come into view. Dates, names, amounts. Facts, figures but no clues. She didn't know for sure what drew her attention to one of the dates in particular. Maybe it was just the feeling she had that something was wrong somewhere. Or perhaps her memory had triggered something in her subconscious mind. With suspicion nagging at her, Carly got up. She approached the counter and cleared her throat to get the woman's attention.

The woman looked up. "Find what you were looking for?"

"Uh, yes, I did. There's just one other thing. Where are the death records?"

The woman wrinkled her nose. "What would you want with those?"

"It's my grandfather," Carly lied. "I'm not certain exactly when he died, and I need the information to fill out some papers. You see, my mother says they're filed in Shannon County, but my grandmother says they're filed in Washabaugh County, and it would make it a lot easier for me if I could—"

The woman waved away the rest of what was sure to be a long and boring explanation. "Never mind. They're over there."

It was just a hunch, of course, but there was something about the date on Mary Yazzie's deed that bothered Carly. She sat down before another microfilm machine and began to scan the records of all the deaths in the past three years. Then she found it.

According to the records of the county clerk of Shannon County, Mary Yazzie died of a coronary thrombosis on September 6, six days *before* she signed the deed with BMI. Carly knew now what had drawn her attention to the date on the deed, for the day following Mary's death, September 7, was Carly's birthday, a day she was not likely to forget. When she had gone by the place and had tasted the foxweed, she remembered thinking what an awful birthday it had turned out to be.

A sick feeling crept into Carly's stomach. Was the discrepancy in the dates just a typographical error made by some tired, overworked secretary who had rushed through the papers so she could get home on time? Carly searched further into the death records but found nothing amiss.

"You're gonna have to finish up," said the woman from across the room. "We're closing up now."

Carly glanced down at her watch. It was five o'clock. She rose from the chair, switched off the machine, thanked the woman and walked from the building.

A host of questions pecked at Carly. A feeling deep down in her gut told her that something was terribly wrong. Whoever or whatever BMI was, someone had some explaining to do. Carly was oblivious to everything except the suspicions that fluttered madly in her mind like a flock of startled birds. She was oblivious to the heat that beat down upon her head when she stepped outside into the sunshine, oblivious to the car that was parked parallel to the curb, waiting.

She stepped from the curb. The first place to start, she was thinking, was to find out everything she could about the corporation called BMI.

The car lurched forward. Carly heard it only an instant before she saw it bearing down on her. In that fraction of time she knew the numbing cold of fear.

She reeled from the force of the car as it swerved sharply, hitting her and propelling her back onto the sidewalk. It happened so fast, yet Carly was aware of falling, spinning and striking the pavement with a thud that jarred her. A pain tore through her shoulder as the tender flesh met the concrete. There were the sounds of ripping cloth and a shrill scream. Only later did Carly realize that the scream had come from herself.

The squeal of tires rushing away, the screech of brakes and the patter of running feet could do no more than marginally penetrate Carly's frozen mind. She blinked several times and opened her eyes, surprised at finding herself still alive. Directly overhead a ring of strange faces looked down at her. Beyond them was a circle of bright blue sky. What was going on? Who were all these people? Why were they looking at her like that? It took a few minutes for Carly to realize that they were looking at her because she was lying flat on her back on the sidewalk. She heard their anxious voices asking how she was.

Suddenly, George appeared at her side. "My God, Carly, are you all right?"

She raised confused, bewildered eyes to him.

"Are you all right?" he repeated.

She nodded. "I—I think so," she said in a weakened voice. She attempted to raise herself up and grimaced when a red-hot pain seared through her shoulder from the effort. "My shoulder," she groaned. Her hand moved instinctively to the wounded area.

George slid his hand beneath her and helped her to sit up. The sleeve of her shirt was torn at the seam and hung loosely about her arm. Beneath the jagged tear the skin was abraded and raw. He pulled a white handkerchief from his pocket and dabbed at the oozing blood. "Here," he said. "Hold this over it."

Carly obeyed and winced at the sting of the soft cloth as it made contact with her raw and tender flesh.

"Can you move your shoulder?" he asked.

She bit down hard on her bottom lip when she tested her arm. The pain was acute, but at least there were no broken bones.

"Can you get up?" He placed his hand on her uninjured arm and pulled her gently to her feet.

Carly's eyes were wild and bright. She grasped fiercely at the lapel of George's jacket and said in a desperate whisper, "I didn't see it. I didn't see the car until it was right on me. What happened, George?"

He swallowed hard and turned to the people who looked on eagerly all about them. "Did anybody see what happened?"

A few mumbled noes and several shakes of the head from the crowd of curious onlookers answered the question.

Trying to make some sense of what had happened, Carly said, "Do you think the driver was drunk?"

With a grim expression, he answered, "Probably. Come on. Let's get you to the car. Can you walk?"

She fit snugly into the crook of his arm as he helped her walk to the Lincoln, which was pulled up to the curb as if it had been parked there in a hurry. A thought suddenly occurred to Carly. "George, shouldn't we call the police?"

"Don't worry. I'll take care of it."

She stood, one hand holding the handkerchief in place, the other braced on the open car door for support. Her legs felt weak and threatened to buckle under her.

George helped her into the car, then walked quickly around to the driver's side and climbed in. "I'll get you to the hospital right away."

"No," she said. "No. Just take me home, please."

"But Carly, that's an ugly bruise you have there. Don't you think you should have the cuts cleaned and dressed?"

Carly eased herself back against the black leather seat. Her shoulder throbbed without mercy, and the handkerchief was all wet and sticky with blood. She pulled it away from her shoulder to look at the lacerated skin. "It'll be all right."

"Are you sure?"

She laid her head back against the seat and closed her eyes. Managing a faint smile, she said, "I'm a doctor, George, remember?"

"And a stubborn one, too," he complained as he eased the car away from the curb and drove down the street.

By the time they pulled up before Carly's house in Broken Bow, the pain in her shoulder had subsided to a dull ache. George got out and went around to the passenger side to open the door for her. "Here, let me help you."

She was still a little shaky on her legs and was grateful for the support. She took a clean shirt with her into the small examining room and closed the door, leaving George standing in the living room.

When the wound was dressed, she shrugged gingerly into the clean shirt and left the room. She sank onto the sofa next to George.

"Does it hurt?" he asked.

"A little," she answered. "It's not serious. Just a surface wound." But even as she spoke Carly was beginning to feel the dull aches that sprang from other places on her body from the fall she had taken. Tiny lines of discomfort edged her mouth when she turned to him and said, "Thanks, George."

"Forget it. It's just a lucky thing I happened to be driving by."

Lucky, yes. "What were you doing driving by?" she asked.

"Coming to get you. I had my business with the tribal spokesmen wrapped up, and I figured you had yours wrapped up, too. In all the excitement, I forgot to ask. How'd it go at the county clerk's office? Did you find what you were looking for?"

Carly chuckled softly. "That's hard to say, since I didn't know what I was looking for in the first place."

George nodded knowingly and said, "What did I tell you? A blind alley, right?"

"Not exactly. This alley leads somewhere."

He arched an inquisitive brow at her. "Oh? Where?"

"It leads to BMI."

"What is it with you and this BMI?" he asked. He seemed somewhat annoyed at her persistence.

"George, in every case in the past three years where someone had died under mysterious circumstances, their land was purchased shortly before their deaths by BMI." All except for Mary Yazzie, she did not say, who had somehow managed to sell her land *after* she had died. "BMI," she

HIT·THE JACKPOT WITH SILHOUETTE

THE JACKPOT

Scratch off the 3 windows above to see if
you've HIT THE JACKPOT

If 3 hearts appear, you get an exciting
Mystery Gift in addition to our fabulous
introductory offer of

4 FREE BOOKS PLUS
A FOLDING UMBRELLA

PEEL UP STICKER AND MAIL TODAY

IT'S A JACKPOT OF A GREAT OFFER!

- 4 exciting Silhouette Intimate Moments novels—FREE!
- a folding umbrella—FREE!
- a surprise mystery bonus that will delight you—FREE!

Silhouette Folding Umbrella— ABSOLUTELY FREE

You'll love your Silhouette umbrella. Its bright color will cheer you up on even the gloomiest day. It's made of rugged nylon to last for years, and is so compact (folds to 15″) you can carry it in your purse or briefcase. This folding umbrella is yours free with this offer.

But wait . . . there's even more!

Money-Saving Home Delivery!

Subscribe to Silhouette Intimate Moments and enjoy the convenience of previewing new, hot-off-the-press books every month, delivered right to your home. Each book is yours for only $2.25—25¢ less per book than what you pay in stores! And there's no extra charge for postage and handling.

Special Extras—Free!

You'll also get our free monthly newsletter—the indispensable insider's look at our most popular writers and their upcoming novels. Now you can have a behind-the-scenes look at the fascinating world of Silhouette. It's an added bonus you'll look forward to every month. You'll also get additional free gifts from time to time as a token of our appreciation for being a home subscriber.

TAKE A CHANCE ON ROMANCE—
COMPLETE AND MAIL YOUR SCORECARD
TO CLAIM YOUR FREE HEARTWARMING GIFTS

If offer card below is missing, write to:
Silhouette Books, 120 Brighton Road,
P.O. Box 5084, Clifton, NJ 07015-9956

DETACH AND MAIL CARD TODAY

PLAYER'S SCORECARD

MAIL TODAY

4 FREE BOOKS

FREE FOLDING UMBRELLA

Did you win a
mystery gift?

Place sticker here

Yes! I hit the jackpot. I have affixed my 3 hearts. Please send my 4
Silhouette Intimate Moments novels free, plus my free folding
umbrella and free mystery gift. Then send me 4 books every month
as they come off the press, and bill me just $2.25 per book—25¢ less
than retail, with no extra charges for postage and handling.

If I am not completely satisfied, I may return a shipment and cancel
at any time. The free books, folding umbrella and mystery gift
remain mine to keep.

CJM 037

NAME _____

ADDRESS _____

APT. _____

CITY _____

STATE _____

ZIP CODE _____

SILHOUETTE "NO-RISK" GUARANTEE
• There is no obligation to buy—the free books and gifts remain yours to keep.
• You pay the lowest price possible—and receive books before they're
available in stores.
• You may end your subscription anytime—just let us know.
Terms and prices subject to change. Offer limited to
one per household and not valid for
present subscribers.

PRINTED IN U.S.A.

Mail this card today for
4 FREE BOOKS
this folding umbrella and
a mystery gift ALL FREE!

repeated. "Listed in the records of the county clerk as a New York corporation. BMI, which then coincidentally happens to lease the land, which it has purchased under dubious means, to Laramie Fork Power Company. Now, don't you find that just a bit peculiar?"

"No, Carly, I don't. In the first place, you're the only one who thinks those deaths were mysterious. And besides, if the sales were legal and the leases are legal, what's the problem?"

She shook her head slowly. "I don't know. I just keep wondering why this BMI is so interested in reservation land."

George expelled a breath of impatience. "People have been interested in Indian land ever since they knew it was there. Sort of like the Mount Everest syndrome, I guess."

"I don't think so," said Carly. "Men climb mountains because they're there, but corporations don't do anything unless it's to make a profit. If anyone should be making a profit from leasing the mineral rights to our land, it should be us. The companies that lease directly from our people pay below-average royalties for the coal they mine, and companies like BMI that come along and buy the land outright offer insulting prices for it. Why is BMI leasing to Laramie Fork? It's our land; why aren't *we* leasing it? And why not land on the other reservations? Why is BMI interested only in Pine Ridge? Why such interest in the land that surrounds the Black Hills? Doesn't that strike you as odd or suspicious?"

"When you put it like that, sure it does. But you're forgetting something, aren't you, Carly? The hills are rich in minerals, not to mention the aesthetic value. They've even made a national park out of them. I don't find it all that surprising that a company like BMI would want the land surrounding the hills. Frankly, I'd be even more suspicious if they started buying up worthless land. Now, *that* wouldn't make sense." He got up and stood for a moment looking down into her pale but beautiful face. "Look, Carly, you must be tired. Why don't you get some sleep. Don't get up. I'll show myself out. Good night."

She was only dimly aware of him moving toward the door or of it closing softly behind him. He was right; she *was* tired, desperately so. Her mind and body ached with a weariness that infiltrated every corner of her being. She was tired, and yet she knew she wouldn't sleep. She was too overwrought, too scared, to find any solace in slumber. Perhaps a sedative would help. She took a couple of pills, then trudged back into the living room and flopped back down on the couch.

She lay there, trying hard not to think, waiting for the pills to take effect and transport her away from the terror of this day. Just some crazy drunk behind the wheel of a car, that's all it was. She had simply been in the wrong place at the wrong time. Her timing had always left something to be desired. Grant Hastings was testimony to that fact. And now Jesse.

Tears welled in Carly's eyes and overflowed onto her cheeks. She fought down a sob, then gave way entirely as sobs shook her whole body. A terrible loneliness engulfed her. She was so scared. She could have been killed by that car this afternoon, yet now as she lay on the sofa in the safety of her own home, a different kind of fear settled over her. It was the fear of loneliness, of not having a strong shoulder to lean against, nor strong arms to wind around her while a soft voice whispered that everything would be all right. She had a sudden, intense longing to feel Jesse's lips moving over hers, to lose her breath in the warm, wet hollow of his mouth, to feel wonderfully drugged by the taste of him. Oh, Jesse, she cried softly in her mind, how I need you tonight...how I need you at this moment. If only he were here, she would not fight his strong dominance; she would lose herself in it, embrace it, give herself up to it.

It all came back in a heated rush, the touch of his lips, the heat of his hands, the strong, pulsing beat of his heart. He had wanted more that night on the porch . . . that last night before he had disappeared from her life. She had wanted it, too. But something she had not dared to name had stopped her. She'd been dreadfully tired. She had felt drained of all physical energy in the aftermath of that nightmarish day. But then his lips had awakened her, had erased from her mind all thoughts of reality, had set her heart hammering in her chest. It was her own emotions that had frightened her and led her just shy of giving to him what he'd wanted and taking from him what he'd been so eager to give. Her own fears of falling in love. And now, here she was, needing him, yearning for the sanctuary of his arms and for the sweet pain of his lips to take her far away from where she was.

Her eyelids began to droop, and she was never quite certain when she passed from wakefulness into unconsciousness. Deep into her dreams she carried the image of his handsome face, his dark, obsidian eyes. He was there beside her, his long, lean body pressing against the length of hers, covering it, sealing it in warmth as his mouth moved in a slow seduction over her lips. He was there, loving her, wanting her, telling her that everything would be all right.

Chapter 9

The offices of BMI were deserted. The switchboard was dark; the typewriters were silent. Only the hum of the photocopy machine infiltrated the dense solitude on the forty-fourth floor of the building in midtown Manhattan.

A figure stood at the machine, hands braced on the top, head bowed, shoulders hunched with weariness. The final copy popped out of the slit in the side of the machine. When the cycle was completed, Jesse lifted the stack of copies from the tray and shut the machine down. With long strides he made his way back down the dimly lit corridor to his office.

He kicked the door shut behind him and sat down at his desk. He had gone over the files with a fine-tooth comb, even those bearing the remotest connection to Laramie Fork. So far he had found nothing unusual. Nevertheless, his shrewder side made him take the extra precaution of photocopying everything. Tomorrow he would pack up the copies and send them by messenger to his attorney, Jerry

Klein, for safekeeping. For now he slipped them into a manila envelope, closed the metal clasp and shut them away in the desk drawer.

He eased himself against the high back of the leather chair and sat there for several minutes, staring at nothing in particular, feeling tired and edgy. Why was he going through all this trouble for something he did not fully understand? It was as if he were being activated by an invisible hand. That manipulative hand urged him now toward the telephone, and a familiar voice from some dark corner of his mind prompted, Go ahead, call her.

Jesse reached out to the phone but stopped and pulled his hand back sharply. No. Why should he call her? He had already dialed her number more than a dozen times in the past few weeks without anyone answering. Each time he had let the phone ring much longer than it really needed to, when it was apparent after half a dozen rings that no one was home. Where was she? Out with that Lightfoot guy? Something tightened in Jesse's gut at the thought of it. Pure stubborn pride would keep him from admitting what it really was—jealousy, plain, simple and red-hot. It was something he had never experienced before, because he had simply never cared before. His weariness turned to a slow, simmering anger. He'd told himself it would pass, but it hadn't. It had only grown stronger as the days went by.

There was a restlessness within him, emanating from somewhere deep inside, a restive feeling that could not be assuaged. The closest he came to appeasing it was when he was thinking about Carly and what it would be like to make love to her. He could almost taste the sweetness of her skin, smell the heady ambrosia of sweet grass, feel her warm, pulsing body all over his. Her limbs were long and smooth, muscles toned and supple; that much he had discovered when he had held her in his arms. She tasted incredibly sweet and smelled divine, but it was not enough, not nearly enough. He wanted to know more. He wanted to know what it would feel like to move within her, to feel her velvet softness all around him. He wanted to hear her soft gasps at that precise moment when she was over the brink, to experience the grasping of her fingers, the pleasures of her mouth. He wanted to know her most intimate places as well as he knew the sound of her laugh. He wanted to know what it was that pleased her most, and then he wanted to drive her crazy with it until she lay breathless and panting beneath him. There was a distinct hardening of his desire the stronger the fantasy became, a quickening of his pulse as he imagined what it would be like.

His eyes wandered again to the phone. The distinct possibility that she did not answer because she was out making rounds was something he had considered and then abandoned. That would have been the logical explanation and, sadly, logic had been the first thing to go out the window the moment he'd set eyes on Carly McAllister. He thought of sending her a wire. *Urgent that I speak with you Stop Answer your damned phone Stop.* No, that wouldn't do. He sighed, feeling angry and frustrated.

But it was not only the beautiful Indian woman out west that threw Jesse's emotions out of synch these days. He felt segmented. It was as if he had left a part of himself behind in South Dakota. What was it about that place that had his thoughts returning to it at odd moments? *This* was where he belonged, not out there, in that godforsaken place.

Jesse lifted his gaze and stared at the handsomely paneled office in which he spent so much of his time . . . too much, it suddenly seemed. It was the power of the position that had always appealed to him, just as the awesome power of this city had never failed to impress him.

He swiveled his chair around to face the window behind the desk. The glass ran floor to ceiling, wall to wall, exposing a massive panorama to Jesse's view. The tall skyscrapers blinked like stars against a velvet backdrop of ebony sky. Ribbons of light from city traffic streamed up and down the avenues, which were busy even at this time of night. Into the air rose the shrill blare of an ambulance as it zigzagged through the traffic. New York, it had everything. No, Jesse thought, that wasn't right. Something was missing.

Jesse's mouth became a hard, taut line, and the handsome planes of his face took on an ominous appearance as he stared out the window at the Manhattan skyline. Ever since he'd returned home he had felt distinctly ill at ease. He argued constantly with his father. They found little to agree on these days, least of all how to run BMI. The board of directors' meeting had gone poorly for Jesse. Russell did indeed have them where he wanted them, squarely under his thumb. A carefully worded reminder as to who owned controlling interest in BMI intimidated them sufficiently. Every one of them owed his position to Russell Blackmoon. None wished to oppose him and risk losing the life-style afforded a director of BMI.

But Jesse was not without his own persuasive qualities. One look from his chilling black eyes had given the directors something to fear in him, too. In the end they had agreed to postpone signing the deal with Laramie Fork for two weeks. Caught as they were between two opposing forces, they managed to oblige the president without outrightly disobeying the chairman.

Well, at least it had bought him two weeks. But the past two weeks had produced nothing. Jesse had put a call in to Washington to a friend in the Justice Department, and a few members of various other federal agencies owed him some favors. Something would turn up sooner or later. Jesse only hoped it would be sooner, for in just two days, his deadline was up.

The telephone rang, jolting Jesse out of the private thoughts furrowing his brow. He swiveled back around to the desk.

"Hello? Hi, Jerry. I see you're working late, too, tonight. Yeah, I know, but what's your excuse? You've got a beautiful wife to go home to. Have you got anything for me?" He rubbed his eyes as he listened. "I see. No, no, that's all right. Keep working on it. Do what you can to get this thing blocked in court. Okay, pal, I'll check in with you tomorrow. Go home and get some rest or you'll be mush when I meet you on the racquetball court this weekend. Me? Oh, sure. Right."

He hung up and glanced down at his watch. It was ten-thirty, but it felt more like the wee small hours of the morning. He pushed himself away from the desk and got up. He picked up his jacket lying over the back of a chair, slung it over his shoulder and left the office.

Jesse waved to the cleaning woman who had just come off the elevator with her cart. "Hi, beautiful."

"Mr. Blackmoon," said the woman upon seeing him. "You working late again tonight, sir?"

"I'm afraid so, Millie."

She shook her head. "That's not right, spending so much time all by yourself working late. You look like you're going to fall dead asleep. Just like that Miz Wilson upstairs. Told her the same thing just a few minutes ago."

Jesse thrust his hands into his pockets and turned to go. "Goodnight, Millie." He strolled down the corridor to the elevator and pressed the Up button.

He rode the elevator one flight up to his father's office. There was a light shining from beneath the door as he approached.

"Working late?"

The sound of Jesse's deep voice from the doorway startled the woman behind the desk. Her head snapped up. "Jesse. What are you doing here?"

He walked into the room; her eyes followed him. There was a smoothness to his gait, a silent symmetry of muscles. Something quick and dangerous simmered inside him. One word always came to mind whenever she saw him: Indian.

"Same as you, Helen," he said, smiling. "Just a couple of workhorses, I guess. I can understand it with me, though. After all, I own the company. But you? Don't you have anything better to do? Say, aren't you missing your favorite show tonight?" He knew of her penchant for the weekly television series, but he also knew of her steadfast devotion to her job, so her answer came as no surprise.

"I'll catch the reruns."

"Well, I'm calling it quits. How about you? Do you want to grab a cup of coffee with me before heading for home?"

"No thanks, Jesse. I have to finish up here."

He seated himself on a corner of the desk. "Can't it wait?"

She pulled a piece of paper from the typewriter and set it facedown on top of the stack she had already typed. "You know how your father is. When he wants something done, he wants it done yesterday."

"Don't worry. I'll take care of him. Come on. I insist." He leaned over to grasp her by the hand and pull her lightly to her feet despite her protests. "Boss's orders," he warned.

Helen hedged. Casting an uncertain look down at the stack of papers, she said, "I don't know."

"I do." He led her around to the front of the desk, then leaned over to turn off her typewriter. He escorted her from the office, flipping off the overhead light on the way out.

They waited for the elevator in silence. Helen's gaze was glued to the floor indicator over the doors. Jesse's eyes were fixed on Helen. He sensed a certain tenseness about her. "Is it my imagination, or have you been avoiding me lately?" he asked.

"You know how it is, Jesse. There's so much paperwork to do on this new deal that I scarcely have the time to go out for lunch."

"Are you sure that's all it is?"

Her eyes met his then. "Of course. What else would it be?"

He shrugged. "I don't know. Everyone around here knows that I've locked horns with my father over this Laramie Fork thing. Maybe he let you know in that way of his that it isn't wise for you to be too friendly to me."

"Your father has been dictating letters and memos to me and giving me orders for the past twenty-five years," she told him. "But he has never once told me how to run my personal life. Who I choose to be friendly with is a personal matter."

"I'm not so sure about that," Jesse muttered.

Her eyes searched his earnestly. "What do you mean?"

"I mean that the day might come when you have to take a side."

"Why should that be necessary?"

He did not answer right away, wondering how best to explain something that she was better off not knowing. "Let's just say that my father and I don't see eye to eye on a lot of things. In the long run that could affect the company."

"But Jesse, you're president of BMI. You wouldn't do anything to hurt the company." Her expression clouded with disbelief. "Would you?"

He avoided the question. "You're right. I am the president, although sometimes I don't think my father knows that. This new agreement, for instance, the one that had you working so late last night. How come I don't know anything about it?"

She looked away. "I assumed you had been told."

The elevator came and they stepped inside. "So? Who's the deal with?"

She replied, "Laramie Fork."

He let out his breath in a sigh of sharp annoyance. "What is it this time?"

"Just a standard contract."

He snorted at that. A standard contract with Laramie Fork meant leasing more Blackmoon land for them to dig up. Didn't they already have enough? "What the hell do they want with Blackmoon land?" he grumbled. "How much of a royalty are we getting for our coal anyway?"

Helen shifted uncomfortably from foot to foot, her eyes following the light on the panel as it counted off the floors.

"Helen? How much?"

"I, uh, I don't know."

"But you must know if you were typing up the papers."

"What I mean is I've forgotten. I have it written down somewhere in my notes, and I haven't gotten to the royalty clause yet."

"Okay, fine," he said. "Then I'll buzz you first thing in the morning and you can read me the figures."

"Yes, of course."

The elevator doors opened onto the lobby. The sound of their footsteps echoed through the vacant corridor as they headed for the exit. They signed out, then left the building, stepping into the balmy summer night. Jesse took Helen by the arm and said, "Come on, how about that cup of coffee?"

She pulled away. "No, I can't. I'm tired. Thanks anyway, Jesse. Goodnight."

He watched her walk off down Park Avenue. What's gotten into her? Jesse wondered as he stuck out his arm to hail a taxi. Whatever it was, he couldn't worry about it. At the moment he had more pressing things on his mind.

In two days, for instance, his two weeks would be up and the board would move to go ahead with the deal. He leaned back against the worn seat of the taxi as it sped uptown. Think, man, *think*, he told himself. There had to be something somewhere, a loose thread he had somehow missed. Ordinarily, Jesse took fierce pride in the fact that he made few mistakes. Now, however, he was desperately hoping he had overlooked something in the files. The prospect of finding nothing, although an unpleasant possibility, was becoming more and more real, and Jesse was growing angry because of it. Let the damned deal go through, then, he thought bitterly. He'd challenge the next one. And if that one went through as well, he'd challenge the one after that and the one after that. He would not stop until the board of directors of BMI—and Russell, too,—realized what it would cost the company in the long run if they went on leasing land to Laramie Fork.

He wondered why he hadn't been told of this latest contract with Laramie Fork. The last one wasn't even signed yet and they were talking about another one. As president of the company, Jesse was prepared to use his power to do whatever he thought was right for BMI, yet to challenge them on this issue would put him in direct conflict with his father. And Jesse knew that if it came down to a fight for control of BMI, without another fifty voting shares to rival Russell's interest, he would lose.

Nevertheless, it was not without a certain what-have-I-got-to-lose attitude that he showed up at his parents' home for dinner the following evening, nerves steeled for a confrontation.

Dinner progressed at a torturous pace. The elegantly set table, the candlelight, the fine wine and food were lost beneath a shroud of tense silence as three figures sat at the table without speaking. Lucy felt sandwiched between two opposing forces, one or both about to go off at any moment. She made an attempt at light conversation but failed miserably when Russell shot her an unappreciating look from under dark brows, and Jesse sat there eating with a perturbed look on his face, eyes carefully fixed on his plate.

It was obvious to Lucy that these two were at odds about something again. She knew they hadn't been getting along lately, and she had foolishly thought that a pleasant candlelit dinner in a relaxed atmosphere might help relieve some of the tension that always seemed to grip her family these days. But she'd begun to regret her insistence that Jesse drive out from the city to join her and Russell for dinner as she picked at the impeccably prepared veal cordon bleu on her plate. At last, unable to bear the taut silence any longer, she put her fork down and said, "I don't suppose you two could confine your differences to the office."

Russell looked up, and in the same efficient tone with which he dictated memos at the office, said, "Your son seems intent upon prolonging the issue. Perhaps you should address your request to him."

Jesse rolled those dark eyes with annoyance. "Why is it that whenever I do something you don't like, I'm *her* son?"

"What issue?" Lucy looked to Jesse for an explanation. "Don't tell me you two are still quarreling over that Laramie Fork thing."

"He doesn't think it's necessary for the president of the company to know about the deals it makes," Jesse complained.

Lucy looked bewildered. "But why?"

"That's what I'd like to know." He swung his gaze to his father, saying, "And I'll prolong the issue for as long as I have to in order to make my point."

In a droll tone, Russell responded, "I believe you've already made your point. Several times, as a matter of fact."

"And I've yet to hear a satisfactory explanation to my question of why I wasn't told about this new deal with Laramie Fork."

"I told you," said Russell. "It wasn't necessary to bother you with it. If I bothered you with every minor detail of this operation, you'd complain that you were too busy to deal with that sort of thing."

"And I am," Jesse shot back. "We have a staff to take care of trivial matters. But I expect to be told about something that concerns the family property."

"Why? It's just a standard contract. Like all the others. What's so important about this one?"

"Maybe I don't like the idea of leasing any more Blackmoon land," said Jesse.

Russell sat back in his chair and looked at Jesse for a moment. Instead of a forceful response as expected, he said simply, "You're right. I should have told you, but there wasn't time. It happened while you were away. The boys at Laramie Fork wanted to contract for another couple of hundred acres, so I went with it."

Something inside Jesse came alert. His father never admitted to being wrong, and if he was doing so now, there had to be a reason for it. Jesse's black eyes fixed hard upon Russell's face. "I'd like to see those papers."

"Stop by Helen's desk in the morning and pick up a copy."

The easy compliance bothered him. "Fine. I'll do that."

"Is there anything else?"

"Yes. You can tell me what's suddenly so important about Blackmoon land."

Russell offered an elegant shrug. "I don't ask questions. I just make the best deal I can and sign on the dotted line."

"Maybe it's time you started asking questions," Jesse suggested tersely.

Russell picked up the crystal wine goblet from the table and sipped from it. He looked at Jesse over the rim of the glass and said, "Speaking of asking questions, I hear you've been working late a lot."

"That's right."

"What do you think you're going to find?"

"I don't know," said Jesse. "A way to stop you, maybe."

A thin smile stretched across Russell's lips. "You can't win, you know."

"Maybe not, but it's worth the try. I don't suppose that's something you would understand."

"I understand about making money and about building empires. What I don't understand is why you want to tear it down."

"Tear it down?" Jesse's eyes flared with incredulity. "Is that what you think I'm trying to do?"

"Well, aren't you?"

"Hell no, Dad," Jesse scoffed. "I just thought it was about time someone put a little pride back into the Blackmoon name."

"And how do you propose to do that?" Russell ventured. "By spending tens of thousands of dollars in legal fees to fight your own company? I can instruct the budget committee to withhold the funds for that sort of thing, you know."

"And I can use my personal funds if I have to. I'm way over twenty-one, Dad. I can do with my trust whatever I want, even if it means sinking the entire two million into legal fees to get you to stop leasing land to Laramie Fork."

Lucy fidgeted nervously in her seat during the heated exchange. "Russ, Jesse. Please."

Russell laughed. "Go on, use it all up. What would that get you? You wouldn't even know how to be poor, Jesse. Look at you. You've spent most of your adult life chasing women and driving fast cars. You like eating out at fine restaurants. You like nice clothes, fine wines. All those things cost money, Jesse. And where do you think it all comes from? It comes from making deals, the very deals you find so repugnant all of a sudden. What would you suggest we do then? Sell the company? Shut down our operations? Fire the hundreds of people who work for us and tell them 'Oh, we're terribly sorry, but you see, we have decided to put a little pride back into the Blackmoon name and that means putting all of you on the unemployment rolls?' And what do we tell our business partners? And the banks? And the stockholders?''

Jesse's eyes grew brighter as he listened. ''That's not what I'm suggesting, but if that's all you can think of, then why not? Go on. Scrap the whole thing. Either that or change the name to something else. Blackmoon was never meant to be synonymous with wealth.''

''I have raised this name to the pinnacle,'' Russell declared. ''*I* have made it known in international markets. *I* have given it assets in excess of fifty million. I'd say it was *me* who gave it some pride for the first time in history.''

Jesse stared back at him. ''I don't believe it. You actually view yourself as some kind of god, don't you? Well, let me tell you something, Dad. The name of Blackmoon was something to be proud of long before you came along and pumped it full of money.''

Russell chuckled at that. ''Yes, well, that may have been fine a hundred years ago around a campfire, but these are the 1980s. Men don't ride into battle these days whooping and hollering and wearing war paint on their faces and feathers in their hair. The best you could expect from counting coup was the right to brag about it.''

''Our ancestors did more than count coup,'' Jesse said. ''Your own great-grandfather fought beside Sitting Bull and Crazy Horse. Did you know that even today the Sioux people speak the name of Black Moon with reverence and pride? He's one of their heroes, Dad.''

"Yes, and no doubt a very poor one, too.''

Jesse shook his head disbelievingly. "Don't you ever see beyond the money?''

"What is there to see?''

Lucy sat there, eyes moving from her husband's face to her son's face and back again. It was bound to come, the inevitable explosion that occurred whenever they were in the same room together. But since Jesse had returned from South Dakota it had only gotten worse. She could easily predict whose voice would boom first in fiery anger. It would be Jesse's, for his was the temper that was always quickest to snap. He was just like—No, she mustn't think it . . . she must never think it, lest it show in her eyes.

So, it came as no surprise when Lucy heard Jesse's deep voice disrupt the tense silence hovering about the table as a result of Russell's question. Still, it made her jump in her chair and sent a faint tremor through her from the raw, blistering power resonating from deep in his throat.

Jesse jumped to his feet, snapping his chair back with enough force to send it toppling over. He shouted, "Our heritage! *That's* what there is. How much longer can you go on denying what we are? We're not descended from royalty, Dad. We don't have any Rockefellers or Vanderbilts on our family tree. We're *Indians*, Dad. Our forefathers hunted buffalo and cooked it over an open fire. They fought the cavalry and the immigrants and the government and everything that men like you stand for!''

"I was wondering when you would get around to that," Russell said, sneering. "It only took you thirty-eight years." His vengeful gaze flew to his wife's pale face. "Did you have anything to do with this?''

Lucy opened her mouth to speak, but before any words could emerge, Jesse's strong voice overrode hers. "Leave her out of this. She's not an Indian. She has nothing to do with it.''

But Russell's eyes remained locked on Lucy. "You were always determined to turn him into an Indian, weren't you? By hook or by crook you were going to make him just like—"

Lucy's voice tore from her throat in an agonized scream. "No! It's not true. Don't say it!"

"What's not true?" demanded a confused Jesse. "Mother?"

"Nothing," she nervously answered.

"Go on," Russell prompted. "Tell him." But when Lucy just sat there, unable to speak, he smiled coolly and said, "You always had a thing for Indians, didn't you, Luce? It had to be that wild streak in you. When we were kids growing up in South Dakota, you could ride and shoot arrows just like an Indian. *He* taught you that, didn't he? The fact is, you even fell in love with him. But you married me, and we both know why. It was the money. You knew that with me it would be easy street."

Jesse turned to his mother, noting the pained expression on her face. "What's he talking about?"

In a voice taut with suppressed emotion, Lucy replied, "Your father just likes to remind me that we all make mistakes."

Russell's eyes turned cold and hard like uncut stones in a face twisted with rage. "Mistakes?" he bellowed. "You didn't seem to think it was such a mistake back then. You wanted a ticket out of the wheat fields of South Dakota, and I was it. That's true, isn't it? *Isn't it?*"

"Yes!" she cried. "It's true. My father's health was failing. He couldn't run the ranch anymore. I knew how much he loved that land. I couldn't stand by and let it fall into the hands of the creditors. The only way to save it was to marry you. If it became Blackmoon land, at least it would remain in the family. I'm just glad my father died before he could see what you're doing to it. Jesse's right, Russ. That land is what put you where you are today. It deserves a lot more respect than you are giving it."

"Listen to you," her husband said mockingly. "You even sound like an Indian. Just like *him*."

Jesse's eyes flew from one face to the other. Were they talking about him? It couldn't be, for it was as if he weren't even in the room. The grip on his temper snapped. He brought one strong fist crashing down upon the table. The impact sent the plates and utensils clattering about and snapped Russell's and Lucy's eyes away from each other and up at the fiery black orbs that blazed down at them. "*Who*, damn it? Just like *who*?"

Several tense, silent seconds passed. Then, in a tone reeking of bitterness, Russell said simply, "My brother, Jess, that's who. She was always in love with him." His green gaze slid to Lucy's face, and to her he said, "And I always knew."

Not bothering to deny it, she said, "Then maybe you're the one who made the mistake."

"I don't think so. I knew exactly what I was getting. It was all part of the plan, you see. A Harvard education, a pretty wife, my land holdings sizably increased. I couldn't lose. I don't see what you have to complain about, my dear. I gave you everything you could want, didn't I? Clothes, jewels, furs, a fine home, vacations all over the world. What else could you possibly want?"

Tears began to well up in Lucy's eyes, which were carefully averted. In a soft voice, she answered, "Jess."

"And then what would you have had?" Russell snapped. "A life filled with hard work and nothing to show for it."

"Love," she said. "I would have had love."

He scoffed. "All the love in the world wouldn't have gotten you anything from that man. He was aimless, irresponsible, primitive. All he knew how to do was work the land." He laughed. It was a thick sound from deep in his throat. "With the possible exception of love, which neither of us deluded ourselves about when we entered this marriage, what could he have given you that I couldn't?"

Lucy was crying softly now, tears spilling from her eyes to dot the white linen tablecloth.

Jesse strode angrily to Russell, demanding, "Leave her alone!"

Russell whipped the cloth napkin from his knee and slapped it down on the table as he rose to his feet. "You stay out of this. It's between your mother and me."

"I won't have you speak to her this way."

"She's my wife. I'll speak to her any way I please."

Lucy sprang to her feet and rushed forward to stand between them. "No. Please. Stop!"

"I'll stop," Russell said, sneeringly, "as soon as you answer the question. What could he give you that I couldn't?"

Lucy began to sob. At any second Russell and Jesse would come to blows. She had to say something. The words came tumbling from her lips before she could stop them. "He gave me Jesse!" she cried. "He gave me my son!"

It was as if they had suddenly entered another zone of consciousness. For several desperate moments as time stood still, Lucy's words struck their target and sank in deep. No one moved as the shattering reality came crashing home.

Russell slipped wordlessly back down into his chair. His expression was unreadable. He had suspected, but hearing the confirmation stunned him, nevertheless.

Lucy moved in a trance to the door and disappeared from the room. Upstairs in her bedroom, she went to the window. She drew the curtain back and peered out at the crescent moon. As tight as a bowstring, that's how Jess would have described it. The thought of him brought a smile to her lips and a quiver to her heart. She felt amazingly calm in the midst of the startling revelation and its resulting tumult. It was as if a great weight had been lifted from her shoulders, and now that it was over, she was glad. Ever since Jesse had returned from South Dakota, changed in subtle ways that only her keen eyes could detect, she had known in her heart that it was just a matter of time. How many times she had wanted to tell him, to shout aloud to the world that it was Jess, the Indian, the warrior, the lover, who had given her her dark-eyed son. How Russell must hate her for this. Well, it didn't matter. It wasn't as if she had his love to lose. Rather, it was Jesse who worried her. How was he taking this news? Would he despise her for not having told him a long time ago?

Jesse stormed from the house, slid his lean frame behind the wheel of his car and peeled out of the driveway. He took the expressway at a speed of eighty, not caring who didn't like it, including the highway patrol. His thoughts and emotions collided within him. He didn't hate his mother—he could never hate her. Sure, it would have been easier for him had he known the truth a long time ago. Things would have made sense then, like why Russell hated him so and why he had never felt much of a part of the mold into which he'd always been expected to fit. He despised the circumstances under which the truth had been forced out into the open, but it was better that he'd found out now than never at all.

They used to joke about it, saying that he looked more like his uncle Jess than Russell, but Jesse never would have guessed to what extent it was true. The revelation was a forceful shove into the reality of who and what he really was—an Indian. Suddenly, this thing that had sat nameless for so long within him came into sharp focus, and something Carly had said to him filled his thoughts with a new and powerful meaning. It was about being an Indian and

being one with the land. The two, she had said, were insep-
arable.

The fight for the Black Hills, the one Jesse had told Carly
he had no part in, was his battle, after all. He had never
been more certain of anything in his life. If he had lived 150
years ago, he would have laced feathers into his black hair,
painted his face, mounted his fastest war pony and gone to
war against the enemy that threatened his land. But these
were the 1980s. The enemy did not wear a loincloth and
moccasins and shoot arrows at him. The enemy wore a
three-piece suit and had eyes of green. The enemy was Russell.

Jesse's grip tightened around the steering wheel as he
drove, knuckles whitening from the pressure. It was time, he
knew, to go to war.

Chapter 10

He had no idea whether the telephone had rung just once or several times. His eyes snapped open to the sound that screeched close to his ear. Somehow, he found the strength to move. He thrust out his hand and felt around in the darkness for the phone, knocking the ashtray off the night table in the process. He mumbled a vague "Hello?" into the receiver.

"Jesse? Jesse, I have to speak to you."

His head was killing him. "Huh. Who's this?"

"It's Helen."

"Helen? What the—"

"I can't do it, Jesse. I've tried to tell myself that I owe it to him out of loyalty. Twenty-five years I've worked for that man. I've seen him do some pretty underhanded dealing at times, but there's something about all this that frightens me."

Jesse rolled over onto his back and rubbed his eyes, which were still heavy with sleep. He squinted into the darkness at the clock on the table. Three-thirty. "Helen, what the hell are you talking about?"

He had a right to be annoyed. What she did not know was that after returning home from the fateful dinner at his parents' house, his first thought had been to get stinking drunk. Toward that end he had downed enough Scotch to render himself incapable of thinking... indeed, of feeling. He had fallen asleep fully clothed on the bed, only to be awakened now, many hours later, by the shrill blast of the telephone and Helen talking nonsense.

"I'm sorry, Jesse," she was saying.

"Can't this wait until morning?" he groaned. "Or better yet, late afternoon?"

"No, it can't."

Something in her voice made him pull himself up and listen. It sounded like fear.

"Jesse? Are you awake?"

"I'm awake," he grumbled. "What is it?"

"It's that new contract with Laramie Fork."

"The one for the coal?"

"Yes. But that's not what it is."

Her riddles were beginning to provoke him. "What are you talking about?" he asked roughly. "You mean the contract is *not* with Laramie Fork?"

"Yes, it is. But Jess..." She paused for one uncertain moment, then said, "It's not coal."

"Look, Helen, it's three-thirty in the morning, and I've got a hangover the size of the state of Montana. Whatever you're talking about, you'd better just say it. I'm in no mood for—"

"It's uranium."

He said nothing as the words penetrated his mind, jerking it fully awake. *"What?"*

"I said—"

"I heard what you said, damn it. What the—I didn't know there was any uranium under Blackmoon land." A sudden thought fell into place. If there was uranium under Blackmoon land, then it stood to reason that it was under reservation land as well. "What's going on?"

"I don't know," she said. "But there's more."

"I can hardly wait to hear it," he droned. "All right, let's have it."

She took a deep breath and told him, "Your father is negotiating not only with Laramie Fork for another two thousand acres, but he's been talking to several large energy concerns as well. Something big is going on, Jesse. Something I don't quite understand, but I thought you should know about it."

There was silence on the line, but she knew he was there by his hard breathing. "Jesse," she ventured, "if your father finds out that I've spoken to you about this, he'll fire me."

Jesse snorted derisively. His father. That was certainly a laugh. In a flat tone he told her, "Don't worry, Helen. Nothing's going to happen, because he isn't going to find out."

"What are you going to do?"

Jesse's mind was working fast. "I was going to stop by your desk tomorrow to pick up a copy of the new Laramie Fork contract, but I don't suppose he would chance giving me a copy of the real thing."

Guiltily, she said, "I was instructed to type up a duplicate set of documents substituting coal for uranium and changing the royalty clause to be appropriate for coal."

"Can you get me a copy of the real thing?"

"I think so."

"Good girl. Now look, I want you to do me a favor. I want you to put it in an envelope and send it down to my office first thing in the morning, just as you would any routine papers. I don't want anyone to suspect that there is anything unusual in that envelope, least of all my...I mean Russell. Got that?"

"Yes."

"There's something else. I want to know why you told me this."

She answered honestly. "I don't know. This whole thing scares me. I also happen to think you're right about not leasing any more land to Laramie Fork, and I figured that since your father has controlling interest in the company, you need all the help you can get."

"You're right about that," he said sardonically.

"It's a shame that your father's brother isn't alive."

"Why do you say that?"

"It's just that with the shares he owned, you and he might have had the power to fight your father."

Jesse straightened up on the bed. "What shares? How do you know my, er, uncle owned shares in BMI?"

She replied, "You don't work closely with a man for twenty-five years and not learn things about him and his family. I know, for instance, that those shares are just sitting there."

"How do you know that?" he fired at her.

"Once, many years ago your father tried to get control of them, but as I recall, his attorney advised him that they could only go to his brother's heirs. It seems that when your grandfather left his land to his two sons, it was under the stipulation that neither could get control of the other's shares, that they were meant to be passed down to their respective heirs. But since your uncle Jess died without leaving any heirs, his shares have remained inactive."

That was it! The ammunition Jesse needed to fight Russell had just been dropped into his lap by an unwitting Helen. Jesse let out a loud whoop of triumph. "Helen, have I ever told you how wonderful you are, especially at three forty-five in the morning?''

"I don't understand," she said, confused at his sudden turn of mood.

"Never mind. Get some sleep. I'll see you bright and early in the morning."

"I thought you said late afternoon."

"Forget what I said before. Things are different now. I'll be in early. And Helen, hold on to your hat. Things are about to blow wide open."

"Jesse, you don't mean—"

"I sure do."

"Oh, dear." She sounded troubled. "You were right, then, when you said that the day might come when I would have to make a choice. But how can I?"

"Helen," he said, "I think you already have."

Jesse hung up and reached in the darkness for the pack of cigarettes that sat beside the clock on the night table. He hadn't had much luck in cutting down. The funny thing was that while he'd been out in South Dakota, he hadn't thought much about smoking. It must have been that hot, arid air scorching his lungs like cigarette smoke. He lit the cigarette, searched around for the fallen ashtray and set them down while he undressed. He climbed back into bed and pulled the white sheet up over himself. A shaft of pearly moonlight slanted through the open window to fall across his bare chest. With the sheet resting just below his navel, he smoked in the darkness, inhaling the smoke deep into his lungs and letting it out slowly through pursed lips.

He lay there, the red glow of the cigarette like a tiny beacon in the darkness. Uranium, so that's what it was all about. He'd known it had to be more than coal, but he'd had no idea it was anything like this. Uranium, he knew, meant only one thing. Nuclear power.

Jesse got no sleep that night. The next morning he was up early. He showered and shaved, dressed in a cool cotton suit and left for work.

The contract with Laramie Fork was waiting on his desk in a plain brown envelope just as he had instructed. He slipped the document from the envelope and studied it. Damn them, he thought bitterly. Damn them all!

Things moved swiftly after that. It was time to call in those favors. The only reason he had not done so before was because he simply had not known where to begin looking. Knowing what he now knew, he put his first call through to the Energy Department, in Washington, D.C. Many phone calls and several hours later, Jesse had the whole picture before him, and it was worse than he would ever have guessed.

The power companies wanted the land because the Black Hills and the surrounding country, including Pine Ridge Indian reservation and Blackmoon land, contained extensive uranium deposits. It was a veritable mother lode of nuclear power. Collectively, several large energy concerns, among them the Laramie Fork Power Company, had plans to construct thirteen coal-fired, ten-thousand-megawatt plants and a nuclear "park" with up to twenty-five reactors.

Jesse was aghast. They were going to turn the Black Hills into a nuclear playground complete with waste-reprocessing and disposal facilities. Such intensive energy development would surely destroy the beauty of the hills forever and wrench from the Sioux people their most sacred places. They had to be stopped.

Jesse swiveled his chair around toward the window and looked out at the skyline for a long time, thinking, plotting. The shares. He had to get hold of those shares Helen had told him about. Of course, it would mean coming forward with the truth, and a family scandal would become public. No doubt the press would have a field day with the news, and Russell would be furious. So what if he didn't like it, Jesse thought belligerently. There were plenty of things he himself didn't like. Hangovers, for instance, like the one he had this morning. Somehow, though, he managed to deal with them. Russell would just have to do the same.

But first, before he did anything else, there was something very important Jesse had to do. He turned back to the desk and picked up the phone. To the voice that answered, he said, "Operator, I want to place a call to Broken Bow, South Dakota, person to person to Dr. Carly McAllister."

Carly could hear the telephone ringing as she fumbled with the front door, arms laden with bags of groceries. Inside, she hurried through the living room, past the clamoring telephone to the kitchen, where she deposited the groceries on the table before racing back to the living room to answer the phone.

"Hello? Hello?" she panted into the receiver.

It was too late. The sound of the dial tone forced a sharp oath from Carly's lips. She slammed down the receiver and returned to the kitchen. One of these days she would have an answering machine installed, she swore to herself as she unpacked the groceries and put them away. She shuddered to think that someone might need emergency medical care and she would not be there to receive the message. She fished her checkbook from her handbag and scanned the balance. With her funds dipping dangerously low, an answering machine was out of the question.

The sound of a car approaching outside caught Carly frowning and brought her eyes up from the checkbook. With a dismal sigh she dropped it back into her bag and went to the window to look out.

A little feeling caught at the edge of her stomach at the sight of the familiar pickup raising a funnel of dust behind it as it neared. The feeling was not a good one. She turned from the window and went outside.

The heat rose from the parched ground in steamy undulations, making the whole countryside look as if it were moving. Carly swept a few loose strands of hair away from her face and ran the back of her arm across her brow, which was lightly dotted with perspiration. She stood on the porch watching the pickup approach the house and come to a halt.

It was two weeks since she had been forced to fight off Luke's misguided advances on the road to Willie Nighthawk's place. From the way he shifted uneasily from foot to foot after stepping down from the cab, it was obvious that the incident was still fresh in Luke's mind as well. "Hi, Carly."

"Hi, Luke."

He gestured toward the red Mustang that sat under the cottonwood where Carly had parked it. "The last I saw your car it was stuck in a ditch about three miles from here."

A flush of hot emotion overwhelmed Carly at the sudden, unexpected reminder of the night she had gotten stuck in the mud with Jesse. "Willie came by the other day and gave me a tow. Then he did a little work on the engine and got it running for me," she explained.

"Why didn't you ask me? I would've fixed it for you." His long black braids glistened in the sunshine as he stood looking up at her. His worn and dusty Stetson dangled from his hand; his dark eyes squinted into the light.

"I know. But Willie didn't have the money to pay for his office visits, so I figured we would simply trade services."

"The barter system, huh?"

"I guess you could call it that."

He walked onto the porch, the old timbers creaking from his weight, and came to stand beside her. She could smell the heavy scent of male perspiration that ringed his shirt. "How about me?" he asked. "I still owe you for those stitches you put in my head when I fell off my horse a couple of months ago. Remember?''

"Forget it," said Carly. "It's on me."

"No, really, what do I owe you?"

"I said forget it, Luke. It was nothing."

In a disgruntled tone he replied, "No, I don't want to forget it. The others don't forget. They pay you back however they can. What about me? I don't need your damned charity."

Perhaps it was the heat that had gotten the best of both of them. Carly whirled to face him, planting both arms akimbo. "All right, Luke, be pigheaded about it. If you insist on paying me, that'll be forty dollars, please." She held out an impatient hand, palm up.

Luke thrust his own hand deep into the pocket of his jeans, but when he pulled it out, it was empty. "Uh, Carly? I'm a little short of cash this week."

She had to laugh at the ridiculous front they were both putting up, for his chances of having any money to pay her were as remote as Carly's chances of taking it. "I seem to recall you were a little short of cash when I stitched you up, too. One of these days, Luke, you're going to have to get yourself a job."

"How do you know I haven't been looking?" he shot back.

"Have you?"

"Yeah," he said with a burst of anger that died to dismal resignation when he added, "But no one's got any work for an Indian."

Carly's smile drooped. There it was, that expression on his face, that hopeless ring to his voice that echoed the plight of so many of his kind. "Listen, Luke," she said, "if you really want to pay me back, maybe there is something you can do for me."

His eyes seemed to brighten a little at that, and he took a tentative step toward her. "I knew you'd change your mind!"

Carly's hand came up to halt his advance. "I haven't changed my mind about *that*."

Dejection dulled his eyes once again. "Oh," he muttered. "What is it?"

"I need some information, and I thought someone like you probably has better access to it than I do." It was reasonable to assume that Luke's aimless wanderings brought him in contact with more people. A few questions asked in the right places might produce some answers. "I'd like you to find out who in these parts has been approached to sell their land."

"And where am I supposed to do this asking?"

"The canteen in town, maybe. Frank's Café in Pine Ridge. You should have no trouble hitting most of the bars on the reservation." The remark was not without its foundation, for even now Carly could smell the alcohol on his breath.

"Why don't you just call George and ask him?" he suggested. "He's bound to know."

"I already have, and he doesn't."

"Or so he says," he muttered.

Carly looked at him curiously. "What's that supposed to mean?"

Luke gave a careless shrug and replied, "Lately he doesn't seem to have the time for anything but those meetings of his. He doesn't even like to play poker with the guys anymore."

His remark reminded Carly of George's promise to help her get to the bottom of the killings and of the persistent feeling she had that he was merely placating her. It was a small measure of comfort to know that she was not the only one to get a taste of George's seeming indifference. "Oh, well," she said, "you know George. He's a busy man with a lot on his mind these days."

"Yeah, right," he grumbled. "Okay. I'll do what I can." He walked back to the truck with a loping gait, kicking up the arid dust with his cowboy boots. He swung his lanky frame behind the wheel, slammed the door, then leaned out the open window and said, "By the way, I came by today to ask if you're going to the ceremony this year."

He was referring to the annual Sun Dance ceremony that took place each August at Pine Ridge. Many Sioux from other reservations and other plains tribes from hundreds of miles away came to participate in the days of feasting and the nights of dancing. Although the ceremony also attracted its share of tourists with their inquisitive cameras, it also brought a strengthening of tradition among the proud Sioux people. "I wouldn't dream of missing it," said Carly.

"Yeah, well, I was thinking that maybe you'd like to go with me."

She hesitated, not quite knowing what to say. What could she do with a man who refused to take no for an answer? Tactfully, she said, "You know how it is, Luke. It's hard for me to make definite plans. Tell you what. Why don't I just see you there?"

He slapped his Stetson back on his head and thrust the key into the ignition. Without another word between them, he drove off.

Carly stood there for several minutes, watching the pickup disappear down the winding road. The hot breeze played with the ends of her hair, whipping them about her face as the dust swirled in small eddies about her legs. She turned to go back inside, but froze in midstep. Something caught in her mind. Her thoughts flew back to the day she had been run down in Pine Ridge. She remembered seeing a flash of blue pass swiftly before her eyes just as she hit the pavement. Funny that she should remember that now. It was only when Carly realized what triggered the memory that her hand flew instinctively to her mouth and she gasped. She turned back to the pickup disappearing from view. It was blue.

She walked slowly back into the house, shaking her head with disbelief. Surely her rebuff of Luke's advances had not angered him to the point where he would try to run her down. She dismissed the notion as preposterous. Besides, the accident had happened so swiftly she was not even sure it was a pickup truck. It could have been a sedan or a station wagon or a go-cart, for all she knew.

Nevertheless, two days later Carly's heart gave a little shudder when she answered the phone and heard his voice.

"Carly? It's me, Luke. Listen, I may have something for you. You know what you asked me to find out for you? Well, it seems a lot of people have been approached to sell their land, but no one's saying very much about it. Makes me think maybe they've been told to keep their mouths shut. There's something else, too. When I asked who's making the offers, I found out it's a company called BMI."

Carly had already guessed that BMI was at the bottom of this thing, so it came as no surprise to hear it confirmed by Luke. Rather, it was what Luke said next that set her to wondering.

"The way I hear it, something big's going on. Even the Blackmoon land up north is somehow involved. I drove by there a few weeks ago. You should've seen all the rigs."

"Blackmoon?" she questioned.

"Yeah. Blackmoon's the family that owns all that land up north. As far as I know, the other private owners in the area haven't been affected by it, but who knows? . . . Carly, are you there?"

"Yes, Luke, I'm here. I hear you. Thanks. Thanks a lot."

When Carly hung up, she stood there for several minutes, her mind working furiously to form connections out of loose threads. From the deeds she had seen on the microfilm she knew that BMI was buying reservation land and leasing it to Laramie Fork. Luke's mention of the name Blackmoon had sparked something in her mind. Suddenly she remembered. On the microfilm records, under the typed name of BMI had appeared a sprawling signature; the name penned on behalf of the corporation had been Blackmoon.

She picked up the phone and dialed New York City information. "Operator? Do you have a listing for Blackmoon?"

After a short wait, the operator told her, "Sorry, ma'am, but that number is unlisted."

"I see. How about a listing for BMI?"

"One moment, please." In about thirty seconds an automated voice responded with the number.

Carly hit the hook switch on the phone to summon the dial tone, then dialed the number. She could hear the static on the line as the call raced through the wires. A voice at the other end answered with crisp efficiency. "Good morning, BMI."

Carly took a deep breath and said, "Good morning. I'm calling from Laramie Fork Power Company. I'm addressing a letter to Mr. Blackmoon and I would like to confirm the address."

"Certainly. That's 305 Park Avenue, 10022."

She thanked the woman and hung up. Her heart was racing, her thoughts forging full steam ahead. Somebody at BMI had a lot of explaining to do. The president of the company, no doubt. Thinking to call him, she reached out to dial, but pulled her hand back. No, she would tell him to his face exactly what she thought of him and what he was doing. She would show the powerful head of BMI that she was not afraid of him and his millions!

With a determined glint in her blue eyes, Carly picked up the phone and booked a flight to New York City.

When that was done, she marched back into the kitchen, where she had left her bag dangling from a cane-backed chair. She dug her checkbook out again and reexamined the balance. The answering machine would have to wait, but her trip to New York could not.

Chapter 11

New York City lay trapped in the grip of a heat wave. Steamy vapors rose from the cracked pavement, mingling with the humidity to make the mere act of breathing laborious.

The heat only intensified the rank smells of the city. The garbage that lay in bags alongside the curb awaiting pickup and attracting summer flies emitted a foul odor. The noxious exhaust fumes belched out by the weekday traffic bleared the eyes of pedestrians. The sweet, sticky smell of the hot pavement mixed with the pungent aroma of boiling franks and tart sauerkraut from a corner stand.

The streets of the city were rushing rivers of traffic. Masses of bodies rushed this way and that, all moving at the frenetic pace typical of the city.

But along with the disagreeable smells and the frustrating congestion came the lovely fragrance of green grass and summer blossoms from Central Park, that oasis in the midst of the Manhattan desert. Street musicians played to appreciative onlookers everything from Mozart to rhythm and blues. The hansom carriages pulled by clopping horses lent an air of charm and quaintness to the thoroughly modern metropolis, helping to create the paradox that was uniquely New York.

Carly sat forward in the seat of the taxi, staring out the window with the wide-eyed wonder of a child. She had forgotten how mighty and wonderful this place was, but then, she had not seen very much of it during her days at New York University Medical Center. During her internship she had shared a Greenwich Village studio apartment with another intern. The long hours she had put in at the hospital left no time for sight-seeing or nightlife. Only an occasional movie broke the monotony and kept her from going totally insane. That had been years ago, and as Carly looked out the window now, absorbing all the colors, sights, sounds and smells, it was as if she were seeing the city for the first time.

In a curious way the city reminded her of Jesse. Maybe it was the raw, unharnessed power and the throb and hum of electricity sizzling in the August air that lent a certain strength to the beauty. It was not surprising that she should think of him, for in looking around her, she knew why this was his home. Somewhere in this steel forest of a city was Jesse, but Carly's chances of finding him, even if she wanted to, which, of course, she didn't, were remote.

The thought of Jesse did unsettling things to her. Nothing these past few weeks had distracted her from the intense longing that had taken hold of her. Somewhere inside of her was a vast empty space begging to be filled. To Carly's dismay, she was discovering that nothing could relieve the perpetual ache.

Every black-haired stranger who passed on the street set Carly's heart thumping. Was it possible that she missed the possessiveness of his arms and the audacity of his kiss? Yes, she thought miserably, that and all the other things about him. Did she actually fancy herself in love with a man she scarcely knew? She railed against the possibility, but in the end she was forced to admit that his presence was there in her blood like a dangerous drug. That very first kiss he had presumptuously helped himself to had hooked her to the taste of him.

Don't think about him, Carly told herself. He's gone, and that's that. She slid back in the seat, no longer interested in the sights around her, hopelessly mired in the realization that she had seen Jesse Black for the very last time.

The taxi pulled up before a building on Park Avenue. Carly paid the fare and got out. With people rushing past her, she stood on the sidewalk looking up at the black marble letters atop the revolving doors. BMI. The name sent a faint shudder of foreboding down her spine. Pulling in a deep breath for support, Carly straightened her shoulders and walked inside.

Jesse sat in a high-backed leather chair behind his desk, hunched over a stack of file folders. Helen was at his side, making occasional comments and jotting down notes as Jesse dictated them. She had made it clear that her loyalty to Russell would not permit her to swing her allegiance entirely over to Jesse. Nevertheless, she was willing to help him in whatever way she could. Knowing the differences that existed between the two men, however, she wisely confined her visits to Jesse's office to those times when Russell was out, as he was today. The matter of the uranium contract remained a secret between her and Jesse—for the time being, at least.

"And what about this?" Jesse pointed to a document in one of the folders.

"That's just a standard deed between BMI and someone named Mary Yazzie. As you can see, everything is in order, right down to the price per acre."

"When did we start stealing people's land?" he growled.

"Stealing?" She looked at him quizzically. "I don't understand what you mean."

"This price per acre. Look at it. It's highway robbery, that's what I mean."

"But Jesse," Helen said gently, "you yourself approved this deal."

"That was before I knew what I know now."

She studied him from above. In his own way he could be as exacting and demanding an employer as Russell, and certainly as intimidating with that deep voice and those fierce black eyes that fairly screamed Indian. Yet beneath the surface Helen sensed an acute vulnerability that she suspected even Jesse was unaware of. Despite the efficient way he masked it, something was hurting him, something that went far deeper than he would allow anyone to see.

"And this?" he wanted to know.

"That's the lease agreement between BMI and Laramie Fork covering the Yazzie land. Again, a standard contract."

Jesse shook his head in disgust. "Why are we leasing so cheaply to Laramie Fork? It's as if we're giving the rights away. Call Fred Santini in Legal and find out everything you can about the men who run Laramie Fork. We must have a file on them. Who are those bastards, anyway?" He sat back and tossed his pen onto the desk with an aggravated gesture. "Nothing. Absolutely nothing. No mention of uranium anywhere in these papers."

"Maybe that contract is the only one," Helen suggested.

But Jesse wasn't so sure about that. Something deep down in his gut told him there was more to these coal leases than met the eye. People didn't die for coal, he reminded himself. He'd been over these files until he knew each word by heart. There wasn't even a typographical error anywhere to be found. It was as if everything were *too* perfect. There had to be a connection, there just *had* to be, and if there was, he would find it.

Just then a commotion from the outer office drew their heads up in unison. Jesse heard his secretary's frantic voice. "Miss! Miss, you can't go in there!"

The door swung open on its hinges and in burst Carly, blue eyes fired up with angry determination. "I don't care if he *is* busy," she said angrily to the secretary, who ran in after her. "I have business with Mr. Blackmoon, and I damned well intend to—" The rest of the words caught in her throat, and Carly's heart struck painfully in her chest when she saw a familiar handsome face behind the desk. It was Jesse! What was *he* doing here? And then it hit her, with the impact of a Mack truck, even before she heard the secretary say, "I'm sorry, Mr. Blackmoon, I tried to stop her, but—"

Jesse was already in motion, rising from his chair and stepping around to the front of the desk, eyes fixed apprehensively on Carly's face, which had gone all wooden and white. "That's all right, Susan. I'll take care of this."

For several stricken moments they stared at each other. When Carly found her voice, it emerged ragged and incredulous, scratching roughly at the back of her throat. 'Blackmoon? *You?*"

He took a cautious step toward her but stopped at the warning look in her eyes. "Carly, I know what you must be thinking, but—"

Somehow she found the strength to move from that spot. With a strangled sob she whirled and ran from the room. With hot tears stinging her eyes, blinding her vision, she ran down the corridor. She could hear Jesse calling out behind her in a strained voice. "Carly, wait! Let me explain! *Please!*"

He chased her down the hallway, heedless of the heads that turned and stared. The elevator doors were just closing when he reached them. He slammed his hand angrily against the door and muttered a fierce epithet as he punched the Down button. When the car finally returned, he rode it down to the lobby and raced out into the street. He looked in all directions for a sign of Carly, but she was gone, vanished into thin air. A constricting fear welled up inside of him as he walked back inside, making him feel sick to his stomach. Oh, God, he thought desperately, what have I done?

Many hours later a pale moon shadowed the big city. The stars were strung like Christmas lights across the dark sky. A saffron-tinted cloud floated above the skyscrapers, hanging for a while atop the Empire State Building as if snagged on the spire before moving on.

The moonlight tapped at the window of the high-rise apartment on the east side of Manhattan, reflecting on Jesse emerging from the bathroom, naked except for a white terry-cloth towel wrapped about his midsection. With brisk motions he rubbed the moisture from his hair with a towel, then walked barefoot to the bar and poured himself a drink.

The hot shower had done little to ease the tension that had been building up in his body all afternoon. Maybe a stiff drink would help.

But the drink did not help either to shake from Jesse's mind the look on Carly's face just seconds before she had run from his office. He had seen...what? Disbelief? Anger? Pain? Yes, all that and more. Written all over her beautiful face he had also seen fear. How she must hate him. If only he had told her who he was that very first day. If only she had not found out this way. If only there was some way to make her understand that he had never meant to hurt her. If only. . . if only. The words ticked like a crazy clock inside his mind—useless words, meaningless words.

Jesse downed the brandy in his glass. The liquor fired its way down his throat but did little to quell the anger building up inside him like steam in a pressure cooker. Jesse reached again for the crystal decanter and poured himself more of the amber liquid. He contemplated it for a few moments as he swirled it around in the short-stemmed glass, then swallowed it. He poured himself another.

He carried the glass to the telephone and dialed Carly's number in Broken Bow. He let her phone ring longer than it had to before he slammed down the receiver. Surely she'd had enough time to hop the first flight back home. He waited five minutes and called again. The sound of the doorbell elicited a sharp expletive from Jesse as he dropped the receiver back into its cradle. Feeling testy and frustrated, a dangerous combination when fired up with brandy, he stalked to the door and yanked it open with a gruff "Yeah, what is it?"

All thought screeched to a halt the moment he saw her. He stepped aside for her to enter.

Carly walked past him into the apartment. She looked pale and tired, Jesse thought as his eyes swallowed her up. His deep voice spiked the tension that was strung tautly between them. "I thought you would have been on a plane back home by now."

The truth was she had taken a taxi to the airport, intent on fleeing with all possible haste, only to be informed by the ticket agent that there would be a three-hour wait. Those three hours had been the longest in her life. The waitress at the airport coffee shop had looked at her sympathetically as she sat in a corner of the booth, spilling tears into her coffee.

But as she sat there, Carly's pain had begun to take on different proportions. Three hours and many tears later she had ceased feeling sorry for herself. She began to grow angry and indignant. She was furious at Jesse for the way he had betrayed her, but mostly Carly was angry at herself for the way she had run away like a coward. Once before, she had run away from a broken heart. She was tired of running, damn it. After that she had returned to the city to wander the streets, thinking hard about what her next move would be. She remembered looking up from her tortured thoughts to find that night had fallen. Feeling lonely and afraid, she'd arrived at Jesse's; for what reason she was not entirely certain. She could have told him all this, of course, but she was still smarting over his betrayal and was not about to give him any more than he deserved. Flatly, she said, "I nearly was."

"What stopped you?"

She met his gaze without flinching. "There was something I had to do first."

He watched her closely, searching for a sign that she did not hate him. "Can I get you something to drink?"

"Sure. Why not?" She was trying hard to hate him. Maybe a drink would give her the courage to see beyond that handsome face and nearly naked body to what he really was underneath, a calculating scoundrel. Yet in spite of herself Carly could not prevent her eyes from following him when he walked to the bar. She noticed the way he moved, with easy, confident strides, and the play of muscles across his broad back, the flexing cords of his legs and the damp black hair curling at the nape of his neck.

He returned and placed a glass in her hand. Assuming a cool air, she said, "Thank you," and took a sip of the brandy.

"You must have charmed the pants off of Ernie for him to let you up without announcing you," said Jesse.

"If you mean that nice man downstairs in the red uniform, yes, he was very obliging."

He had no doubt that poor old Ernie had been putty in Carly's hands. Not that she flaunted her assets. That wasn't her style. Rather, the seductive grace that enhanced her every movement came as naturally to her as breathing. She seemed truly unaware of the effect she had on men.

"How did you know where I live?" he asked.

"I saw some mail on your secretary's desk this afternoon," Carly explained, grateful for the conversation to take their minds off his nakedness. "I recognized a phone bill, and I noticed the return address on the envelopes of what looked to be other personal stuff. I assumed it was yours."

"You assumed right."

"So I see," she responded dryly. Her glance flicked over him, permitting a quick wordless comment on his state of undress. "Do you intend to stay like that?"

Jesse looked down at the towel that hugged his middle and said, "To tell you the truth, I wasn't expecting company, but if it bothers you, I'll put something on."

It did, but not in the way he thought, for instead of offending Carly's sense of modesty, it only provoked the most scandalous thoughts. She cleared her throat nervously and said, "Please."

"Sure. Make yourself comfortable. I'll only be a minute."

Comfortable? she thought after he had disappeared from the room. There was little chance of that, for as soon as she had set foot in this apartment, Carly had felt as if she'd walked into the lion's den. His absence did, however, give her a chance to look around.

She was struck by the unpretentious air of the place. It certainly didn't look to her like a den of seduction with its uncluttered furnishings and straightforward look. There was no flash of wealth in these warm earth tones, just an honest comfort with a distinct masculine feel. The room made no attempt to mask its primordial appeal or disguise its earthiness. It echoed Jesse in every corner.

Several minutes later he was back dressed in a pair of jeans, a T-shirt that spanned the broad expanse of his chest, and sneakers. His hair fell in damp, dark strands across his forehead. Noticing her empty glass, he asked, "Can I get you another?"

"No, thank you. One more and I might forget what I came here for."

"Would that be such a bad idea?"

Carly struggled to harden herself against the warm, seductive tone of his voice. Don't be misled by his friendliness, she told herself. "Yes," she answered. "It would."

"What *did* you come here for anyway, Carly?"

She placed her glass down carefully on the table, drew in a deep breath and faced him. "I came to New York to tell the president of BMI just what I think of him and the way he does business, but since you and he are apparently one and the same, I may as well address my comments to you, Jesse Black, or Blackmoon, or whatever your name is."

Jesse grimaced. "Sounds bad."

"It's not so much what you've done to me," she said. "In a way it was my own fault. I should have seen it coming. I should have seen you for the kind of man you really are. I suppose a man as good-looking as you really can't help himself. It must be in your genes or something. But you must pardon me if I object to becoming just one more notch in your belt. Or should I say one more coup for the brave Sioux warrior."

The remark stung. Jesse winced, not only at her suggestion that he was some kind of notorious womanizer but at the reference to his Indianness, which had taken on a whole new meaning to him these past few days that Carly could not know.

"It's the others," she went on. "All those people killed for something you stand for. Something you are."

"And just what am I, Carly?" he asked, his tone faintly threatening.

"You're a slick businessman who can't see beyond the figures to the emotions underneath. You think you can use your charm and looks to get what you want, and if that doesn't work, you'll use your money."

"So? Does that make me a killer?" he demanded.

"Of course not. I don't think you did it with your own hands, but a man as wealthy as you can buy anything, even someone to do the killing for him."

Jesse's black eyes grew fiery bright, and Carly thought she had gone too far when he took a menacing step toward her. Instinctively she back away. Her blue eyes went wide. "How could you?" she cried. "Have you no conscience?" Teardrops glistened at the corners of her eyes, threatening to spill from her lashes. Her cheeks were flushed.

She was right to be angry with him. He deserved her wrath for the way he had hidden the truth from her. And she was right; he was a slick businessman who was not above using his charm to get what he wanted. But he was no womanizer, and certainly no killer! He swallowed the rest of the brandy in his glass. This time he did not bother to refill it. He was suddenly cold sober, and no amount of alcohol would rectify that. He turned to face her. Running a hand through his dark hair to sweep it from his eyes, he said, "You're right. I should have told you who I was, and for that I apologize. But I'm not the one you want."

"You're the president of BMI, aren't you?"

"Yes, but it's the chairman of the board you're looking for."

"You mean your father?"

There was an imperceptible wince behind his eyes before he snorted contemptuously. "I guess you could say that."

"Then I want you both to understand that I intend to fight you in whatever way I can."

"I'd advise you against tangling with him," Jesse warned. "You don't know what he's like."

"If it runs in the family, then I already have a fairly good idea." She missed the sharp look from those dark eyes as she turned away to leave. She was halfway to the door when Jesse came up swiftly behind her. He clamped a hand over her arm and spun her back around. "I've let you say some things I wouldn't take from anyone," he growled, "because in some respects you're right. But you don't seem to understand what I'm telling you. He's unscrupulous. He'll eat you up alive. He'll do anything to get what he wants—anything."

Carly glared up at him, refusing to back down despite the way his fingers bit into her flesh. "Does that include murder?" she challenged.

It was a question Jesse had asked himself. He did not want to believe that the man he had called father for thirty-eight years was capable of such a thing, but neither could he completely dispel the notion. "What do you intend to do?"

"I intend to see him and tell him what I think of him."

"What can I do to make you change your mind about seeing him?"

"Nothing."

Jesse knew by the stubborn tilt of her chin and by the spark of angry determination that brightened her eyes as she squirmed to break free of his grip that she would not listen to reason. He watched her struggle for a moment more, then he said, "You still haven't answered my question."

"What question?"

"I asked you why you came here."

"I told you. I came to New York to—"

"No, not to New York. *Here.* To my apartment."

"I told you—"

"Yeah, I know. You came to tell me what a snake I am. But you could have called me at the office to do that. If you really hate me so much, why would you even want to see my face again?"

"You're absolutely right," she said. "I should have gone back to Broken Bow at once."

"Why didn't you, then?"

She struggled not only against his grip but with her own swirling emotions. She was angry and hurt by his betrayal, but the very nearness of him was causing her not to think clearly and producing a predictable tightening in her belly. His clean, fresh, just-showered smell mingled with the natural ambrosia of his skin to infiltrate deep into Carly's being.

A half-muffled groan spilled from Jesse's lips as he pulled her hard up against him. He didn't need to hear her answer. Whatever words she might have uttered could never express as clearly the unspoken language of her body or the silent words written in her eyes.

His kiss was hot and punishing, devouring her with the craving that was in him. His mouth was wet and wild as it came down over hers, seeming to suck the breath right out of her lungs. He kissed her until she had no breath left, and when he pulled his mouth away, Carly drank in deep gulps of air as his lips seared across her cheek to her ear. His voice was deep, ragged. "Later," he murmured hoarsely. "Tell me later what you think of me. Right now, show me."

She closed her eyes to the sound of his voice. God, how she wanted to hate him. When she opened her eyes, she found herself looking into desire-narrowed black orbs in whose depths she felt herself drowning. She could see the hunger in them. She scanned his face, exploring, memorizing the lines and curves, committing to memory those predatory eyes, that seductive half smile, the I'll-do-whatever-I-want three-day growth of beard that added a dash of ruggedness to the extraordinary perfection of his looks. His eyes were so black, so intense, as they searched hers. "Tell me you don't hate me, Carly. Not now...not at this moment."

How could she hate a man who filled her with such incredible desire? "No, Jesse," she whispered brokenly against his lips. "I don't hate you." Not at this moment, she was thinking. Not ever.

Her lashes fluttered down as she melted against him, pliantly, willingly, until their bodies were crushed close. She didn't resist, but went with him as he eased her slowly back and onto the floor. The thick pile of the carpet at her back cushioned their fall. Softness at her back, the hard, immobile wall of Jesse's chest on top of her, created a stirring contrast of sensations. She wanted this, the triumph and the weakness of being in his arms, the glory of letting herself go. *This* was why she had come here...to this place...to this man.

She felt him tugging at the buttons of her blouse until the soft, silky fabric slid from her shoulders and fell away from her body. She knew he would not be an easy lover—that he would fill her to overflowing and that he would demand as much in return. She could tell by the impatience of his hands as they moved over her bare shoulders, grazing her flesh with heated fingers, up and down the length of her arms, over her ribs, across her midriff. His touch slid easily over the lacy fabric of her bra, teasing her nipples erect underneath. In one deft motion the bra was unhooked at her back, lifted easily from her and tossed aside without another moment's thought. His hands moved over her bare breasts, lifting, cupping, caressing, teasing, stroking the soft, sensitive undersides, thumbs working in slow, seductive circles over her tender nipples.

There was no time to experience individual sensations, to luxuriate in each stroke of his fingers or flick of his tongue. Masses of emotion swirled all around her, picking her up like Dorothy in the funnel of a tornado and dropping her in some far-off place of multicolored fantasies. She tried to concentrate on what was happening. The taste of his lips, of his skin, strong, flavorful upon her lips. The scent of him, warm and sexual. The nap of the carpet rubbing provocatively against her naked back, the hard brush of his palms. The sound of his breath ragged at her ear, matched by her own that pounded in her temples. Through half-opened eyes she could see moonlight shafting in through the terrace glass doors and the excited gleam in his eyes as his mouth took hers again. It all collided into one explosion of passion that left her breathless and trembling beneath him.

It was the sound of her moan that made him linger when he could have driven on. She was so smooth, so soft, so slender. The amber glow of the lamplight played softly against her flesh, drawing his lips downward to the warm, white mounds that strained beneath him, hardened little peaks pricking his chest with desire. The scent of her was driving him wild. Sweetgrass, sensual, tempting, invading his senses. He felt his control slipping away from him. He took one swelling peak into his mouth and kissed it deeply, fully, seeking its nourishment like a starving man.

His hands moved rapidly now over the fabric of her skirt, palms pressing against the hollow of her waist, the swell of her hip, coming to rest upon the soft V-shaped mound between her legs that burned with expectation and anticipation. Carly sucked in her breath, arching her body in response. He ran his hands up under her skirt and tugged the panty hose down past her knees until they wound up lying on the carpet beside her blouse and her bra. The sound of her skirt zipper being forced down barely penetrated her thoughts. Moments later she was naked and waiting beneath him.

At the sight of her nakedness, Jesse's breath quickened perceptibly. A moan escaped him, at the exquisite torment of his own body. His eyes locked on her, he rose to his feet and ripped the clothes from his own body. When he was naked, he stood over her for one excruciatingly long moment. He was even more boldly masculine than she could have imagined, more powerfully aroused than even he had thought it possible to be. Without a word he lowered himself to her.

She writhed beneath his touch. Her skin was hot and somehow softer with the heat. Her scent seemed intensified by it. As he covered her waiting mouth with his, his fingers moved to the warm wetness between her legs. Her legs parted willingly, eliciting a strangled groan from deep in his throat. "Carly..."

His gentle, probing touches sent Carly beyond reason. Her mind and body coalesced to form one strong union. All these long weeks of suppressing her needs had taken their toll on her. She needed him to ease the ache, to quench the fires that were burning out of control.

His own passion wildly out of control, Jesse sensed her need and matched it with his own. It was basic, elemental, primitive. "Jesse," she whispered, her fingers grasping his thick, black hair and thrilling to its softness, "make love to me. Now, Jesse. Now..." She opened herself up to him, lips parting, legs widening, arms embracing.

He surged against her, his lean and limber body answering her heated demands. Energy and passion raced together. She touched him, kissed him, enticed and weakened him. She demanded when he had expected surrender. It thrilled him in a way he had thought only existed in his wildest fantasies. But this was no fantasy. This was real and honest. No pretenses, no excuses. Their need was not just of the flesh; it was for each other. This woman had seduced not only his body but his mind and his soul as well, leaving no part of him untouched or unchanged.

His touch was like hot embers against her flesh. The feel of him filling her up, taking her higher and higher until she craved sweet release. And what had begun as a gentle melody in her blood grew into a symphony resounding throughout her entire being. She closed herself around him, pulling him deeper into her warm moist softness, and, her own pulse thundering in her ears, Carly loved him back with a desperate hunger of her own.

Chapter 12

The stars found them lying naked in each other's arms in his bed, her head curled against his chest, the brush of her breath warm and soft upon his flesh. He ran a finger along the contours of her face, gently tracing the delicate lines before reaching over the side of the bed for his pack of cigarettes. He slid one out, placed it between his lips, lit it and settled back against the pillow. He felt her shiver and pressed his body closer to hers in order to warm her with the heat that fired him up inside.

Carly opened her eyes and tilted her face up at him. "I didn't know you smoked."

"It's a habit I've been trying to break," he said. Sort of like you, he was tempted to add. In just a few short weeks this woman had become an addiction with him, something he seemed unable and unwilling to do without. At a time when he could afford no weaknesses, no distractions from the thoughts and feelings he was trying hard to come to terms with, she had walked onto the shifting sands of his life, leaving a trail of footprints on his very soul. Jesse took a deep drag of the cigarette and exhaled through pursed lips, sending the smoke curling into the moonlit darkness. Flicking the loose ashes into the ashtray, he tightened his arm around her.

Carly nestled in the crook of his arm, feeling warm and protected and content in the aftermath of their lovemaking. She should have hated him for what he had done, but in truth, she could not. There were so many things about him she did not know but was slowly finding out. In these past few hours, for example, he had proven himself capable of great tenderness. He had made love to her as if she were the only woman in the world. He had not only taken but given, making her pleasure as complete as his. Yet Carly also knew him to be hard and unyielding. Along with the desire that narrowed his dark eyes, there was also a hint of danger that sometimes frightened her. He was a paradox, a dark and brooding mystery whose secret lay close yet carefully guarded. He was a man who took what he wanted with the confidence of a white man and the fierceness of an Indian. His voice even had an ominous ring to it when it infiltrated the tense silence, and though it was scarcely a whisper, Carly shuddered.

"I called you several times these past few weeks, but you weren't in. Do me a favor, would you, and buy yourself an answering machine?"

"If my chances of getting an answering machine were remote before," she said, "they're nonexistent now. This trip to New York has eaten up a good portion of my funds."

"The doctoring business is that bad, huh?"

"It is on an Indian reservation."

"Did you ever think of practicing somewhere else?"

"Like where?"

He shrugged. "I don't know. Here, for instance."

She raised her head to look at him. "New York? Are you kidding?"

"No. Why would I be?"

She laid her head back down on his arm and sighed. "I don't belong in a place like this. There's not enough . . . I don't know . . . freedom, I guess. Wide-open spaces, good clear air to breathe."

But it was more than that and Jesse knew it. "New York has a pretty big Indian community, you know. Up on 155th Street at the Museum of the American Indian, we've got the biggest collection of artifacts in the world. And if that's not enough reason for you to move here . . ." He paused to nuzzle her ear and whisper, "I'm here."

Still, Carly was not convinced that that was enough reason to pack up and move to New York. She was kidding herself to think that they could ever be right for each other. His place was here, in the midst of this steel and glass forest where people pressed in all around you, while hers was out upon the open prairie, where you could ride for days without encountering another human being. And no matter how passionately they felt about each other, nothing could change the fact that they were from two different worlds.

Her silence spoke volumes, and Jesse knew it was useless to press the issue. "Did you get the supplies I sent?"

"Yes. Thanks. They came in handy."

"Forget it. I'll have more sent whenever you want them."

"Uh, no, I don't think that will be necessary."

"Why not? You can't treat sick people without medicine."

"I have enough to last awhile, and when that runs out, I'll use roots and plants."

"Yeah," he scoffed, "and you can always shake a rattle over them and chant to the Great Spirit. Did they teach you that in medical school?"

She let his remark pass. It was true that she needed the supplies, but she didn't need his charity. Carly was beginning to understand how Luke had felt when she'd refused his payment. The fact that he hadn't had the money to pay her was, she knew now, inconsequential. His pride had been the source of his anger that day, just as hers was now getting in the way of accepting Jesse's offer.

"What is it?" he wanted to know. "Why don't you want me to help you?"

"It's hard to explain," she said.

"Try me."

She took a breath and began to speak, not sure just what she would say or whether he would understand. "Throughout the course of history, our people have suffered enough from the handouts they received. The once proud and mighty Sioux nation has been reduced to dependency upon the very enemy they once fought against. Call it pride if you want, but I just can't accept your handout, Jesse." She sat up, drawing the sheet up to her chin. "If you want to help, why don't you stop buying up Indian land and leasing it to Laramie Fork?"

"I'm working on that," he said.

"How? By having the mining rigs moved onto Emma Huggin's land?"

"Don't worry about the rigs. They can't be used until the lease agreement is signed, and so far it hasn't been. I've managed to hold off my board of directors. First they gave me a two-week time limit to come up with some proof of wrongdoing by Laramie Fork. When that ran out a couple of days ago, my attorney came through with a way to block the thing in court. So you see, Carly, at the moment they're stalemated."

"But the rigs," she insisted.

"Forget the rigs. That's just blind optimism on their part."

"You mean pure, unadulterated greed, don't you?"

"Yeah, that too." He pushed the sheet aside and swung his legs around to sit on the edge of the bed. He ground out the butt of his cigarette in the ashtray, got up and walked to the bathroom. She could hear the water running in the sink. The moonlight played across the planes of his body when he returned a few minutes later to lie back down beside her. The cold water he had splashed over his face washed the tiredness from his eyes and revived him temporarily. Nevertheless, there was a tightening of his muscles and a hesitation to his voice when he said, "I've been checking into things. I think you should know what I've found."

Carly listened speechless as Jesse told her about what his search had turned up. When he finished, she gaped at him, blue eyes wide and incredulous. "Uranium?" she breathed.

"Yes. And there's more. The man behind it is Russell Blackmoon."

Carly gasped. "Your father?"

No, he wanted to shout, *not* my father. But the words froze on his tongue. His feelings were too raw. He needed time to come to terms with it. He turned his face away, the darkness hiding his expression, and said, "It doesn't matter. We can fight him."

She expelled a hopeless breath. "Where would we even start?"

"Right here. With BMI."

She dropped the sheet and scrambled over to him. "What are you saying?"

"I'm saying that I plan to do everything in my power to prevent my company from buying any more Indian land and from leasing any more Blackmoon land to anyone."

"Do you have the power to do that?"

He smiled coolly. "I do now." Careful not to reveal too much too soon, he said, "Recently I came into some additional voting shares, giving me equal controlling interest in the company. I can do whatever I want."

"But, Jesse, that means you would be fighting your father for control of the company. Are you sure you want to do that?"

His tone hardened like steel with a fine edge. "There's nothing I'd rather do." He turned to look at her then, his tone softening and a spark of mischief igniting his eyes. "Except maybe make love to you again." He reached for her, strong arms encircling her and trapping her against the hard wall of his chest as he pulled her down on the bed and quickly covered her body with his. She winced and let out an involuntary yelp of pain. "What is it?" he asked. "Did I hurt you?"

Carly adjusted her body beneath his and smiled at his concern. "It's nothing. I had an accident a couple of weeks ago and my shoulder's been a little sore since then."

Jesse chuckled softly. "What did you do, fall off your horse?"

She wound her arms around his neck and brought his face close to hers. "No," she said against his lips as she kissed him. "I got run down."

His head jerked up, snapping her arms apart. "What?" Alarm sprang into his features. "Carly, are you all right?"

"Yes. A little stiff, but fine." She sought his lips again, not wishing to speak of the frightening incident, seeking protection from its memory in his kiss. But Jesse would not let the matter lie. "What happened?" His face hovered just inches above hers. "Well?"

"You mean you want to know right now, at this very moment?"

He rolled off her and sat back, one leg stretched out straight on the bed, the other knee drawn up, an arm draped across it. His gaze was intent upon her face. "Now."

"Your timing leaves a lot to be desired," she complained as she sat up and crossed her legs beneath her, Indian fashion. Her long hair fell in raven-dark waves over her shoulders, brushing her breasts and spilling into her lap. "There isn't much to tell, really. One day I drove into Pine Ridge with George, and as I was coming out of the county clerk's office, this vehicle came from out of nowhere. It swerved sharply into me as I was stepping off the curb and knocked me down. When I looked up, it was gone."

His features tensed into a mass of worry. "Did you see it?"

Carly shook her head.

"Did you report it to the police?"

"What was there to report? I didn't even see it."

"Maybe someone else did."

"I don't think so. George questioned the people at the scene, and nobody saw a thing. George thinks it was a drunk driver."

"Is that what you think?"

She heaved an uncertain sigh and said, "It's possible. The Pine Ridge town dump contains an extraordinary number of beer cans."

"Was George with you when it happened?"

"No. He happened to be driving by."

Jesse snorted derisively at that. "How convenient." His disdain for the other man was blatant.

"I'm lucky he *was* there," said Carly in George's defense. She had tried to avoid thinking about it, but Jesse could be so persistent at times, like now, the way he fired questions at her as though she were on the witness stand. A shudder coursed down her spine at the memory of that frightening day in Pine Ridge, as it invariably did whenever the occurrence slipped without warning into her mind.

"Does George know you came to New York?" asked Jesse.

She answered with a shake of her head and a dull "No."

"Does anyone know?"

"Luke."

His tone turned decidedly belligerent when he asked, "Why should *he* know?"

"Because he's the one who gave me a lift to Rapid City, where I caught the flight to Cheyenne and from there to New York."

The next question came with the force of a command. "Have you been seeing much of that guy?"

She smiled at him through the darkness. "Jealous?"

"Don't be ridiculous," he said. "There's not a jealous bone in my body."

She did not fail to notice that he said it a beat too quickly, or his eagerness to change the subject. "So, what were you doing at the county clerk's office?"

Carly hesitated, uncertain just how much to trust him. She knew it was useless to hide the truth from him, though, for he would just hound it out of her. Drawing in a breath, Carly straightened up and said, "Well, I got to thinking. I figured that since all land deals must be recorded at the county clerk's office, maybe there was something in all those deeds that was the same."

"And was there?"

Her tone soured. "Yes. In every instance where someone died under mysterious circumstances it was shortly after selling their land to you."

His look hardened, splicing the night. "If you're insinuating that I—"

"I'm not insinuating anything, Jesse. I'm *saying* that your company's name is on every one of those deeds. And for every deed there's a lease agreement between BMI and Laramie Fork."

Glumly, Jesse said, "Yeah, I know." He was thinking of the company files he'd been poring over the past few weeks.

"Now you're telling me that uranium is somehow involved, and I'm wondering how many more people are going to die. Maybe you're not the one behind it, Jesse. Maybe it is your father. All I know is we've got some maniac running around Pine Ridge, killing innocent people. That means that someone at BMI has blood on his hands as well."

"Do you think it's me?"

She answered honestly. "I don't know what to think anymore."

"Think about it, Carly," he urged her. "Whoever killed those people would have to be someone they knew. Someone who could come and go without arousing much attention. Someone who could gain their trust enough to swindle them. Does that sound like me?"

She had to admit it did not. A stranger would certainly arouse suspicion on the reservation if seen coming and going. Yet homes were far enough from one another that it was possible that one could come and go without being seen. And while it was true that the people were reluctant to trust strangers, Carly knew herself just how persuasive Jesse's charm could be. Hadn't she fallen for it like a ton of bricks despite her own inner warnings?

"Great," Jesse grumbled. "We have absolutely no proof of anything, and on top of that, you think I'm some kind of mad killer."

"I didn't say that," she objected. "I also didn't say there wasn't any proof."

His eyes lit up. "You mean you found something."

"I found something, all right, but I don't know what it has to do with BMI or Laramie Fork." She paused for a moment, as if at the edge of a lake testing the water with one toe. It was too late to turn back now and she knew it. Like it or not, she had to trust him. It was an uneasy alliance, to be sure. Nevertheless, without thinking further, Carly dived right in. "Do you recall seeing in your files a deed between BMI and Mary Yazzie?"

"I remember it," he uttered.

"The date on that deed is September twelfth."

"So?"

"So, I also checked the death records, and Mary Yazzie died on September sixth, six days before signing the deed."

His muscles tightened. "Are you sure?"

She nodded slowly.

He tried not to let himself get too carried away, lest this be just another dead end. First thing tomorrow he would check the original in the file. If Carly was right, this could be the thing he'd been looking for. A strange light came into his eyes and a triumphant smile spread slowly across his full lips. His pulse quickened. Maybe he had finally found the ammunition he needed to fight Russell and win. So wrapped up was Jesse in thoughts of victory that he was unaware of the way he was being watched until he heard her voice with its echo of doubt.

"Why, Jesse? Why are you suddenly so interested in our side of it?"

For several minutes he did not answer. Finally, he said, "I've spent most of my life running away from the very thing I was running toward. I don't know if that even makes any sense. All I know, Carly, is that I'm through running."

He did not explain further, and she did not ask him to. She moved instead into the wide arc of his arm that closed gently around her. "Jesse," she whispered, "I'm scared."

His arm tightened around her shoulder, drawing her protectively to him. "Shhh," he murmured. "I'm here, and there's nothing to be afraid of." He kissed her on the mouth to silence her fears.

Carly shivered. Yes, he was here for now, but what about tomorrow and the day after that? After knowing the protection of his embrace and the heat of his passion, could she ever live without them? She sighed inwardly as she kissed him back. She could fight to protect the sacred places of the Sioux, but what about the sacred places of the heart? Lost in his embrace, they were vulnerable to his plunder.

"Jesse." She let her hands move over his body, thrilling to the incredible softness of his skin. The sound of his name spilling from her lips rekindled the fires that simmered deep within him. He could not read her thoughts, but he could read the desire in her eyes, and for now it was enough. His lips were waiting for hers when they came. Her kiss was deep and long while her hands created a frenzy of excitement as they touched him intimately, hungrily. Her mouth was softly yielding and demanding at the same time. The brush of her long hair against his flesh was a sensual experience, tickling the tiny nerve endings that screamed just below the surface.

She tossed her head back, whipping her magnificent mane of dark hair away from her face. There it was, written in her eyes, which danced over him, mirrored in her features, the thing that told him she was reachable, ready. He drew her close, wanting her beyond endurance, needing her. Only her, he thought dizzily as he rolled her onto her back and began a slow, seductive exploration of her body. "I fantasized about making love to you," he admitted.

"Disappointed?" she murmured as her lips grazed the tanned flesh of his shoulder.

"Oh, no," he breathed. How could he describe the pitiful inadequacies of his fantasies compared with the pandemonium she unleashed in him? "Were you?" he asked.

She smiled, the darkness concealing a blush. "Stunned. Shaken. Overwhelmed. But never disappointed."

"For a minute there I thought you might be. I mean it was all so quick."

"Not too quick to tell."

He had promised himself, as he'd consumed her in a mad rush earlier, that the next time he would take it more slowly, allowing them to experience every maddening sensation, to discover each layer of passion. Lacing his fingers in her hair, lifting the silken strands to his face, he inhaled its fragrance deep into his being as he set about fulfilling his promise. He wanted to prolong the sweet agony, to make every moment last forever, but Carly's desire was sweeping him along and he was powerless to hold back any longer.

She exchanged each masculine stroke with a feminine response, and when she felt his rhythm accelerate, heard his breath grow raspy, she demanded it all, now. He scooped her buttocks into his hands and thrust without thinking, all instinct now as they reached a peak of uninhibited pleasure, of give and take, of tangled legs and mingled moans and heart-stopping passion.

She awoke the next morning to a ray of sunlight slanting across her eyes. She reached her hand out for Jesse, but the place beside her on the bed was empty. Rolling over, she buried her face in his pillow. The scent of him was still fresh, clinging to the soft cool cotton. The sheet was still warm from where he had lain. In a luxurious state of contentment Carly closed her eyes, daring to recall in her mind's eye the intimacies they had shared last night and into early dawn when he had awakened her in those still hours before first light with softly caressing hands and she, eyes still half-closed with sleep, had opened herself up to him. The sound of the shower was strangely comforting to Carly as she lay there now, indulging in the fantasy. After a spell she got up, shrugged into a shirt of Jesse's that she found hanging over the back of a chair and went to the bathroom, where the partly open door invited a peek inside.

Jesse was standing before the mirror in the steam-filled room. He was naked except for the white towel draped over his neck. His handsome face was covered with shaving cream, which he carefully stroked away with a razor.

"Good morning," said Carly from the doorway.

He smiled at her in the mirror. "Hi, sleepyhead. I was beginning to think it would take a sound dousing in the Hudson to bring you around."

Carly made a grim face at the prospect. "From what I've heard of the Hudson, I'm not sure I'd come out alive."

Jesse laughed. It was good to see mirth in his eyes, instead of the icy, impenetrable look that so often clouded them.

"How come you're up so early?" she asked.

"We're going to the office," he said.

"We?"

"That's right," he replied, eyes twinkling. "As in you and me. You know. The same you and me as in last night."

She could not help but blush at the reminder of their intimacies.

"As fetching as you look wearing nothing but my shirt," said Jesse as he shaved, "I would suggest something a little more appropriate for Park Avenue. You'd better get into that shower and get dressed or we'll be late. But first—" He dropped his razor into the sink and turned toward her. She slid into his arms. He smelled of soap and spicy shaving cream. When he finished kissing her and drew away, Carly's face was dotted with the white foam. Jesse laughed softly. "Go on, get into that shower or I'm going to need another one myself—this time a cold one."

An hour later they emerged from the taxi in front of the BMI building. Hand in hand they walked inside. Jesse's secretary looked at them a little oddly when they passed her desk on their way to his office. Carly was feeling slightly foolish for the sight she must have presented yesterday when she had demanded to see Jesse, only to run away with tears in her eyes.

"Susan, bring me in the Laramie Fork files," said Jesse to the pretty blond woman.

"Yes, Mr. Blackmoon."

Blackmoon. The name sent an unwelcomed shiver down Carly's spine as they entered Jesse's private office. But no sooner had the door closed behind them than he drew her into his arms and pressed a hungry kiss to her lips, and all else was forgotten when the sound of his urgent whisper was at her ear. "I thought I'd go crazy keeping my hands off you in the cab. I want you."

"Forget it," Carly teased. "You had your chance earlier, but you blew it."

"Where's that cold shower now when I really need it?" he groaned.

Carly laughed, spinning out of his arms just as the door opened and his secretary came in, file folders in hand. She glanced at the two, only to find Jesse grinning broadly and Carly blushing furiously. She placed the folders on his desk and made a hasty exit.

When they were alone again, Carly expelled a sigh of relief. "That was close."

"So, she would have caught us kissing," he said as he strode to his desk. "Big deal. I think it's safe to assume that Susan has done that sort of thing herself. There must be a man in her life. After all, she's an attractive woman."

"So I noticed."

He arched a dark brow at her as he sat down. "Jealous?"

"Don't be ridiculous," said Carly, mimicking his deep voice of the night before. "There's not a jealous bone in my body."

"Touché," he laughed. "Now, get that pretty fanny of yours on over here and take a look at something."

When she was standing beside him behind the desk, he said, "These are the Laramie Fork files, the ones I was telling you about. Now, what was that name you mentioned last night?''

''Mary Yazzie.''

He shuffled through the files. ''That's funny,'' he muttered. ''It was here yesterday.''

''What was?''

''The Yazzie deed. It's gone.'' He hit the button on the intercom to summon Susan and said brusquely, ''Ring Helen and tell her I'd like to see her in my office right away.''

Five minutes later an older, gray-haired woman in a neatly tailored suit walked in. Her eyes went briefly to Carly, then settled on Jesse. ''You wanted to see me, Jesse?''

''Helen, this is Dr. McAllister. Carly, this is Helen Wilson.'' With the introductions performed in a perfunctory manner, Jesse got right to the point. ''Helen, did you remove the Mary Yazzie deed from the file?''

''No, Jesse, I didn't.''

''Who did, then?''

She looked momentarily befuddled. ''I don't know.''

''Would anyone have any reason to?''

''No. Why? Have you found something? Does it have anything to do with—'' She stopped, eyes shifting warily to Carly.

''That's all right, Helen,'' Jesse assured her. ''Carly knows what's going on. Do you recall the date on the Yazzie deed?''

''Not offhand.''

''How many copies of a contract do you usually make?''

''Well, there's the original, of course, and I keep one copy for my own files upstairs, and one copy goes to Legal.''

''Okay, fine. I would like you to get the copy from your file and bring it to me as soon as possible.''

When Helen had retreated from Jesse's office, Carly asked, ''What do you suppose happened to the original?''

Jesse offered a haphazard shrug. ''Beats me.''

A short while later their heads came up from the files when the intercom buzzed. Jesse picked up the phone. "Yes? Yes, Helen. You're sure of that? Okay. Thanks." He hung up and looked at Carly with a scowl on his face and said grimly, "Her copy is gone. She called Legal, and their's is missing as well."

The carefree mood of earlier was rapidly disintegrating as evinced by Carly's exclamation of surprise. "Who would have taken them?" And by Jesse's sharp annoyance when he replied, "How the hell should I know?"

"We've always got the microfilm record of the deed back in Pine Ridge," she said. "That's better than nothing."

"Yeah, but at the moment that's out there and we're here. I need that proof, and I need it in my hands, where I know it will be safe." Just then a thought occurred to him. He grabbed the phone and hit the buttons with swift precision. "Hello, Jerry? Hey, pal, it's me, Jesse. I'm in a bit of a bind and I think you can help me out. Remember those papers I sent over by messenger a couple of weeks ago? Do me a favor, would you, and see if there's a copy of the deed between BMI and Mary Yazzie. Yeah, I'll wait." He glanced up at Carly and gave a small shrug to signify the helplessness he felt as he waited for his attorney to get back on the line. Then, "Yeah, Jerry. It's there? Great! Guard that thing with your life, buddy. I'm coming right over."

He jumped to his feet and grabbed Carly's hand. "Come on, let's go," he said as he strode to the door. "Did you bring anything pretty to wear with you?"

"What?"

"Preferably something black and sexy."

"Of course not!" she exclaimed. "I didn't plan on hitting the night spots."

"All right, then, while I'm over at Jerry's, I want you to go shopping and get something to wear for this evening."

"Jesse, what are you talking about?" she protested as she half ran down the hallway to keep pace with his long strides.

"I'm talking about our date."

"What date?"

"The one you're going on with me tonight."

When they reached the elevator, Carly pulled back. "There you go again, presuming too much."

The doors opened and they stepped inside. "Are we back to that again?" complained Jesse. "All right, how's this? Would you like to go out with me tonight?"

"Well," she said, turning coy, "since you put it that way instead of in your usual primitive fashion, yes, I would."

"Good. I'm glad that's settled."

"Where are we going?"

"To my parents' house for dinner."

Carly's visions of a hot time on the old town fizzled like bubbles in leftover champagne. That didn't sound like a date to her and she told him so.

He said simply, "So, I lied. Cheer up, kid. You'll like my mother."

"And your father?" Despite her threat to confront Russell Blackmoon, Carly was not at all thrilled with the prospect of meeting the man.

"My father. Yes, well, that's another story. Someday I'll tell you about it. For now, just concentrate on looking your best."

Out on the sidewalk Carly drew back. "Jesse, I don't know about this."

"Look," he said, "you said you wanted to meet him, and I'm not about to let you near him without me there."

"It's not that. It's the dress. I can't afford it."

He looked at her as if she'd gone daft. "This isn't the time to be worrying about money."

"When you don't have it, you worry about it," she hotly replied.

"I know, I know," he said. "All right, tell you what. You've got a credit card, haven't you?"

"Yes, but—"

"Well, charge the thing and send me the bill. And don't give me any speeches about handouts and pride, Carly, because I have neither the time nor the patience for them. Consider this a favor to me, okay? Just go buy something pretty." He hailed a taxi and ushered her into it before she could issue another protest. Leaning into the open window, he said, "I'll see you back at my apartment in a couple of hours. Here, you'll need this." He delved into his pocket and came out with the key to his apartment, which he pressed into Carly's palm. A brief yet thorough kiss on the mouth, a curt "Driver, take the lady to Fifth Avenue," and he stepped away.

"Jesse?" she called through the open window as the taxi slowly pulled away. "Is the black and sexy for him?"

He smiled sheepishly and admitted, "No, that's strictly for me." He watched the yellow cab disappear, then he thrust his arm out and hailed another for the ride across town to Jerry Klein's office.

Chapter 13

Wow! That's not a dress; it's a weapon!''

He stood in the doorway to the bedroom, watching as she clipped an earring to her lobe. Carly felt a rush of pride at the compliment. She had given a lot of thought to the selection of this dress. After trying on half a dozen others, she had finally chosen this basic black shirtwaist in silk crepe de chine. From the tiny pleats at the padded shoulders to the long, full sleeves that buttoned at her wrists, to the brush of the hemline just below the knee, the dress cried elegance in its simplicity.

Jesse's eyes traveled a slow route over her, narrowing with typical male appreciation. She was, in a word, beautiful. But as much as he was taken by the visual impact she created, he was also secretly delighted by that mercurial nature of hers that had, at first, balked at the idea of buying the dress, only to go full tilt, it seemed, once she had gotten to the store. Her unpredictability was evidenced by her black high heels, also new, which enhanced the shapely curve of her legs, and by the single strand of pearls, which cast a luminescence over her sun-browned skin and did more to excite him than all the diamonds in the world. Her long black hair was swept upward and coiled into a soft, uncomplicated knot on top of her head. Several tendrils had come undone to fall softly to her shoulders.

One might have expected the expensive bite of a French perfume to trail in her wake, but Jesse found himself smiling when the scent of sweet grass drifted into his nostrils. What other women paid small fortunes for in crystal bottles this woman achieved by burning the aromatic leaves of the sweet-grass plant over an open fire. The scent had become so much a part of her that it emanated from her raven-dark hair even now, when there was no sweet grass around. The aroma, so alien to the cosmopolitan world of New York City, took Jesse back to the prairies of South Dakota.

Jesse eased his index finger around the collar of his white shirt and gulped. Even the sound of her voice did crazy things to him, as it did now when she flashed a smile at him and said, "Thank you." Her own blue eyes caressed him tellingly. "And you don't look too bad yourself."

The dark suit and white shirt lent a somber elegance to his appeal, refining those good looks to just shy of devastating. He laughed in a sound that spilled rich and mellow from his throat, and said, "This sounds like the mutual admiration society."

"Yes, it does."

For several long moments they remained motionless facing each other as if locked in a spell. Carly felt her cheeks burning beneath Jesse's lusty stare. And Jesse, afraid to speak lest his voice betray the trembling in his knees, took a deep breath and said, "We should be going, I guess."

She was standing so close that she could smell the stirring scent of his after shave and feel the tension crackling in his muscles. Softly, she said, "Yes, we should."

Neither made any move to leave. His black eyes caressed her lovely face, and there was no mistaking the seduction in his deep voice when he said, "Because if we don't leave right now, we may never make it out of this bedroom, and you may not get another opportunity to confront him."

"I know."

"So?" he urged her gently. "Just say the word and we'll forget about tonight. We'll spend it here, just you and me."

Carly wanted nothing more than to drown in his passion, to experience all over again the incredible thrill of being in his arms. This man aroused feelings in her that she had not known existed. In his embrace she was like white heat, burning up from the inside out with the sweet and savage pain of desire. In his own way he was as dangerous to her as his father was. It frightened her. Tearing her eyes from his, she muttered, "We don't want to be late for dinner," and moved past him through the doorway.

He could have reached her in two long strides and told her to hell with dinner. It was not dinner he was hungry for. He was torn by the impulse to make love to her, whether she liked it or not, to show her that nothing mattered except the searing attraction that existed between them. But he made no move to stop her, for as much as he craved the feel of her soft flesh pressed to his, he knew that he would never be completely free to love her until he had settled his score with Russell.

Jesse's car was waiting for them at the curb, where Ernie had had the garage attendant park it. Jesse held the door open, and Carly slid gracefully into the leather seat of the low-slung Porsche. Minutes later they were winding their way through the Midtown Tunnel.

It was a warm summer night. The moon, nearly full, appeared over the tops of the trees as they sped eastward on the Long Island Expressway. Jesse pressed the buttons on the radio until he found some mellow jazz. His hand then slid across to reach for Carly's. Enveloping her fingers in his, he drew her hand from her lap and, without speaking a word, placed it on his thigh. Then he settled back to drive.

Half an hour later they arrived at the Blackmoons' stone Tudor home on a quiet tree-lined street in Great Neck. They got out and went up the flagstone walk. At the front door Jesse gave Carly's hand a squeeze. "Are you ready?"

She smiled up at him. "As ready as I'll ever be. And you?"

With this woman at his side there was nothing he could not do, including challenge Russell. He bent his head and kissed her lightly on the lips.

Russell had met a couple of Jesse's women in the past when he and Jesse had attended company-sponsored benefits. This was the first time, though, that Jesse had ever bothered to bring one home. It was easy to see why. She wasn't like the others. He knew right off that something about her was different, but he could not put his finger on it. Perhaps it was her uncommon beauty. The stark blue eyes set against golden skin, the coal-black hair, the unconscious grace with which she carried herself, all combined to undermine a man's senses. But it was more than her looks that caused Russell to scrutinize her in a curious way when the introductions were performed. Maybe it was because she was a doctor. Smart women were a pain in the neck, he had always thought, and intelligent ones were downright dangerous. This one, he sensed, was both.

It was not until they were seated for dinner, however, that Russell realized what it was about her that he found so unsettling. It was Lucy who provided the unwitting clue when she smiled at Carly and said, "Jesse tells me you're from South Dakota, Carly. I'm from South Dakota myself."

Russell's gaze came up from the duckling Rouennaise on his plate. He was not so much surprised that Lucy knew more about this young woman than he did—no doubt Jesse had told his mother all about her—as he was by the mention of South Dakota. "South Dakota?" he questioned. "Ah. I take it, then, that your family are landowners?"

"Oh, yes," said Carly. "They have been for quite some time."

Russell seemed favorably impressed and nodded his head approvingly. "What's the name of your spread?"

"I beg your pardon?"

"Your property."

Smiling sweetly, she replied, "We call it Pine Ridge."

"But isn't that—"

"It's the Sioux Indian reservation."

"I see. But a moment ago you said that your family owns land in South Dakota."

"They do. Indian land."

Realization was rapidly forming in those emerald eyes, turning them icy. "Then you're—" He paused, seemingly unable—or unwilling—to utter the word.

"Yes, Mr. Blackmoon," said Carly, "I'm an Indian."

A tense silence settled like dust over the table. Lucy spoke up, partly to combat the moment of awkwardness, partly out of curiosity. "Then you must be Sioux. What a coincidence. Jesse's grandfather was half Oglala. Tell me, do they still have all those wonderful ceremonies? My father used to take me to see them when I was a child. They always filled me with such terror and awe."

Carly found Lucy Blackmoon to be a gracious woman, with clear, intelligent eyes and a gentle manner. It was easy to like her for that, and also for the way she seemed unintimidated by her husband's frosty demeanor and the look he shot her way. "As a matter of fact," said Carly, "they're preparing for the Sun Dance ceremony, which takes place in a week."

"I can remember the story Jesse's grandfather told us kids about the time he returned from the war overseas and traveled to the Wind River Reservation to take part in the Sun Dance," said Lucy. "You remember, don't you, Russ? He said it was to rid himself of the white man's war and to become Indian again. His chest bore the scars of that Sun Dance for many years after."

"If you ask me, it's barbaric," said Russell. "I remember those stories my father used to tell, of men piercing the skin on their chests with skewers that were attached to long thongs, of how they dragged buffalo skulls around by the thongs until the skewers tore loose from the skin. And for what?" He laughed abruptly. "For some disgusting scars on your chest?"

"It's much more than that," said Carly. "To the Indian the flesh represents ignorance. When a man dances in the ceremony and breaks the thong loose, it's as if he were being freed from the bonds of the flesh. It's like breaking a young colt. At first a halter is necessary, but later when he has become broken, the rope isn't needed. The dancer is like a colt when he starts to dance, but soon he becomes broken and submits to the Great Spirit."

"Yes, well, that's very interesting, but this *is* the twentieth century."

"Yes, it is. And perhaps the Sioux people need the Sun Dance now more than they ever did. The Sun Dance is a means to strengthen the circle of life, to reinforce all that is Indian. Contrary to what many people think, the Indian has not disappeared into the American mainstream. We are alive. We embrace not only what is new, but what is old. The old ways will never die as long as there are those of us who believe strongly enough in keeping them alive."

"Nevertheless, it sounds like a hell of a way to worship," said Russell disapprovingly.

"It's no stranger than any other form of worship. Frankly, I find worshiping the Great Spirit infinitely more human than the worship of . . . money, for instance. I have seen men do all kinds of things for the sacred dollar, including kill their fellow human beings for it."

Jesse's dark eyes swung in Carly's direction. Her calm and level voice did not fool him, nor did the pleasant smile she aimed at Russell as she spoke, for beneath it he knew she was boiling with indignation.

"It certainly sounds fascinating to me," chimed Lucy.

"It is," said Carly. "Of course, to those who don't understand it, I can see how frightening it must appear." She paused to look at Russell and add deliberately, "Still, one should not condemn something one knows nothing about."

A muscle jumped in Russell's cheek, the only evidence that her remark had struck a nerve. "I would advise the same thing of you, Doctor. If you do not understand the business of making money, you should not be so quick to judge those of us who do."

Jesse watched the exchange between Russell and Carly, ready to jump in if he had to. But she was doing just fine on her own. She was a formidable adversary in her own right, as Russell was finding out, and Jesse derived a secret pleasure in seeing Russell being backed into an uncomfortable corner.

"On the contrary," Carly said. "Being the only doctor within a hundred-mile radius on the reservation, I understand only too well the business of making money and what it does to people."

"Of course," he scoffed. "I'd forgotten how much money you doctors make."

"A popular misconception," she said, laughing. "I assure you, practicing medicine on an Indian reservation is considerably less lucrative than practicing on Park Avenue. My bank account currently has a balance of three figures. But that's not what I meant when I said that I understand the business of making money. I was referring to all the people I have treated in the past three years who have died."

"Sick people have a way of doing that."

"It wasn't sickness that killed them, Mr. Blackmoon. It was someone's love of money."

Russell removed the linen napkin from his knee and wiped his mouth on a corner of it. "Dr. McAllister," he said, "perhaps you should explain to me what it is you are trying to say. I dislike evasion."

Struggling to keep her tone level in spite of the way she was trembling inside, Carly said, "Very well. People on my reservation are dying. Eleven at last count."

"Come now, my dear, you cannot expect one thing to have anything to do with another."

"When all of their land falls into the hands of Blackmoon Industries, I can."

"I have very astute financial advisors whom I pay a great deal of money," Russell explained. "If they tell me to purchase land on an Indian reservation for the purpose of leasing the coal rights, then I do it. It is their job to seize the opportunities when they arise."

"Seize the opportunities, or make them?"

"If someone dies and their land is up for sale, I would call that seizing an opportunity. It's standard business practice."

"And if I told you that every one of those people died under mysterious circumstances, would you call that standard business practice also?"

Russell stiffened. "I don't know what you're talking about."

"I'm talking about people being poisoned, shot, blown up in their homes."

The fork dropped from Lucy's hand with a clatter. "Russell," she said with a gasp, "is that true?"

"Of course not."

"Perhaps you should look into it," Lucy suggested.

"I will," her husband replied.

"There's no need," said Jesse, breaking his long, taut silence. "I've already looked into it. Carly's right. BMI is somehow involved in a string of murders on the reservation."

There was no disguising the hostility that blazed in Russell's green eyes when he fixed them on Jesse. "Do you know what you're saying?"

"I know exactly what I'm saying. BMI is involved up to its neck. Someone is killing people out there, and my guess is he's getting his orders from here."

"Who would do such a thing?" demanded Russell.

"I don't know...yet."

Russell eyed Jesse coolly. "That's a pretty big assumption without proof."

With a touch of familiar arrogance, Jesse replied, "I never said I didn't have any proof."

"Good. I'll have my men working on it first thing in the morning."

"No need," said Jesse. "*I'm* working on it."

"Look, Jesse, be reasonable about this. If something like what you're suggesting is really going on, then we have to proceed with all possible caution. We wouldn't want whoever's responsible to think that we suspect anything."

"Whoever he is, he already knows we're on to him," said Jesse.

"What makes you think so?" asked Lucy.

"Some papers have been removed from the files... incriminating papers," Carly explained to her.

"That's right," said Jesse. "And until I find out what's going on and who's behind it, I'll do everything in my power to suspend all acquisition of Indian land by BMI. While I'm at it, I've also issued instructions that no more Blackmoon land is to be leased to Laramie Fork."

Russell's green eyes narrowed with contempt. "You're walking on thin ice, Jesse," he said. "Don't you know what this could do to the company?"

"To hell with the company!" came Jesse's sharp response. "I'll see BMI go under if I have to, but I won't have it be the cause of people's deaths!"

"Don't you think you're overreacting?" scoffed Russell. "It's only coal!"

"That's what I thought, too," said Jesse. "Until I found out what's really under the land. You went through an awful lot of trouble to keep that latest Laramie Fork contract under wraps, and I couldn't imagine why. Now I know. It's not coal at all. It's uranium."

The word echoed off the walls of the room. From where she sat in silence Lucy turned a stricken look at her husband. Carly's blue eyes were riveted on Jesse. Something far more sensitive than coal or uranium was at the root of this confrontation between these two men. There was too much hatred in Russell's green eyes and too much hostility vibrating in Jesse's deep voice for this to be a mere company matter. What was it, she wondered, that could cause such bitterness between a father and son?

"You'll ruin everything we've worked for!" stormed Russell.

"Wrong!" Jesse snapped. "Everything *you've* worked for. I never worked to make BMI a machine that eats up people, and I won't stand by and let that happen."

"You're insane. You can't do it. I won't let you."

Jesse's face went white with rage. He sprang to his feet and took a menacing step toward Russell, fingers flexing as if to ball into a fist to strike him. He stormed to within a foot of Russell and stopped. The breath shot out of his nostrils in furious bursts. With teeth tightly gritted he said in a low and threatening voice, "You're not my father, or my guardian, or my conscience. I'll do whatever the hell I want, and God help the man who tries to stop me."

Lucy gasped.

Carly's heart struck a painful chord for Jesse, for she knew now what it was that stood like a lance between them.

For several furious seconds Jesse's gaze locked with Russell's in silent combat before Jesse tore his away and stomped over to where Carly sat frozen. Grabbing her hand and pulling her to her feet, he said brusquely, "Come on, we're going." With Carly in hand, he walked around the table to place a kiss on his mother's cheek before leaving without another word.

The drive back to the city was fraught with stress. Carly could feel Jesse sizzling beside her in the cramped space of the car. Her heart went out to him. What a heavy weight he had been carrying around inside of him. "Jesse? What you said back there ... I had no idea."

Bitterness rang like a distant bell in his tone. "Yeah, neither did I until a week ago."

"I'm so sorry."

"For what? For discovering that that bastard isn't my father? Hell, it's the best thing that's ever happened to me. Now I can challenge him without feeling guilty about it."

Carly studied him through the darkness. The glare of the oncoming headlights cast a hard edge to his features. There was something cold and unyielding in that handsome face. How clear everything suddenly seemed to her. She bit back a sob and said, "That's all that matters to you, isn't it, Jesse? Beating Russell."

His eyes left the road to seize hers with a cold, brief stare. Gruffly he said, "You don't understand."

What was there to understand? He needed something with which to fight Russell, and he had found it in the Sioux people. Carly turned her head away to look at the dark terrain that zipped past the window. Just when she thought she was getting to know this man, he was more of a stranger than she could have imagined. Her voice split the dense silence between them with a ring of sad resignation. "I'll be leaving in the morning."

If she had been looking, she would have seen the flash of genuine surprise in his dark eyes. "But I thought—"

"You thought what, Jesse? That I would stay here with you forever?" She had foolishly half thought it herself.

Yes, damn it, that's exactly what he thought. But instead he said sullenly, "No. Why should I think that?"

"I have to get back to my patients."

"Fine."

"And there's the Sun Dance next week."

"Hey, listen, you do what you have to do."

"And you?" she ventured. "What are your plans?"

"To tell you the truth," he replied, "I wasn't thinking much beyond tonight. I guess I'll give Jerry a call tomorrow and see where we go from here."

She hesitated, then asked, "What about . . . him?"

"For the time being he's powerless to countermand my instructions, although I don't know how long that will last. He's not used to losing. But that's not what worries me. He's never before shown a willingness to cooperate, and now he wants to get his guys working on it as soon as he can. He knew weeks ago that people were dying out there. Why is he suddenly so concerned about getting to the bottom of this thing?"

"You must admit, Jesse, that it could cause some pretty bad publicity."

"Yeah, and maybe ruin his chances of getting any more Laramie Fork contracts. But I'll tell you this, Carly. Whatever it is he's after, he's not about to stand by and let you and me ruin it for him. He's got far-reaching influence in places you wouldn't even know.''

"Like an Indian reservation?"

He made no reply, although they both knew the answer. Someone at Pine Ridge was murdering innocent men and women, someone whose connections seemed to go far beyond the bounds of the reservation, all the way to Blackmoon Industries. A grim shudder went down Carly's spine. The two days she had been in New York had seemed like a whirlwind. Two days could seem like an eternity on the reservation. She only prayed that no more innocent souls had met their own eternity in the time she had been gone.

Jesse's voice echoed Carly's fears when he said bluntly, "I don't like the idea of you going back there."

"Jesse, it's my home."

"I know, but there's some jerk running around out there killing people."

"New York City has some pretty staggering statistics of its own," Carly countered. "Aren't you afraid of being mugged or stabbed or even killed? Come on, Jesse, we both know you can't be afraid of everything all the time."

He knew she was right. Still, any of the gruesome possibilities she had suggested seemed somehow less frightening to him than the cold, calculating crimes at Pine Ridge. "I want you to promise me something," he said. "If anyone approaches you about selling your land, I want you to call me."

"I see no need—"

"Just do it!"

She thought better of arguing. "All right, Jesse. I promise." There was no sense in telling him that she had already received a phone call from a man who had not identified himself asking if he could speak to her about her 240-acre tract. The call had come the day before she left for New York. She had not recognized the man's voice, and when she had asked for his name, he'd thanked her for her time and quickly hung up. She had no doubt that she would be hearing from him again. She thought it best not to worry Jesse with it. It could be nothing. Then again . . .

Carly searched Jesse's face by the passing beams of the expressway lights, and even though she knew what his answer would be, she gathered up her courage and said, "You could always come back with me."

There was an expectant pause before he answered. "I can't leave, Carly. Not now with this thing coming up in court. I'm so close to beating him . . . so close."

There it was, the sudden, sharp reminder that there was something more important to him than her. They rode the rest of the way in silence.

The next morning she was gone, and it was Jesse's turn to feel the acute sense of aloneness that accompanies the departure of one you cannot live without. He dressed sullenly and took a taxi to the office, but he'd been crazy to think he could get any work done when his thoughts were sixteen hundred miles away. Somehow he made it through the day. He returned home that night feeling edgy and tense. He lay awake in bed unable to sleep, praying for the sleep that would take him away from this longing, which lay like a rock in the pit of his belly. He turned his head on the pillow and drew into his being the scent of sweet grass clinging to the cool sheets. It stirred in Jesse the memory of last night, when he had held her in his arms and they had made love without speaking. He had loved her in a fever pitch, with the same thrill as if it were the first time and a desperation as if it had been the last.

In the days that followed, the city seemed like a prison to Jesse. He longed to be free of this place of noise and concrete and pollution. His thoughts came and went in a relentless pattern, all converging upon a dark-haired Indian woman. He was at a stalemate with Russell for control for the company, and things with Jerry Klein were in a state of limbo. "These things take time," Jerry assured him of the lengthy court proceedings that blocked the leasing of Blackmoon land to Laramie Fork. But one thing Jesse did not have was time. It was rapidly running out for the Black Hills, for no matter what Jesse was able to do to prevent his own land from falling into the hands of the power companies, there was little he could do about preventing others from converging like scavengers on the sacred hills.

Four days had gone by without any word from Carly. His calls to her went unanswered. He told himself that she was busy with her patients and with preparations for the Sun Dance, but nevertheless, thoughts of Luke Lightfoot lurking in the background sat like tiny vultures in his mind, picking at his reason, destroying his logic. He was feeling sullen and cross on the fourth night when the telephone rang. Jesse seized the kitchen extension, expecting to hear Carly's voice at the other end of the line. "Hello?" he said eagerly, followed by a dull "Oh, hi" when he recognized the voice of the caller and it was not hers. "No, I'm not busy. What is it?" He looked out the window with benign disinterest as he listened. But those dark eyes that brooded beneath heavy lashes snapped to attention, alert at what he'd just heard. "What?" His whole body tensed, muscles going rigid and nerves standing on end. He listened hard, seizing every word and reeling from the impact. At length he spoke. "Thanks. I owe you one."

For several minutes after he hung up he just stood there. His breath came hard and fast through his nostrils as though he'd just come in from a brisk jog. But it was not exercise that had the blood pumping hot through Jesse's veins. It was anger, rising to his surface like warrior birds taking to flight.

Finally he reached for the phone on the wall and dialed his attorney's number. "Jerry? It's me, Jesse. I'm sorry to bother you at home, pal, but there's something I need you to do for me. I want you to get me the name of every rancher and farmer in the state of South Dakota. I know, I know, but it's important. And Jerry, I'll need that information as soon as possible. Thanks. 'Bye.''

He hung up. There was a dangerous glint in his eyes as he strode into the living room. Jesse went straight to a painting hanging on the wall. He swung it forward on invisible hinges to reveal a wall safe behind it. Deftly he spun the dial right, left, then right again. The safe opened, and he reached inside. Along with an assortment of stocks and bonds and personal papers was a copy of the Mary Yazzie deed, which Jesse unfolded. A triumphant smile turned up the corners of his mouth, although it did not reach his eyes, which were fixed upon the document. With this and the news he had just been told, perhaps, just perhaps, he could beat Russell at his own game.

Chapter 14

On a sun-baked hillside in the shadow of the Black Hills, hundreds of people were assembled. It was an eclectic gathering of tribal elders, the new left, a few sixties' activists, environmentalists, socially conservative farmers and rich white ranchers who were somewhat bemused to find themselves fallen in with the reservation Indians they had always scorned. They had all come together over one common concern, the Black Hills, for the purpose of saving them from ruination.

Trailers and recreational vehicles dotted the terrain. A tent city had been set up complete with health-food kitchen, food co-op and a refreshment stand. The conical tepees of the Indians, once made of tanned buffalo skins and now of stiff white canvas, ringed the meeting ground.

Beneath the hot prairie sun a succession of speakers expounded on matters of varied importance, from Indian history and treaty rights to alternative technologies and antinuclear strategy. Several disgruntled Minnesota farmers whose property had recently been traversed by a four-hundred kilovolt power line had made the trip to speak against the encroachment of the power companies. But mostly the talk was of the land and its interconnection with life, of its value to the farmers and ranchers, who made a living from it, of its beauty to the environmentalists, of its sacredness to the Indian.

Carly shielded the harsh sun from her eyes with her hand as she gazed out over the throng. "George," she exclaimed, "it's wonderful! How'd you do it?"

The man standing at her side, his dark eyes fixed upon the scene, only half heard her. "Huh?"

"This turnout. I've never seen so many people at the Sun Dance before. It's great, isn't it?"

He removed a white handkerchief from his pocket and dabbed at the perspiration that dotted his brow, muttering, "Yes, it is."

Something in his tone summoned her attention. "What's the matter? You planned all this, didn't you?"

"Of course I did. Who else would have done it?"

"Then why the glum look?"

"It's nothing. I expected a bigger turnout, that's all."

Despite George's full-blooded heritage, at times he was like the assimilated mixed-bloods who looked upon such celebrations as backward. For George they were a reminder of how far his people still had to go. Friction often developed between the true believers, who came to participate in the religious observance, and men like George, who considered it merely a reenactment, a means of attracting the tourists, who brought in the big bucks. Why couldn't he see beyond the business of it, Carly wondered sadly, to the true significance of the ceremony?

To her the Sun Dance was proof that Oglala society continued to exist. This was a time for the sentiments of Sioux nationalism to be given their fullest expression, a time for the Oglalas to prove that they were fully American while continuing to be distinct. The dual nationalism was evident in the American flag that flapped in the breeze within the Indian encampment beside the sweat bath and the sacred Sun Dance lodge, traditional symbols of the Sioux. Carly's heart swelled with pride at being an Indian.

"Numbers are important," she told George, "but understanding is more important." Judging from what she saw as she looked around, it seemed there were many others like her who understood what this particular gathering was all about, for it had taken on the aspect of an antinuclear rally, prompting her to ask him, "How'd you find out?"

"Find out what?"

"About the uranium and the nuclear park?"

"I did some checking." His gaze shifted to her and appraised her with mild suspicion. "The question is, how did *you* find out?"

With a noncommittal shrug Carly answered, "I did a little checking of my own."

"Is that what you went to New York for?"

"How did you know I went to New York?"

"There's very little that goes on around here that I don't know about, Carly."

Dryly, she responded, "So I see."

"You'd be surprised at the things I know," said George. "I know, for instance, that the guy you brought around a few weeks ago isn't who he said he is. His real name is Blackmoon."

Carly experienced a sudden constricting knot at the back of her throat at the mention of that name. "So? I don't see what that has to do with anything."

"I thought you would have been eager to find out who's at the bottom of this thing. You've been pestering me about it long enough."

She looked at him blankly. "What do you mean?"

"I mean that the man responsible for the killings is Jesse Blackmoon."

She laughed, but it was a strained sound that issued from her throat. "That's ridiculous. Besides, I thought it was you who didn't believe that anyone had been murdered."

"I've come to think differently," he said.

"So, what makes you think it's Jesse?"

"All the evidence points to him."

"Evidence? What evidence?"

"Look at what he was doing here in the first place," George urged her. "What kind of man would kick an old woman off her land? And he came to our meeting, didn't he? Think of the things he could have learned to use against us. If that's not enough, there's his name. Blackmoon. They're the richest landowners in the state. What better motive than to become even richer?"

She shook her head, saying, "I don't believe it. That's not evidence, George; it's suspicion."

"Did you mention anything to him about your land?"

"Yes, but—"

"I wouldn't be surprised if someone approaches you about selling. You've got something he wants, Carly. I'd be real careful if I were you. What's the matter? You're looking a little pale."

She was thinking about the phone call she had received. "It's nothing," she lied. "The sun, that's all." She was feeling suddenly weak and confused and a bit faint. "I think I'll go lie down for a while. See you later."

She left him and went straight to the tepee she had erected earlier that morning the way her grandmother had taught her a long time ago. The canvas, no longer spanking bright, and the poles, worn smooth with age, were heirlooms as precious to Carly as priceless objects were to others. What memories these conical walls held, of sitting around warm fires and listening to legends, of learning how to quill in the

old way, of reaffirming her Indian heart in a white world.
She lay down on a stack of buffalo hides tanned by some
ancestor. One arm crooked behind her head, she stared up
at the circle of blue sky overhead where the lodgepoles met.

George was wrong. He *had* to be. He had never liked
Jesse, and he made no secret of it. The so-called evidence he
had presented was circumstantial at best. Nevertheless, it
made Carly wonder. Her mind went back to the day she and
Jesse had driven out to see Emma Huggins. Before they left,
Jesse had been alone with her medical bag in the living room
while she'd been in the kitchen finishing her coffee. If he'd
worked quickly, he could have tampered with the insulin
solution. What's more, it was Jesse who had found Emma's body. Could he have been the last person to see Emma
alive? A strangled sob caught in Carly's throat. It wasn't
true! She could not love a man who was a killer. To hell with
George's suspicions. Something in Carly's heart told her
that Jesse was no killer. Firm in the belief of his innocence,
she drifted off into a sleep void of dreams, free of haunting
memories.

She had no idea how long she'd been asleep. When she
awoke, the heat of the day had dissipated to the balm of
early evening. She rolled over and looked up. Stars twin-
kled down at her from beyond the smoke hole at the top of
the lodge. Beyond the canvas walls she could hear the stir-
rings of excitement as night blossomed and the dancing began.

A slow, steady drumbeat summoned Carly to her feet.
From behind the stack of hides she lifted a tissue-wrapped
package. Carefully she opened the folds to reveal an elk-
skin dress, tanned to whiteness, whose yoke was heavily
beaded in the geometric designs typical of the Sioux, in reds
and whites and yellows against a sky-blue background. A
double band of blue beadwork ran along the hem, which
was heavily fringed. Tin cones jangled from the ends of the

fringing when Carly removed the dress from its wrappings. Her hands moved reverently over the supple hide, whose seams were sinew-sewn and whose original owner, Carly's great-grandmother, had worked long and hard to create. She set the dress aside and removed a set of intricately beaded leggings, followed by a pair of moccasins done in a four-winds pattern and a set of hair ties made of buffalo hide and decorated with superfine plaited quillwork and laced with eagle feathers.

From beside the doorway Carly picked up two sticks and placed them outside in a crossed position to indicate that the one inside wished privacy. The first thing she did was make a small fire. Into the flames she tossed a few leaves of sweet grass. The lodge filled with sweetly scented smoke that curled into the waiting night through the smoke hole. Deftly she plaited her hair into two long braids, over which she slipped the quilled hair ties. The eagle feathers flicked about as she stripped out of her jeans and cotton shirt. She strapped the leggings over her legs and slid her feet into the soft moccasins. The dress was heavy, a good ten pounds, making it necessary for Carly when she put it on to walk with a straight back to keep from tottering under the extra weight.

The moon, two days past full, was bright when Carly emerged from the lodge. A trail of pearly light lit her path through the lodges and out of camp to where everyone was gathered around a huge campfire that fired the night. The celebration had drawn a crowd of several hundred curious onlookers. The speechmakers of earlier in the day now stood on the perimeters watching Indians dressed in full regalia by the light of the campfire in a scene reminiscent of the great encampments of the nineteenth century.

Several men sat around a large drum made from a smoked buffalo hide, beating a slow rhythm with stout drumsticks that were covered at the end with buffalo hide, the hair side out. The drum was a sacred instrument to the Sioux, its roundness representing the universe, its strong beat the pulse, the heart throbbing at the center of that universe. It was the very voice of the Great Spirit stirring those who heard it.

The campfire sent fiery pitches of light shooting high into the night. There was a sense of fevered urgency in the warm summer air. Carly felt a quickness enter her blood as she watched the dancers. Her own body swayed and her feet moved to the intoxicating beat of the drums, and for the time being her suspicions were lost amid the colorful night-time ceremony. Her eyes were drawn to one who danced with particular flair. She recognized Luke Lightfoot by the light of the fire. He was dressed in a buckskin shirt and dark blue leggings. A red breechcloth hung in long, quill-worked ends. Atop his head he wore a feather headdress. Bells tinkled at his ankles. In his hand he gripped a tomahawk. With knees bent, body crouched, feet moving in time to the drums in a rapid toe-heel step, he worked his way around the dance circle to where Carly was standing. When he looked up and saw her, a slow smile spread across his mouth. He left the circle and approached her.

"Hi, Carly. I see you made it." His flesh glistened with perspiration from the heat of the night and the exertion of the dance. She also recognized the unmistakable odor of alcohol on his breath.

"Hi, Luke."

He whistled through his teeth. "You sure look like something else, Carly."

She stood straight beneath his consuming gaze. "Thank you."

"When did you get back?"

"A few days ago."

"What do you say we go get something to eat?" he suggested. "All this dancing's given me an appetite."

Carly drew back, not certain that food would quench this man's appetite. "Luke, I—"

He was feeling hyper from the dance and testy from too many beers and quickly lost patience with her. "What is it now?" he asked belligerently. "You always find some excuse not to be with me. If being an Indian offends you so much, how come you're dressed like one?"

Carly rolled her eyes and groaned. Were they back to that again? "That's not fair, Luke, and you know it."

"Well, what is it, then?"

It's the alcohol and the aimlessness, she wanted to answer. It was the sick feeling that she was just a tool for him to prove his manhood within a cruel system that tended to emasculate all but the strongest of men. She gave him a withering look and said, "Go back to your dancing, Luke. There's nothing for you here."

"That's not how I see it. You and me, Carly, we'd be good together. We're alike. We're both Indians. No white man could ever understand the things going on inside of you the way I do."

Carly's nerves were on the verge of fraying, her patience being tried to sore limits. "We may both be Indians, but that's the *only* thing you and I have in common." She pivoted sharply to stalk away, but Luke's grip came down swiftly over her arm to prevent her from getting very far.

"Don't walk away from me when I'm talking to you," he ordered.

She turned back to him, an expression of surprise and anger firing up her blue eyes. "Let go of me," she demanded.

"No. Not until you—"

"You heard the lady. Let go of her."

The voice that spoke from behind them was deep and resonant and familiar. Carly's head whirled in its direction. Their eyes met across the flames. He moved toward her with inborn grace and a smoothness of muscles that quickened her pulse. Was it really him? The sound of his voice, uttered through lips whose taste she remembered so well, set her heart beating a wild, erratic rhythm in her chest.

"You heard her, Lightfoot. Let go of her."

Luke hesitated at the low warning, but slowly his fingers relaxed their grip until Carly's wrist fell free. "Well, well, well," he said with undisguised contempt, "what do we have here? What are *you* doing here, city boy?"

Jesse smiled, a mere uplifting of one corner of his mouth. "I'm here for the same reason you are."

"Oh, yeah? Then where were you this afternoon when I was busy getting these?" Luke pulled his buckskin shirt open to reveal fresh wounds on his breast. He wasn't sure why he had taken part in the flesh-piercing ceremony that afternoon when he had never done so before. Maybe it was the need to feel a part of something greater than himself or a way of atoning for past transgressions. While the precise meaning of his actions eluded him, the need had been crystal clear, and it was with a sense of uncertain pride that he bared his wounds to their startled eyes.

Jesse grimaced at the sight of them. It was easy to see why the Interior Department had once banned the Sun Dance and its self-torture rites. Things not easily understood were often condemned. Jesse felt no particular compunction to tear his own flesh apart in supplication to the Great Spirit. Although he understood Luke's need, he needed no scars upon his own breast to remind him of his Indianness.

Carly gasped. "Luke! Are you all right? Here, let me have a look at those."

She moved to touch him, but he brushed her hand away and let his shirt fall closed. Sullen and childlike, he said, "Don't worry about me, Doc. I'll be fine." With that, he raised his tomahawk high over his head and, letting out a piercing whoop, darted off to rejoin the dancers.

For several minutes Carly and Jesse stood there without speaking. A strong and powerful desire stirred within him at the sight of her. She was more beautiful than he had ever seen her. A multitude of emotions swelled his breast as his eyes swept over her, consuming her in a mad, desperate rush.

Carly's breathing faltered. Struggling to maintain a modicum of composure, she said, "Well, Jesse, I'm surprised to see you here."

In a deep voice he replied, "You shouldn't be."

She supposed he was right. He was just full of surprises, not the least of which was his startling metamorphosis. He was dressed in traditional Sioux costume. Buckskin leggings hugged his muscular thighs, the long side fringes moving in the night breeze. He wore moccasins on his feet and a loincloth at his belt. A quilled armband encircled one well-defined upper arm. About his neck he wore a necklace of bear claws. Other than that, his smooth-skinned chest was bare, muscles flexing beneath the glow of the fire. There was something primal about him, something dangerous running in his blood, something distinctly Sioux in those fierce black eyes.

Carly cleared her throat and asked, "Where'd you get the clothes?"

He smiled down at his garments in a way Carly did not understand until he explained, "The day after you left, my mother called and asked me to stop by the house. When I got there, she took me up to the attic and pulled these things out of an old trunk. They belonged to my great-great-grandfather." He paused, then added in a low voice, "She also showed me an old photograph of my father dressed in these same clothes."

"She must have loved him very much," said Carly.

"Yes, she did." A chord of bitterness rang in his tone. "She could have had him, but instead she let him go for something that ceased to matter a long time ago. She begged me not to make the same mistake she did."

Carly closed her eyes in anticipation of what she knew was coming. "Jesse, please, you must forget what's happened between us."

"I can't forget," he said thickly. "Tell me you can."

"It won't work. Don't you see? You live in your world and I live in mine. There has never been harmony between them, and there never will be. All we can do is be who we are."

"Look at me, Carly," he said, his voice softly pleading. "Do I look like the enemy?"

His dark eyes gleamed with the ancient belligerence of the Sioux, the seething hostility of their warrior ancestors, the proud arrogance of his own forefather whose Lakota blood ran through this great-great-grandson's veins. He bore no physical resemblance to the enemy. He looked, sounded, even carried the scent of an Indian. How she wanted him. Her bones were melting from the desire she had for him. But it wasn't enough. She wanted more than just the physical release of his lovemaking. She wanted it all. Nervous and confused, Carly stammered, "I—I have to go. I should see to Luke's wounds before they get infected." It was true; she was concerned about Luke, but it was her own fears that prompted Carly to spin on her heels and hurry off, leaving Jesse to stew in his own mounting frustrations.

Having left her medical bag back at the house, Carly went straight to the lodge for a few stems of the prickly pear plant that she kept handy for dressing wounds. She peeled them to expose the soft core, then went in search of Luke. Luke, however, was nowhere to be found, no doubt having gone off in search of another beer, a willing woman and a bit of the trouble he always seemed to get into. With an irritated gesture, Carly flung the prickly pear to the ground.

Turning her back on the brightly lit encampment, she headed for the woods. Her steps carried her out of the ring of light to the dark, dense solitude beneath the trees where the sound of the drums was a faint echo against the night. She inhaled deeply the sweet scent of the pines and the smell of the earth that was rich and damp beneath her moccasins. She found a flat-topped rock to sit on. With night closing in around her, she could not stop the tears from streaming down her cheeks. Inside, her heart waged a bitter struggle. Like a ship lost in a storm she pitched to and fro. No, it was useless. She could not forget what had happened between them, how their worlds had collided, leaving her hopelessly in love and uncertain just what to do about it.

A faint snapping of a twig somewhere in the blackness that enveloped her snapped Carly's head up from her hands, into which she wept in bitter frustration. She stiffened, growing alert, eyes scanning the darkness, ears straining for further sounds. She had not realized how far off she had wandered until this moment, when she looked in all directions but could not see the camp. Another sound sent a bolt of panic through her. She sprang to her feet and started to run, but in her haste to flee she ran smack into the hard wall of a chest. She opened her mouth to scream, but the sound froze like ice on her tongue when she heard a familiar voice.

It was Luke. His eyes were bright and wild-looking. The fever of the dance was still in his blood. The odor of alcohol was heavy on his breath. His lips were forceful when they came down over hers.

He kissed her harshly, possessively. When he pulled his lips away, he laughed deep in his throat at her struggles. Raking his mouth across her cheek to her ear, he rasped, "We're the same, Carly. Admit it." His lips sought hers again, and he was kissing her hungrily when he felt the sudden pressure of a strong hand on his shoulder. It spun him around and propelled him backward, and when Luke regained his footing, he found himself looking into Jesse's angry gaze.

Luke's mouth drew back in a tight, almost ugly line. "You'd better mind your own business," he warned.

"This *is* my business," said Jesse.

"Yeah? Then why don't you do something about it?"

The challenge was answered in less than a heartbeat. Jesse lunged for him, and the two men fell to the ground in a flurry of fast-flying fists.

Carly screamed and jumped out of the way to avoid their flailing arms and legs. They were going at each other like two mongrel dogs, each landing some solid blows. She cringed at their grunts and bellows and muffled curses and at the spine-tingling sound of flesh striking flesh. She pleaded with them to stop, but they were beyond hearing her.

Through startled, frightened eyes Carly watched as Jesse rolled Luke onto his back and pinned him there. She saw Jesse's fist ball into a mass of white knuckles and draw back to gather strength. It made contact with Luke's jaw in a burst of furious energy. The sound sent a wave of nausea through Carly. She shut her eyes tight, but she could not block out the sound of Luke's grunt of pain.

Jesse staggered to his feet and stood over Luke, feet braced in a menacing stance, chest heaving with fury. But it was more than the fists curled at Jesse's side that made Luke think twice about getting up to fight him. It was the rage he saw burning in those black eyes, turning them stark and chilling, that made Luke rise finally to his feet and stumble off into the darkness, muttering vows of revenge.

Jesse watched him go, then turned to Carly, who stood with her back pressed up against the trunk of a tree, looking pale and frightened. "Are you all right?" he asked.

"You mean now that you've come gallantly to my rescue?"

He looked at her, bewildered by her reaction. "Don't tell me you wanted him to do that!"

"Of course not. But was it necessary to humiliate him like that?" She should have been thankful for Jesse's timely arrival, but her tangled feeling for him, not to mention Luke's forceful advances, left little room for thanks at the moment.

"No," he said. "I guess it wasn't necessary." He was feeling suddenly foolish for his violent reaction. She no doubt would have put Luke Lightfoot in his place with either a few well-chosen words or a swift knee to the groin. He hadn't been thinking. It was as simple as that. In that split second he'd been unable to see beyond the searing red rage that blinded him to see her in another man's arms.

Carly pushed herself away from the tree with her foot. "Why did you come back, Jesse? If you were hoping to get me to sell my land to BMI, you wasted the trip."

Confusion darkened his eyes. "You don't really think that, do you?"

No, she didn't think it. If she had learned anything at all about him it was that in spite of his arrogance and forceful manner, there was an honest integrity about him, when it came to both his professional life and his personal one. Did he love her, though? It was the one question that tore through her mind with uncertainty.

When she failed to respond, but just stood there looking down at the dark ground at her feet, he grew impatient and angry. He grabbed her by the shoulders and gave her a rough shake. "Answer me. You can't think that. You're crazy if you do."

"Crazy, am I?" she said, flaring to life. "Yes! Crazy to have fallen in love with you. Oh, Jesse, why? Why did you come back?"

The anger went out of him in a rush. He dropped his hands to his sides and answered in a low voice. "I had to. I

couldn't stay away." There were so many things he wanted
to tell her, so many things to explain, about himself and who
and what he was, about BMI, about his feelings for her. He
scarcely knew where to begin, for there was so much of it he
didn't understand himself. "I had to see you," he said.

A sudden memory of her last night in New York leaped
into Carly's mind. It had been on the drive home from that
terrible dinner at his parents' house, or one of his parents,
at least. How she had ached for him. She had felt his vulnerability throbbing in plain sight beside her. She had
thought him reachable then, and for some crazy reason she
had found herself suggesting that he come back to South
Dakota with her. Even now she felt pinpricks of pain at his
response. "I'm so close to beating him," he had said, "so
close." Carly knew right then that something was more important to him than she was...ever could be. So it was with
painful doubt tearing at her that she said bitterly, "You
mean you left BMI and your consuming battle with Russell
and flew sixteen hundred miles just to see me?"

He moved to within inches of where she stood, but he was
careful not to touch her. Gently he demanded, "Carly, look
at me."

She lifted her gaze hesitantly to meet his.

"Look into my eyes," he urged her. "Tell me what you
see."

In those awesome black eyes Carly saw all over again the
uncompromising quality about the man, the bitterness and
the anger, the tenderness, the regret, the pride. But most of
all, she saw his love. With a cry she melted against him, her
hand clutching for him.

For a while he just held her like that. Then he took her by
the hand and led her to a cool place beneath a shaggy-leafed
tree and pulled her lightly to the ground beside him.
"Carly," he said softly, "there's something you have to
know."

Faintly she muttered, "It sounds serious."

"It is." Cradling her hand in his, he looked into her misty eyes and said, "The other night I got a phone call from Fred Santini, one of my men in the Legal Department. I had asked him to do some checking for me, some *deep* checking. And it seems he found something." He paused to pull in a ragged breath before continuing. "Laramie Fork Power Company is a wholly owned subsidiary of BMI. It was hidden so deeply in the books that no one even knew it was there. It was created as a means to drain off funds that BMI would otherwise have to pay taxes on. No doubt there are others like it, but this is the one that concerns me right now. I can't tell you how ashamed I was when I found out just how deeply my own company is involved in what's been going on out here, the killings, the rape of the land." He shook his head with a mixture of anger and sadness. "It was the last straw. I confronted Russell with what I knew. He denied it, of course, but I've got him and he knows it." Despite the triumph, there was a sadness in his eyes, for it was a bitter, hollow victory.

"You can start all over again," she said to him. "Turn the company into what *you* want it to be. You've got the power to do that now."

He was shaking his head as she spoke. "I don't think so."

"But that company is your life. You've put so much of yourself into it."

He reached up to stroke her cheek with his thumb. "I'll admit it, Carly; at one time that *was* what I wanted. That was all there was until you came along, and then nothing else mattered." He laughed, but it was a bitter sound from deep in his throat. "In a way I guess he's won after all. I don't want the company. It belongs to him. For too many years I played a role I never felt comfortable with no matter how good I was at it. Don't you see, Carly? That wasn't me. That was somebody going through the motions. I used to think that beating Russell at his own game was the only thing that mattered. Now I know that there's so much else that matters more—you and me, this place, who we are—*what* we are. That's why I organized this rally. I thought—"

She bolted upright in his arms. "*You* organized this rally?"

He grinned sheepishly. "It took some doing, but I've got good people working for me. In two days we spoke to every landowner in the state of South Dakota. We told them what the power companies are trying to do to the Black Hills and we asked them to help us in our fight to save the hills."

Carly's mind backtracked to something George had said to her when she had commented on whether he had planned the rally. *"Of course I did,"* he had told her. *"Who else would have done it?"* Who else? Jesse, that's who. How she loved him for it. But why had George lied and taken the credit for it? One more unanswered question was trapped in her mind. Her fingers closed around his arm, the pressure of them signaling her own worst fears. "Jesse," she whispered, "there are still eleven unsolved murders. Russell may have been behind them, but he's not the one who—who actually... Jesse, I'm scared. I think I may be next."

Beneath her trembling he sensed there was more to it than she was saying. "What makes you think so?" he wanted to know.

"I have the land, don't I? Two hundred and forty acres on the outskirts of the hills."

"Yes, but I told you, I've put a stop to that. BMI won't be acquiring any more land."

She told him then about the phone call she had received the day before she left for New York, but he was still unconvinced of the danger. Carly swallowed hard and said, "I got another call, late last night. It was the same man who called the first time. He didn't identify himself, but he said I'd be hearing from him again.''

The muscles in Jesse's jaw tensed as he listened. Somewhere out on the prairie a killer roamed, leaving a trail of destruction behind him. His arms tightened around Carly. "Don't worry. I won't let anything happen to you. I promise.''

He bent his head close to hers and kissed her, tenderly at first, then harder, until his lips were devouring hers. And all the fears and doubts, all the suspicions and accusations, were forgotten in a tangle of arms and legs and seeking lips.

He clasped her to him, drawing deep into his being her warmth, her fragrance, the very essence of her. He ached with feeling for her, but what was that feeling, exactly? He had asked himself that question time and again, but so far he had managed to evade the answer. In spite of the emotions tearing at him now, the rapid little flip-flops his stomach was doing, he wasn't sure he wanted to hear the answer now. But here she was in his arms, and his defenses crumbled easily. He was in love with her. It was as simple as that. Too late to put the brakes on, take a step back and say thanks but no thanks. He was in love with her in a way that was completely mystifying to him. He'd never been in love like that, but then, there had never been anyone in his life like her. She had forced him to take a good, hard look at himself, to recognize the unknown, to embrace it, to claim it. She had given him the courage to see himself for what he was, and he loved her for it. Unselfishly. Unlimitedly.

Looking back, he could even pinpoint the moment it had happened. When he had kissed her in the mud on the deserted road to Broken Bow, he had desired her with an intensity that had overwhelmed him. When he had received the shocking news of his parentage, he had needed her, not her body, but her strength to get him through those first few shattering moments. But when he had stood across a campfire and gazed at her with eagle feathers laced in her dark hair, her blue eyes clear and bright and focused upon him from across the flames, he had fallen in love with her.

They had become lovers, friends, allies in a common cause. Now he had to find a way to tell her that he wanted to spend the rest of his life with her. The words that had been so difficult to say before came easily now to his lips.

"I love you, Carly," he whispered. "I love you."

The words filled her with a warmth she had never known, the warmth of joy in its purest form. "Jesse," she breathed. "Touch me. Love me." Her mouth was avid upon his, hot and open as if she could draw the emotions right out of him and into her own being. Her hands moved over him, taking what she needed, giving what he wanted, until need and want were indistinguishable from each other.

He could smell the sweet grass in her hair, the scent of pine needles from above, the damp, rich earth beneath. He could feel the passion in her as her body pressed against his. Desires, needs, demands. He could taste them all upon her lips. And if that was not enough, there was the sound of her voice, breathless and urgent at his ear, urging, pleading, daring him to break down those final few barriers as she herself was doing.

Carly had never felt Jesse's passion as intensely as she felt it tonight. His hands pulled at her clothes with a desperation that could not help but thrill her. He wanted her, and being wanted this strongly, this feverishly, was thrilling in and of itself. One by one the barriers crumbled, until each of them was descending willingly into those dark, swirling currents of pure feeling.

The night was still and calm. Through the shaggy boughs the stars played a game of hide-and-seek across the sky. The matted grass beneath them was cool against their naked flesh. The forest was filled with the cadence of crickets, the flutterings of tiny wings, the beating of two hearts. Responding to Carly's overtures, Jesse lowered his face to nuzzle her breasts, kissing their firm smooth skin, tickling with the tip of his tongue, then taking each in turn into his mouth with gentle sucking motions.

Carly's breath caught in her throat. "Oh, Jesse... please... now..."

She heard his voice rasp against the stillness. "Not yet." He didn't want either of them to ever forget this night. He kissed her again softly, lingeringly, as if they had all the time in the world. Slowly, teasingly, he caressed and petted, kissed and nibbled, every part of her. And when at last she felt him slide into her velvet warmth, she clasped her arms and legs around him, drawing him in deeper, matching his rhythm with her own, creating one single drumbeat of love and desire.

Chapter 15

The night was warm and calm. Bullfrogs croaked in a nearby stream. Crickets chirped a rising chorus from the forest. With deadly silence the diamondbacks slithered out from daytime dens to sun themselves on the prairie by the light of the moon.

From the peaks of the nearby Black Hills the wind sang through the dark needles of the pines, chanting a song known only to those who listened and believed. The gentle murmur touched the heart in those deepest places where memories are held dear, where the sacred things are remembered and where hope still lingers. Out of the earth and the wilderness, the gurgling waters, the pungent sagebrush, the thunder of the drums came the song of the stillness.

Through the gentle wisdom of her grandmother Carly had learned how to listen. "Listen," the old one would stop and say. "Do you hear it? Listen and be quiet and you will hear a song out of the stillness." Carly lay awake on this night in the lodge in the waning month of August, listening to the hills talking, the blades of grass murmuring with the movement of the wind through them, the strong, steady beating of her own heart. She turned her head to gaze at the man lying next to her on the tanned hides. For many wordless minutes she studied his profile, discovering all over again what a strikingly handsome man he was.

"Jesse?"

"Hmm?"

"I've been thinking."

He opened his eyes and turned to her. "So have I." He was hungry for her again. Taking her into his arms, he began a slow nuzzle of her neck.

Carly squirmed against him, pushing him gently away and murmuring, "Jesse, wait."

His voice was lazy with sleep, husky with desire at her ear. "I don't want to wait."

"Come on, Jesse, this is serious."

He laughed wickedly. "So is this. Ask any red-blooded man." His lips moved over her throat with renewed aggression.

He was exasperating, to be sure, but secretly Carly would not have had him any other way. She endured his maddening kisses, issuing weak protests and offering unconvincing struggles. "I'm worried about Willie Nighthawk," she said a bit breathlessly.

"Why?" he mumbled against her flesh. "Is he sick?"

"No. He's been approached to sell his land. That's what I'm worried about."

His teeth nipped playfully at her lobe. "How do you know that?"

The tantalizing seduction of his tongue made Carly catch her breath. "I saw the deed. That's where I first heard of BMI. The papers were all typed up and waiting for Willie's signature. I'm just afraid that whoever left them there will be back for them."

He ceased his seduction and looked up. "Why didn't you tell me this before?"

"I—I . . ." It would have been easy to say that she had simply forgotten. "Oh, all right, if you must know, I sneaked into Willie's house through his window and saw the papers on the kitchen table. I didn't want you to think I was . . . you know, snooping."

Jesse laughed at her tenacity. She was impulsive, and maybe even a little too reckless for her own good, but he had to hand it to her; she had guts.

"I think we ought to go and have a talk with Willie," she said.

"Fine. We'll do it first thing in the morning."

"But—"

Her protest was lost in the fury of his kiss. The heat of his impatient hands fired her up and she was powerless to deny him whatever he wanted.

Later she lay in his arms, body glistening with perspiration in the aftermath of their lovemaking, listening to the sound of Jesse's breathing. It was deep and steady, signaling sleep. Gingerly she untangled herself from his sleeping form and rose from the pile of hides. Careful to make no noise, she dressed quickly and tiptoed quietly from the lodge.

Carly decided against taking the car, for the noise of the engine was sure to arouse any light sleepers in camp and signal her departure. She went instead to the place where Janey was tethered. Carly had brought the mare along in order to take part in some of the races over the three days of festivities, but Janey was needed for a more important task now.

She gave the mare an affectionate pat on the nose. Without bothering to saddle her, Carly grasped a handful of coarse mane and jumped onto her bare back. With a subtle tensing of her knees, she guided the mare out of camp.

The moon lit the trail through the woods and over the hills to Willie's place. She had to warn him that his life was in danger. Carly knew he wouldn't sell, and she shuddered to think what the others had gotten for saying no.

It was nearly dawn when she arrived at Willie's ramshackle cabin. The eastern sky was tinted pink as the sleepy sun emerged on the horizon. The birds were just awakening, stirring in their treetop perches. Carly slid like rainfall from Janey's back and walked to the front door. She rapped several times on the knotted planks. "Willie? It's Dr. McAllister. Wake up, Willie. I have to talk to you." When her knocking produced no response, she went around back and peered in the kitchen window. A cup of coffee and a half-eaten doughnut on the table told her that Willie was already up. Where could he have gone? Of course, the mine.

She turned from the window and ran to the foot of the hill behind the house. When she reached the top she was panting from the steep climb. There it was, the gaping mouth of Willie's dusty old mine.

Willie had been working this mine for more than fifteen years. Whatever shallow veins of gold he mined, although not enough to raise him above the poverty level, were sufficient to keep him submerged in the black hole year after year on the vague hope that there was more. His lungs were gritty with mine dust. His eyes were unaccustomed to daylight. The flesh on his hands was toughened and grizzled and so deeply embedded with soot that no amount of washing could ever get them clean again. Still he toiled, laboring far beyond the age when men are strong and able enough for this kind of work, always clinging to the faint hope that the mother lode lay just a pickax away.

Carly stood at the entrance to the mine. Cupping her hands she called his name into the black void. There was no answer. She wasn't surprised, for she knew of Willie's habit of wearing his Walkman when he worked, having once even teased him about it. She called again, hoping he might hear her anyway, for she had no wish to enter the dark and dusty mine shaft.

The air in the mine was dank. Carly's lungs strained for breath. The sour odors that invaded her nostrils made her think of what a dungeon must be like. The steady plop, plop, of water dripping from some unseen crevice echoed throughout the granite corridors that led deep into the earth. Carly proceeded with caution, eyes gradually growing accustomed to the absence of light. It was too dark to see, but at least she could make out shadows and varying shades of gray well enough to avoid bumping into walls as she picked her way into the shaft. The sound of her footsteps through puddles of stagnant water followed her along, and she was cursing the destruction of a good pair of jeans when something scudded across her path. A small cry escaped Carly's throat. Through the darkness she could make out the tiny humped shape of a rat dragging its long, skinny tail behind it as it disappeared into a crack in the rock. She shook off a squeamish shudder. She took a step forward but froze at a faint sound from somewhere deep in the mine. It's Willie, she thought with nervous relief. Feeling slightly bolder, she pressed on.

The air grew hot and stifling, but it was no longer foul. At times Carly could feel currents of cooler air upon her face, issuing from half-guessed openings in the rock. This deep in the mine, there was no sound at all save that of her own footsteps. When she halted, she heard nothing. Yet Carly began to hear, or at least to imagine so, something that sounded like the faint fall of footsteps behind her. All about her hung the darkness, hollow and immense. She felt oppressed by the loneliness and vastness of these sinister walls. The wildest imaginings of the mind began to play with her courage, and she was regretting the impulsiveness that had prompted her to come here alone.

She was picking her way along in the dark, softly calling Willie's name, when she stumbled over an object in her path. In the blackness she could not make it out, but when she bent down and reached out, she screamed when her hand touched a body, soft and still warm.

Carly jerked her hand back and jumped away. A sickness crept into her stomach. Screwing up her courage, she put out a tentative hand and felt further. A cold shiver of fear ran down her spine when her fingers touched the cold metal of what was unmistakably a set of headphones. A check of the pulse confirmed what Carly already suspected. She was too late. Willie was dead.

For several stunned minutes Carly remained in that hunched position. A sound from behind brought her head up with a snap. Unholy terror clutched at her now. Unable to go back for fear of whoever was following her, she had no choice but to jump up and run farther into the mine. Her stumbling footsteps took her to a cul-de-sac. An involuntary cry tore from her throat when her hands touched a wall of solid rock. Even in the darkness she could see there was no place to go. She felt around blindly and touched what she took to be a barrel. The darkness she had previously feared was now her ally as she crouched behind the rotting barrel, her breath trapped painfully in her lungs as she listened to the sound of footsteps coming closer. Her heart was beating so violently she was sure it could be heard throughout the corridors of the mine, signaling her hiding place as surely as if she had screamed.

The footsteps drew nearer. Someone was there, standing so close that Carly could hear the sharp intake of breath through flared nostrils. Her mind screamed for her to get up and run. Leaping up from her hiding place, she made a mad dash for it, but a rough hand darted out to abort her flight.

Carly screamed and fought her attacker, but her strength was no match for the strong arms that encircled her, pinning her arms to her sides. Through the panic that seized her she heard a familiar voice issuing a rough command.

"Stop it, damn it! Stop it!"

The adrenaline seemed to go out of her all at once and she collapsed against him, sobbing. "Oh, Jesse, it's you. I thought . . . I thought—"

"Shh." He stroked her hair with his palm. "It's all right."

"No," she said. "It's not all right." Her voice was choked with grief. "Willie's dead. We're too late. Someone's already been here."

His body stiffened, muscles going rigid. "Someone's still here," he whispered. "Did you hear that? Shh. Listen."

It was only when she quieted down and stopped to listen that she heard what Jesse's keen ears had already perceived, the unmistakable echo of footsteps.

"Quick," said Jesse. "Get behind that barrel."

"What about you?"

"Just do as I say." His strong hand on her shoulder forced her to the ground behind the barrel before she could object.

Eyes wide and glassy with fear, Carly watched as Jesse flattened himself against the rock wall. Together they waited as the footsteps grew louder and more distinct. From out of the blackness a shadow loomed. Closer it came, a dark, brooding menace without a face. When it was nearly upon them, Jesse sprang out.

Carly screamed just as Jesse's fist made contact. Through the gloom she saw a form slip to the ground and lie there without moving.

"Give me a hand," said Jesse. "We've got to get this guy tied up. See if you can find something to use."

She groped around in the darkness and managed to come up with some pieces of rope that, combined with the laces Jesse was tearing out of his sneakers, would have to do. "Help me tie him up," he instructed. Carly dropped to her knees to assist him, but gasped when the odor of alcohol wafted into her nostrils. "It's Luke!"

"Tie as many knots as you can," said Jesse.

She followed his orders, and in a couple of minutes they had Luke trussed up like a Thanksgiving turkey. Jesse rose to stand over the body and said with contempt, "This is one killer who won't get the chance to kill again." He reached in the darkness for Carly's hand. "Come on," he said brusquely, "let's get out of here. This place gives me the creeps."

They followed the sound of dripping water until at last they could see a glimmer of light at the end of the long mine tunnel. Jesse quickened the pace. He was eager to get out of this hellhole and into the light of day. He should have been thinking about scolding her for the way she had scared him half to death. When he had awakened and found her gone, he'd known immediately where she'd gone, and he'd been angry. But all he wanted to do now was hold her in his arms and tell her how much he loved her.

They emerged from the mine shaft into the bright daylight and were greeted by the nose of a shotgun. Whatever notions Jesse had of laying Carly down in the grass and making love to her vanished into the still morning air when this newest danger presented itself.

The expression on George's face was one of twisted triumph. "Well, well, well," he said, sneering. "This is better than I expected, finding you both here together. Now it'll be sort of like killing two birds with one stone." He settled his gaze on Carly's pale face. "I knew what you were up to that day we drove down to Pine Ridge. Very clever of you, Carly, checking the county clerk's records. I've got to hand it to you. I knew you were smart, but I didn't realize just how smart. I thought I did a pretty good job of throwing you off my trail, though." The edge in his voice hardened. "But it looks like I underestimated you."

A shaft of realization shot through Carly like a hard-driven nail. Her blue eyes flared wide upon him. Her voice scratched at the back of her throat and emerged in a whisper of shock and sadness. *"You!"*

"Congratulations," he said sarcastically. "You finally figured it out. Of course, I could have gone on letting you think it was Luke. I even found some guy in Pine Ridge with a blue pickup to run you down so you'd think it was Luke. After all, who would believe the word of an unemployed alcoholic?"

As he stood there listening, Jesse's fingers clenched tightly at his sides, flexing with explosive potential. He took a menacing step toward George. "You miserable—" But the muzzle of the shotgun jerked in his direction, warning him against coming any closer.

George was feeling bold behind the weapon, secure in its ability to keep Jesse at bay. There was something in those black eyes of Jesse's that George had always secretly feared. And what he feared he hated.

Carly's mind flashed back to that awful day in Pine Ridge. The realization that George had been responsible for the accident that had nearly killed her stunned her, but what he said next frightened her even more.

"The stupid fool botched the job," he said. "So now I'll have to do it myself."

George's eyes shifted to Jesse, who stood in smoldering silence at Carly's side. "Everything was under control until you showed up. He told me you'd be trouble, but I didn't realize just how much."

Jesse returned George's stare without flinching. "He? I presume you mean Russell."

George snickered, neither confirming nor denying Jesse's suspicion, and returned his attention to Carly. "I admire your determination," he told her. "But don't you see? I was always just one step ahead of you. When you left for

New York, I went to the county clerk's office myself. I figured there had to be something in those records to send you running east. That's when I discovered that stupid error in the Yazzie deed. So I simply phoned to New York and had all the copies removed from the files. Clever, don't you agree?"

A low rumble of laughter spilled from Jesse's throat. "And I made copies of everything before that. Clever, don't you agree?"

George detested that arrogance and the mimicking tone behind it. "It doesn't matter. You aren't going to live to show them to anyone."

"What are you going to do?" asked Carly.

"What I should have done before. Actually, I'm kind of sorry, though. I almost liked you, Carly."

"Oh, George," she cried. "Why?"

He startled them both with a burst of contemptuous laughter. "Do you think we've all had it as easy as you, Carly, with your well-to-do white stepfather paying your way through medical school? Or you?" He turned to Jesse with a sneer. "With all your money and your land? Some of us have had to fight our way to the top. The first thing you learn is how to get what you need. Then you learn how to get what you want—and from whom."

"From your own people?" she exclaimed.

"If need be. It's a sad fact of life that at times it's necessary to sacrifice a few for the good of many."

"And you figure that robbing them of their land and turning it over to a corporation like BMI is for the good of many?"

For all her fiery intelligence it seemed to him at times that she was incredibly naive. He rolled his eyes impatiently and said, "There you go again, thinking like an Indian."

"What's wrong with that?" Carly challenged. "It's what I am. It's what you are, too."

"I haven't forgotten that," said George. "And once I get to where I'm going, who can tell the kinds of things I'll be able to do for our people."

"Where would that be?" asked Jesse.

George shrugged. "Who knows? The Senate maybe. The House. The point is, it takes friends to get there."

"I get it," said Jesse. "You think you're buying yourself some pretty influential friends by killing your own kind."

"We do what we have to do."

Carly eyed George with disgust. "How could you?"

"It wasn't so hard. It was simply a case of the end justifying the means. Look at me. Do I look like some impoverished reservation Indian to you? Not me. I've got money, power—"

"White man's tools," Carly cut in.

"Yes, but necessary in this white man's world."

"I've got news for you," said Jesse. "It's not all it's cracked up to be."

George was unimpressed. "I'll take my chances."

"You won't get away with this," Jesse warned.

"I'd like to say just watch me, but you won't be around to see it." He waved the shotgun at them. "Now turn around and walk slowly to the mine."

With the gun at their backs, George herded them toward the opening. "Go on," he ordered. "Get in there."

They walked into the darkened shaft ten yards or so and turned around to watch in mounting horror as George pulled a stick of dynamite from his pocket and placed it on the ground at the entrance to the mine. He paused to smile coldly at them before lighting it.

Jesse was already in motion before the wick started to sizzle. He grabbed Carly by the hand and dragged her behind him as he raced deeper into the mine to get away from the inevitable explosion. They raced in the darkness, half stumbling back to the place where Luke was still tied up.

"Come on," shouted Jesse. "Help me untie him." Together they worked in frantic haste to free their own clumsy knots.

Luke was just coming to as his hands fell free. "Hey, what the—"

Jesse helped Luke to his feet. "There's no time. We'll explain everything later. Come on, this place is about to blow."

The explosion rocked the ground. Carly screamed and Jesse shouted something that could not be heard over the roar of falling rock.

Luke was screaming something at the top of his lungs. "This way! I know a way out. This way!"

The three of them ran for their lives from the avalanche of rock that was rushing toward them from behind. Down one black mine tunnel to another they went while the underground shaft crumbled all around them. The dust was blinding. They choked on it as they ran faster, deeper into the earth.

"There it is," Luke shouted.

They plunged toward a source of light that came from an overhead ledge where a crack in the rock opened to the daylight. It was just big enough for a man to pass through. Luke scrambled up to the ledge, then reached down and yelled, "Come on, Carly."

With Jesse hoisting her up from behind and Luke pulling from above, Carly made it to the ledge, and then stood aside as Luke reached again, this time for Jesse's hand.

One by one they squeezed through the crevice just as the mine shaft collapsed behind them. They fell to the ground, panting.

Several minutes passed before the shock wore off and Carly realized with a desperate sigh of relief that she was still alive. If it hadn't been for Luke, they would have been dead. She felt ashamed of having suspected Luke of so foul a crime, and guilty because she and Jesse had tied him up. "Luke?" she ventured. "Can you ever forgive me?"

Luke rolled onto his back and looked at her. "Hell, Carly, I can't say I blame you, sneaking up on you the way I did." He cast a furtive glance at Jesse and rubbed his jaw, which was noticeably swollen from having received two blows from Jesse's angry fist. "I can't say I like your friend's style, though."

Jesse sat up and looked at him. For a long moment two pairs of dark eyes clashed before Jesse's softened in a look of grudging respect. "Sorry about that. Under the circumstances I figured it was best to hit first and ask questions later." He thrust out his hand in a gesture that revealed more than he was willing to say.

Luke hesitated, then clasped Jesse's hand in a brief but firm handshake.

"What were you doing here, Luke?" asked Carly.

"Looking for you." His gaze dropped to the ground, where he plucked absently at a blade of grass. "I, uh, went to your house to talk to you, to, uh, apologize. I've been acting like a fool, Carly, and I'm sorry for it. When you didn't come back after I'd waited around for a while, I looked inside. It looked like you hadn't been there. So I went back to the camp. No one I asked had seen you this morning, so I took a chance. I don't know. Something told me maybe you'd be here." He shrugged as if to suggest that maybe it was better not to question one's inner voices.

Carly smiled tenderly at him. "That's all right, Luke. I think I understand."

"Yeah," he said. "I think you do."

There was no need for him to explain. He wasn't even certain he could, anyway. It had to do with yesterday's ceremony; that much he knew. To the throb of pain and drums he had danced before the sun in the climax of a solemn rite once performed by his ancestors. He had taken the test of faith and courage, and he had passed. And the disillusioned man had found something to believe in at last.

"What I don't understand is why you came here, to the mine, I mean," he said, puzzled.

It was time to tell Luke what she and Jesse already knew. Carly took a deep breath and began the incredible tale of murder that had taken her all the way to New York City and back. When she finished, Luke shook his head with a mixture of sadness and disbelief. "George, a murderer. I just can't believe it. And you suspected *me*?" He seemed genuinely hurt.

"Only because you lied about the poker game, the one in which you claimed to have won the money for the pickup."

Luke's expression turned guilty. "Yeah, well, I guess I did lie about that. The truth is I sold a big chunk of gold that I dug out of Willie's mine without telling him. I've done some dishonest things in my life, Carly, that I'm not especially proud of and..." He shrugged helplessly. "I guess that was one of them." He pushed himself to his feet and stood looking down at her. "What's gonna happen to George?"

Carly glanced over at Jesse for the answer. "I don't think he'll get very far," Jesse told them. "To his knowledge, Carly and I are the only ones who know about him, and he no doubt thinks we're dead by now. My guess is he'll be pretty surprised when I show up at his door."

"Don't you think we should let the police handle this?" said Carly.

"We will . . . after I've finished with him."

Luke shifted nervously from foot to foot, for he was well acquainted with the ferocity of Jesse's fist. "Well, uh, I guess I'll be going. If you need me for anything, let me know. I'll be seeing you around, Carly." He looked briefly at Jesse and gave a quick nod of his head before turning and starting down the hillside.

They were alone now on the hill. Overhead, the sun was inching its way higher into a deep blue sky. Jesse reached for Carly's hand and pulled her lightly to her feet next to him, and together they walked away from the scene of death and destruction. He started for the car, but she pulled in the other direction, saying, "Let's take Janey. I feel like riding."

"I thought you told me once that Janey's not sturdy enough for the two of us."

She smiled impishly up at him, blue eyes flashing, and confessed, "I lied."

So they left the red Mustang parked beneath a tree where Jesse had left it earlier. They would be back for it tomorrow. Jesse placed two strong hands around Carly's waist, hoisted her into the air and set her down on the mare's back. In a fluid motion he jumped in place behind her. His arms went around her to grasp a fistful of coarse mane and settle tightly at Carly's sides. With a subtle movement of his knees he set the horse in motion.

The sun shone with crystal intensity in a boundless blue sky on this August day. Carly's head slipped back onto Jesse's broad shoulder. Her eyes closed to the warmth of the sun and the gentle rhythm of the horse's steady gait. She looked so calm, so at peace within herself with that reflective expression on her face. Who would have guessed that inside she raced like a locomotive out of control at the nearness of this one special man?

"Jesse?" she murmured. "Where do we go from here?"

His voice was deep and rich at her ear, like thick maple syrup dripping with mouth-watering sweetness. "The first thing we do is build you that clinic."

It was not so much his mention of the clinic, nor the naturally seductive tone of his voice that made Carly's eyes snap open. She looked over her shoulder and questioned, "We?"

He smiled that devastating smile of his and said, "Of course we."

"You're not going back to New York, then?"

"Sure I am."

Her look turned crestfallen, and her shoulders slumped for having misread him. Disappointed, she muttered, "Oh."

"There are loose ends to be tied up at BMI," he said. "I figure it will take me a week, maybe two, before I'm back."

"You're coming back?"

"Of course I'm coming back," he laughed. "Did you think it would be that easy to get rid of me?"

A feeling stronger than joy stunned Carly. She laid her head back against him. No, in her heart she knew it would never be that easy to rid herself of him. His presence was embedded deeply in her soul, far too deeply for her to ever be the same again without him. Their paths were inextricably entwined, destined by fate to cross, bound by desire never to part again. And even if they were forced apart in distance from time to time, nothing could separate their hearts, which had become one. For them it would be one step at a time.

Was it over at last, Carly dared to think, the long terror of these past three years? So much had been lost—innocent lives, precious time, maybe even the sacred places. But as Carly's grandmother used to say, "In every ending there is a beginning. In death there is life, for there can be no beginning and no ending in the Circle of Life." Surely it must be so, for she and Jesse had gained in ways that otherwise would never have been.

For Jesse the gain was an awareness of who and what he was, the fulfillment of a being too long denied. For Carly it was the courage to love again, to trust, not blindly but with eyes wide open. For the people it was a strong and powerful new leader in Jesse, a leader who was prepared to fight for the land as fiercely as their Lakota ancestors had fought.

The air was warm and languid with the fragrance of sweet grass and sagebrush. Carly inhaled, breathing it deep into her lungs. Something barely perceptible captured her attention. She straightened up. "Listen," she whispered. "Do you hear it?"

Jesse listened and smiled. "Yes," he murmured. "Yes, I hear it."

It was the wind whispering through the cottonwoods in a voice scarcely noticeable, save to those who listened and believed. It was the voice of the Stillness, singing a song of hope that the sacred places of the earth, and those of the heart, would live forever.

COMING NEXT MONTH

MIND OVER MATTER—Nora Roberts

Aurora Fields believed she was a modern, practical woman who had no time for romance. But when her work as a theatrical agent brought her up against film producer David Brady, he found a way to change her mind.

EDEN'S TEMPTATION—Susanna Christie

Their government assignment brought them together, but treachery forced them to flee into the desert. On the run, Eden and Jake shared many things: exhaustion, hunger, distrust—and love.

COLTON'S FOLLY—Renee Simons

Abby Colton came to the reservation as an outsider, but she won acceptance from everybody—except Cat Tallman, the man she was beginning to love. Cat's mind was sure Abby had no place in his life, but his heart had other ideas....

BAYOU MIDNIGHT—Emilie Richards

Sam Long knew what he didn't want: a relationship that would interfere with his first, last and only love—police work. Then he met Antoinette Deveraux and realized just how wrong a man can be.

AVAILABLE THIS MONTH:

SACRED PLACES
Nancy Morse

WITHIN REACH
Marilyn Pappano

BEAUTIFUL DREAMER
Paula Detmer Riggs

SEPTEMBER RAINBOW
Sibylle Garrett

FOUR UNIQUE SERIES
FOR EVERY WOMAN YOU ARE . . .

Silhouette Romance

Heartwarming romances that will make you
laugh and cry as they bring you all the wonder
and magic of falling in love.

6 titles per month

Silhouette Special Edition

Expanded romances written with emotion and
heightened romantic tension to ensure
powerful stories. A rare blend of passion and
dramatic realism.

6 titles per month

Silhouette Desire

Believable, sensuous, compelling—and
above all, romantic—these stories deliver
the promise of love, the guarantee
of satisfaction.

6 titles per month

Silhouette Intimate Moments

Love stories that entice; longer, more
sensuous romances filled with adventure,
suspense, glamour and melodrama.

4 titles per month

Silhouette Romances
not available in retail outlets in Canada